Sometimes In December

A Novel

Sometimes In December

A Novel

Dorian Mendez-Vaz

Bellflower, California

Masquerade an Imprint of Hawkins Publishing Group
P.O. Box 447
Bellflower, CA 90707
www.hawkinspublishinggroup.com

This is a work of fiction. Names, characters, businesses, places, events and incidents are either the products of the author's imagination or used in a fictitious manner. Any resemblance to actual persons, living or dead, or actual events is purely coincidental.

Copyright ©2015 by Dorian Mendez-Vaz

All rights reserved, including the right of reproduction in whole or part in any form. No part of this book may be reproduced or transmitted in any form or by any means, electronic or mechanical, including photocopying, recording, or by any information storage and retrieval system, without prior written permission of the publisher, except by a reviewer, who may quote brief passages in a review.

Winter Poem by Nikki Giovanni reprinted with permission. All Rights Reserved ©1972 Nikki Giovanni.
Author Photo Courtesy: Wil Hardmon
Cover photo: Rose in Snow © Oleh Marchak | Dreamstime.com
Cover design and layout: Hawkins Publishing Group Design Team

ISBN: 978-0-9835356-7-6 (Softcover)
Library of Congress Control Number: 2015940174
Manufactured in the United States
10 9 8 7 6 5 4 3 2 1

To my mother for everything.
To all the magnificent women in my life-past and present.

Acknowledgements

My deepest appreciation is extended to Patti Beck, Alyson Brown-Johnson, Ardelia Deeble, Mrs. Betty Graham, Solange Jorge, Deborah Taylor and Tammy Tull for taking the time to read the progressions of my manuscript and give invaluable feedback. You helped confirm that this is a story for all women.

Thank you Yolanda Harris for loving the part that stayed to the end even as Quinza became Geri. Perhaps Quinza will still have her say.

Thank you to Ludi Fort who edited for grammar when the book was still a journal entry. Blessed thanks to Lucille Mendez-Vaz my mother, Natalie Stevenson-Stewart and LaShena Reynolds for their final stage editing. Natalie and LaShena, your margin comments were priceless!

To Wil Hardmon, thank you for taking the photos that you believed would be used for my first novel. Thank you Audrey White, my aunt, who encouraged my writing and kept me supplied with paper and ink cartridges.

I would be remiss if I did not thank Nikki Giovanni for inspiring me from afar to become a writer as a teen and for responding to my letter regarding the use of Winter Poem (1972) at the onset of writing this novel.

Special thanks to Cheryl "Inahlai" Powers who directed me to Hawkins Publishing Group. It is interesting how chance conversations can become life changing events. Another special thanks to Felicia Y. Thomas for her encouragement when this book was just an idea.

Last but not least, thank you to all of my incredible girlfriends across the country who fit so well within my life story, making it easier to write Geri Michael's story. You have been my earthly "cloud of witnesses"! You are a testament to the "marvelousness" of Godly women! Selah!

Winter Poem

once a snowflake fell
on my brow and i loved it so much and i kissed
it and it was happy and called its cousins
and brothers
and a web
of snow engulfed me then
i reached to love them all
and i squeezed them and they became
a spring rain and i stood perfectly
still and was a flower.

Nikki Giovanni
February 3,1972

Prologue

Geri frowned as her fingers rested on the computer keyboard. This was the second night she edited the same pages and still she was not satisfied with how the story was moving. She could not understand why she was having such difficulty writing beyond her new protagonist's pain. The words were clear in her mind, but for some reason they were not transferable to the page. A few of the notes she had written were scattered across her kitchen table. That in itself was telling about how unsettling her writing attempts had been. She normally kept her work space clutter free.

Looking around the room as if to search for a clue about her writer's block, her eyes became fixed on the clock sitting on the counter. The almost inaudible sound of its synchronized ticking interrupted her thoughts about the book. Hands still on the keyboard, she sat up straight and took a deep breath. As she exhaled she felt a rush of longing for Christian. The clock was a gift from him. As always with his gift he had enclosed a special note. His words came rushing back to her mind. "In real time, in all time, I'm there with you." The irony of recalling the phrase on that evening was not lost on her.

Geri felt the tenseness in her body relaxing as she remembered why she placed the clock in the kitchen. It was where she did most of her work and too often lost track of time. Christian gave her the clock as a reminder to take time for herself. It was not just any old clock either. He had seen it in an antique store in London on one of his travels. He said the flower petals around the clock's face were so gracefully set that it made him think of her. The idea that he wanted to remind her not to work all the time was an added bonus. Christian was one of the reasons she so desperately wanted this to be the best book she had written. He had inspired her. Recovering her focus, Geri leaned forward to begin reading what she had written the night before.

G.M. - 11/12/09 - Title Unknown

What do you do when the end comes and you're not ready? For weeks Jasmine asked herself that question while holding on to an unbridled hope that there would be no need to reply. Tonight was the first time she allowed herself to consider that the loss was inescapable.

The optimism that had kept her grounded in the belief that he would return was now fleeing from her very soul. Someone once told her that when death begins your life flashes in front of you. Although she knew the expression did not literally apply to her situation, she wondered if it was why the imagery of their time together seemed to be moving across her window like a movie screen. Was she giving in so completely that her mind was projecting what her heart was afraid to accept?

The snow had fallen heavily all day reminding her of the season. Winter had captured the brittle landscaping in front of her home. A cold white blanket was now covering the evidence that there was ever a slither of grass or the red gold of autumn leaves skipping across her lawn.

As she stared out the window the scene seemed to imitate her life, signifying that the fertility and swelling of the pregnant ground – their ground – had been put to rest. She touched the window pane and felt its frostiness. The coolness mocked the warmth of the room. Jasmine stood quietly giving way to the chill that ran through her body. Her hope that he would return was unceremoniously released into the cold wind.

To think that just weeks ago the balmy breezes of Indian summer streamed through the window causing the silky white curtains to dance in the air. There were children playing on the sidewalk and cars driving by with their tops down. The curtains blowing in front of her were directed by her arm to rest behind her back as she anxiously awaited his arrival. Music came from her neighbors' open window and she moved without realizing it to the beat. It had been days since she heard from him and Jasmine knew that something was terribly wrong. The last time they spoke he said he would be there later, but later never came.

Remembering it all tonight, she leaned closer to the window and let her breath cast an icy film on the glass. She drew a circle in the mist and placed her lips in its center. "I miss you so." Allowing the lightness of her love to push away the heaviness of her loss, she envisioned how it would be to step through the circle, right at that moment. Would the snow feel like it was cascading over her or would it gently caress only her face? Whichever occurred she knew that if she caught the snowflakes on her tongue they would melt and vanish into the air. The warmth of her body would momentarily control the icy crystal, and instead of feeling helpless, she would feel a sense of power. She would turn everything around.

As if to will the snow and the wind to stop, Jasmine pressed the palm of her hand firmly against the window, covering the circle and the imprint of her lips. The wind pushed snow continued to flog the lamp post mercilessly until it piled and hardened around the base. Releasing her hand, she contemplated how something that moved so freely could at once have no movement at all. Although she felt she was handling it, her pain had created an unmovable pile at her very core.

He was simplicity laced with a stark contrast of complexity caused by painful life experiences. His presence was illuminated by the fiery passion he felt about many things and a gentle compassion that seemed to conflict with his no nonsense self-confidence. In time, she understood that the difference between him and some of the other men she knew was that they chose rage in place of passion and selfishness in place of self-confidence.

Jasmine had felt at home with him. Every "good morning" they spoke was like an echo of years past, causing her to feel like they knew each other in another life. They would dance to the smooth sounds of music she had forgotten, music he reintroduced. The dance would begin in the middle of anything.

A glance across the room was a signal to celebrate with the twirls and head tossing that took on the magic of music heard and not heard. Joy filled memories now moved in the dust particles of the rooms in her house reminding her of those times. Sometimes she still felt them playfully bouncing across her bed when she climbed in alone and shifted to get comfortable. Waking after sweet dreams, she could feel his arms around her and hear him whisper, "It will be fine."

As she walked in places they had frequented, she could smell him in quick breezes that moved across her face. It was the clean earthy scent she pulled through her nostrils the first time she held him, vowing never to forget it.

Moving beyond the disquieting pain, the memories now flooded through her mind. She could almost feel the warmth of his touch and desired him the way she did the first time. It was as if she was standing in the center of everything she experienced with him, painfully considering that theirs may have just been a journey that had to end. She knew the risk – the risk she would someday talk about with those who had no idea. Until then she would wrestle alone with whether it had been worth it to give so much only to be left with so little.

The phrase 'it's better to have loved and lost, than never to have loved at all' ran fleetingly across her mind. "Right." She smiled to herself and let the curtain fall from her hand.

Jasmine walked to her bed willing the tears in her heart to fall as gently as the curtains had fallen in the warm breezes and as heavily as tonight's falling snow. What a relief it would be to feel the tears burning her cheeks and melting the pain that seemed to cover every part of her.

She wished she could curse the love they shared with each tear, but they would not come. Just as she could see but not hear the snow fall outside her window, somehow all she continued to experience was the calm quietness of grace. Grace, the contradiction to sorrow and the conqueror of pain swelled deep within her. It was a calmness that did *not seem real. Her fear was that the quietness would go away in the middle of a room full of people. That it would be in that moment of exposure she would scream and cry and indeed curse their love. But in truth the spirit of grace had silenced the screams coming from her heart.*

Like the coldest snow, grace had somehow put her pain to rest. Grace had kept her from losing her mind. Grace had become her closest friend and tonight "Grace" was still there. She turned out the light believing that someday it might all make sense. But for now...

"But for now – what?" Jasmine's question spun off the page onto Geri's lips. Was it a rhetorical question or did she not have the answer?

"Enough for tonight." Geri sighed heavily. It was not a sigh of resignation. With it came the feeling that she was releasing something other than what was holding her attention in that moment. She did not stop to consider what it was. What she had written over the past couple of days was better than she remembered, but still she had nothing else to add.

Turning off the computer she contemplated how time had moved so quickly over the last several months. Had time run out for the book just as it had run out for her? Was there even a story to be told? Would any of her readers benefit from it if it was told? Not wanting to think about it anymore she repeated "Enough for tonight" and got up from the table. Before heading to her bedroom Geri glanced at the clock again. A shiver ran through her body causing her to wrap her arms around herself. Trying not to think anything of it, she turned off the kitchen light. The lingering scent of unlit jasmine and juniper candles rested lightly in the air. Geri breathed in deeply with the hope that the aroma would begin to transform her confusion into peaceful rest. The timed light on the side of her bed was still casting a glow but would shut off soon. Sitting on the edge of the bed she wondered if being able to end the story in the book the way she wished hers had ended might have been the reason she wanted to write it in the first place. There had been constant changes in her life for three years. Some were great things and some really difficult. Some she had control over and others were completely out of her control. Like Jasmine's story, it all seemed to be the mere cycle of things. Tomorrow was the anniversary of one of the most difficult in her life cycle. Tomorrow would once again mark the date of hearing about Christian's death. As the thought pierced her mind, the bedside light went dark. Fully dressed, Geri pulled the comforter over herself and got into her usual sleeping position. It was always facing the other side of the bed where he once slept.

Geri closed her eyes and ran her hand across the pillow. Familiar nighttime tears filled the corners of her eyes as she wrapped herself in her arms the way she did a few minutes before in the kitchen.

Recalling the feel of Christian's embrace she whispered "Good night, my love." Her nightly prayer – the one taught to her by her grandmother – came next. "Let my spirit rise and meet You in my being even as I lay my head in slumber. Let me be what is good and faithful in You. Give me love and rest in the belief that all of these things are true. Give me strength and courage when I meet You in the next day. Amen." Sleep came softly.

Chapter 1

Geri Renee Michaels was named after her grandfather Gerald Reynard Dixon who was killed in a horrible car accident three days before she was born. They say that when someone close to you dies there is often the birth of a new loved one waiting to soften the experience. Geri remembers her mother once telling her how significant it was that she was born three weeks early. It was a short labor. There were no complications and no concerns about her health. Perhaps the stress of losing her father had caused the premature birth. No matter. Geri Renee was perfect.

Appreciating being named after her mother's father came easily, but as a little girl Geri was not sure she liked the idea of having what seemed to be a nickname. In her mind "Geri" was merely a nickname for "Gerald" a boy's name at that. She wondered why she could not have her own name, Jennifer maybe, and then she could decide if she wanted to be called Jenny. Or at least she could have been named after someone special like Dorothy in "The Wiz." She saw the movie for the first time on television at seven years old. Although it was a movie about someone's dream, Geri connected with its relevance to her life. She too was dealing with all kinds of obstacles that seemed to be blowing her life apart like a tornado.

Dorothy in the Wiz was quiet, but strong. Also, Dorothy was smart, pretty and at times funny. They were all the things Geri's grandmother said described her. Geri renamed her dolls after the other characters in the movie and like Dorothy's friends they were the ones she turned to in times of trouble. She even had a special pair of shoes to put on if she needed them. They were not shiny and red like Dorothy's, but they would do. Every now and then her mother would ask, "Why don't you wear your new shoes for church instead of those scuffed up school shoes?"

Geri would respond, "I'm saving them for a special occasion."

Soon enough Geri would understand that good friends were to be cherished and that her power was sometimes in her feet no matter what kind of shoes she wore. That power allowed people to walk away from unhealthy situations and walk toward something good and better. One of her sayings was "Sometimes better still ain't good."

Looking back, Geri's fascination with names began when she was seven years old. She asked her mother what the girl name was for Gerald. To her dismay she was told it was "Geraldine". She had just found out that her second grade teacher's name was not just Ms. Hayes, but Ms. Geraldine Hayes. Ms. Hayes had been sending notes home almost every day complaining about her daydreaming in class. She was convinced that Ms. Hayes' name should have been

Ms. Tattletale.

Geri wondered why Ms. Tattletale could not respect that there were things requiring her attentive concentration even in the middle of learning about full sentences. She would lower her head in embarrassment each time the teacher called her out, when all she wanted to do was say,

"Ms. Hayes, I have been writing full sentences since I was five years old."

Such a response might have stopped her teacher from asking that particular question on that particular day, but would have caused a mighty price to pay at home. She could imagine the note reading "Miss Michaels is disrespectful and I need you to come in to talk about it." The visual of her mother's reaction made her cringe and keep her mouth shut until one afternoon she spoke under her breath without realizing the latter part of her thoughts were about to be heard. Before she could stop herself, the words just popped out of Geri's mouth. She said, "Why don't you ever ask what I'm thinking instead of saying, 'Miss Michaels, do you want to tell the class what I just said?'

Geri's eyes got as big as saucers when she realized what happened. Ms. Hayes did not look happy as she walked towards her.

"Excuse me?" Ms. Hayes said in a higher pitched voice than usual.

"Nothing, Ms. Hayes." Geri replied.

An earnest expression that veiled sheer fear covered Geri's face. To her surprise and relief the teacher just looked intently into her eyes for what seemed forever then turned around and walked back to the front of the room. The class snickered until Ms. Hayes caught the eye of Sarah, the little girl sitting across from Geri. Getting the eye always meant 'stop whatever you are doing'. No one wanted to take the chance that they would be next.

Half expecting that she would get another note sent home and thinking she might as well get it over with, Geri lingered after the bell rang for dismissal. As she approached the desk, Ms. Hayes looked up and said, "Be better tomorrow, Miss Michaels."

With another sigh of relief, Geri walked quickly out the room before the teacher could change her mind and send a note to her parents.

"Be better tomorrow" became a phrase that would resonate with her for years. It was the phrase that she eventually extended to her idea that being better did not mean being good. But in the meantime, the experience with Ms. Hayes made her question if a person's name actually was a reflection of who that person was. The notes and frequency of being embarrassed had become synonymous with her teacher's name.

In Geri's young mind, tattling was one of the worst attributes a person could have. A couple of days after the classroom situation, she asked her mother,

"Mommie, would you buy me a book about what names mean?"

Geri was certain that the meaning of her teacher's name would reveal something awful about her.

"Why do you want a book about names, Geri? Don't you have enough books already?" Her mother asked unsuspectingly.

Mrs. Michaels knew that her daughter was really smart, but that kind of book was a little advanced even for her.

"I need it to look up names and the meanings for something I'm doing." Geri explained feebly, letting her mother conclude that it was for a school project. After all, it was a school project of sorts.

"Okay. I'll pick one up as soon as I can." She smiled as she responded.

She also thought, "I know Geri is up to something."

"Thank you, thank you, thank you, Mommie!" Geri shouted as she skipped from the room before her mother could ask any more questions.

A few days later her mother presented the book to her. Appropriately it was called "Names to Live By."

"Here you go, Miss." She held the book teasingly before releasing it into her daughter's hand.

"Thank you!" Geri said, as she gushed with delight at the title and then held the book to her chest. Still holding it as if afraid that someone might take it from her, she walked away anticipating what she might find in its pages.

After dinner that evening she began her investigation. The names Gerald, Geraldine, Victoria which was her mother's name and Elatine, her grandmother's full name, were the ones she looked up immediately. She got the spellings out of the big family Bible. The meanings were in short sentences with words she already knew or could look up in the dictionary. She grimaced when she thought that Ms. Hayes did do something right by helping them learn how to use the dictionary instead of giving the answers about meanings or correct spelling of words.

Geri was happy to learn through her research that the name, "Gerald" meant a mighty spear and "Geri" was short for "Geraldine" which was the feminine version of Gerald. Standing in front of the dining room mirror with book in hand, she looked at herself and said, "My name is Geri and I am a mighty spear."

The mirror hung a little higher than she was tall and she could barely see her whole face. Nonetheless, she gave herself a big grin of appreciation before going back to the seriousness of her discoveries.

She was not sure what to do with how the meaning of the name Geraldine discounted her notion about Ms. Hayes. She was sure that Victoria meaning "victory" was right on target and easily applied it to her mother's personality. At seven and a half years old "victory" was narrowly defined, but she believed that her mother had victory in everything she did. She was especially victorious in making her point in the conversations she would overhear between her mother and father. She knew this because her father would often say, "You win, Victoria" and the conversation would end. She added her mother's ability to make the best birthday cakes on the block to the equation.

The name "Elatine" on the other hand, was nowhere to be found in the book. She decided to define it herself, writing the definition in the right margin next to "Gerald." Elatine "Strong and lovely. Also, Geri Michael's grandmother."

When she considered looking up her father's name, she realized that she did not know what it was. He was "Daddy" and everyone else referred to him as "Michaels." She had not thought it odd until now and wondered why his name was not in the big Bible. She decided to investigate later and that she did.

"Mommie, I have everybody's name but Daddy's. What's it?" Geri asked her mother curiously.

"First, it's 'What is it?' Not, 'What's it?' Your father's name is Samuel." After responding, Victoria wrote the whole name on a piece of paper. Samuel Morgan Michaels was her father's name. Geri immediately looked up the name and was astonished that Samuel meant a name of God. She decided to tuck the knowledge away for some other time. It was too confusing to even think about then. She said to herself, "Daddy doesn't even go to church."

A couple of days had gone by since she found everyone's name. Excited about sharing her discoveries, Geri sat on the edge of the living room sofa until her mother got home from work. Grandmother Ella was there every day she got home from school, but she wanted to tell them both at the same time. In her estimation nothing that exciting had crossed the dining room table that she could remember.

She had placed the book with its marked pages in the center of the table. Waiting patiently but bursting with enthusiasm she sat in what was usually her father's seat. Her news was that important! Finally the moment came.

The two women looked at her and then each other. Grandmother Ella whispered, "What on earth could have this child looking like she just ate the canary." It couldn't be bad because she was beaming.

"Guess what?" Geri belted out.

"What?" Victoria and Ella spoke at the same time.

"Open it. Open to the pages." Geri's tone was shrill with excitement. She slid the book over to her mother. If excitement was measured by the width of a smile, it was clear that Geri's could not have been greater.

Geri held the sides of her face as if to make sure the smile and excitement stayed put. She was proud about her discoveries. It was information she thought no one in the family knew but her. Leaning closer to Victoria, Grandmother Ella smiled and nodded her head. Careful not to correct her granddaughter's belief that no one else knew what she was presenting to them, she looked at Geri and said,

"I have the smartest granddaughter in the whole wide world!"

That moment opened the opportunity for Ella to talk about her husband and share some other things she thought her granddaughter should hear. In the midst of the conversation the idea that a name could tell anything about a person did not hold weight.

"It's the person who makes the name good or bad and not vice versa." Ella began the conversation with these words.

"Character. Good character is a good thing." Victoria chimed in. "Your grandfather had real good character." Ella added as she reached over to hold Geri's chin in her hand.

"Gerald Reynard Dixon was strong with a heart as deep as the ocean." Ella continued.

Right then it was as if no one was in the room but Geri and her grandmother who seemed to be summoning the spirit of Gerald Reynard. She looked past her grandmother to see if her mother was still there. She was sitting quietly with her eyes closed.

Mrs. Ella Dixon was much taller than Victoria, Geri's mother. Unlike Victoria's small slim frame, Ella was plump with perfectly rounded hips and bosoms. Geri thought her skin was the color of the lightly browned Toll House cookies she made for her at least once a week, without the chocolate chips that is.

For as long as Geri could remember her grandmother wore her hair pulled back tightly either in a braid wrapped around the back of her head or falling down the center of her back. Until it changed to gray, Ella's hair was almost jet black and thick as the mane of a well-groomed thoroughbred.

Grandmother Ella always smelled of the patchouli oil she used to keep her body soft. Often the smell was laced with the sweet thing she had made that day. To be hugged by her grandmother was sheer joy.

Now standing in front of Geri, Ella wrapped her arms around her granddaughter and moved them both to a silent rhythm. She whispered softly into Geri's ear, "Little One, I want you to grow up to be just as strong, to have as good of a heart, and to make sure one don't outweigh the other."

"When you are strong, you can afford to have a good heart. Make sure one evens out the other." Ella spoke into the room.

Some of the words she heard that day were ones Geri would hear for years to come. Ella would place her hand on her hip and look directly into Geri's eyes.

"Be strong Little One and have a good heart. Make sure one evens out the other." If placing your hand on your hip and looking squarely in someone's face meant you were serious about what you were saying, Geri got it. It was a little intimidating and obviously a grandmother's right of expression because her mother never did it. Maybe when and if she had grandchildren and it was really necessary, she would do the same. In the meantime, practicing on her dolls had been good enough.

That day Geri found out a lot about names and people. The purpose of getting the book was to justify her ill thoughts about "Ms. Hayes." She had gotten so excited about her family's names that she had totally forgotten about Ms. Hayes. It was her mother who interjected her teacher's name in their conversation.

"Guess whose name has the same meaning almost as your grandfather?" Victoria said.

"Who?" Geri asked.

"Ms. Hayes. Your teacher." Victoria answered and was not surprised when Geri gasped so loudly.

"But she's so mean!" Geri protested.

Placing her hand on top of her granddaughter's, Ella gave it a gentle squeeze and said, "Now. You should be happy that Ms. Hayes cares enough about you to want you to pay attention in class. It shows she has good teacher quality."

Unknown to Geri, Victoria had inquired about the type of book Geri needed through Ms. Hayes who took the opportunity to share her concerns about Geri daydreaming in the class.

"Mrs. Michaels, Geri has been a little distracted lately, but I think she'll be okay. I don't think there is anything to be alarmed about. She is such a smart child."

Ms. Hayes spoke not knowing why her young pupil had requested the book. "As for the book, we aren't studying anything about names." Ms. Hayes continued with,

"Maybe it's just a sign of her inquisitiveness. She is a smart one, your daughter."

The same evening she spoke with Ms. Hayes, Victoria asked Geri if everything was okay at school. Geri responded as usual, "Its okay." And now tonight, after talking it through with her mother and grandmother it was clear to Geri that Ms. Hayes' faults as she saw them had nothing to do with her name. That was easy for her to accept since the name Gerald meant good things.

As much as Geri enjoyed the conversation with Ella, she still held back on the thing that was really bothering her. The truth was that questions about names did not begin to describe the seven year olds concerns. In her childish mind her dislike of Ms. Hayes was due to her calling her out in class. She was trying to make sense of why her teacher did not see that something was really wrong. If she really cared she would have seen that. Why didn't anyone see that something was wrong?

For months the boy next door had been her greatest challenge. He would come outside when he saw her playing with her dolls or reading a book behind the big oak tree in her back yard. All of the houses on her street were attached and most did not have trees.

Not only were there no trees, but most of them had fences prohibiting neighbors to go from one yard to the next without coming through a gate which was usually locked. The Michael's family did not have a fenced in yard and that was fine when they shared Bar-B-Q with the Lewis family next door. Griffy – Griffith Lewis – was not interested in Bar-B-Q.

Weather permitting Geri preferred to go outside to play after school instead of sitting in the house listening to her grandmother's television shows. Griffy seemed to know just when she would be out there and just how to do what he was doing without anyone seeing.

"What you doing?" He would kneel in front of her and ask the question.

"Playing." The first time Griffy asked, Geri thought he was really interested. But even then she wondered why he was asking a question that had such an obvious answer.

"Yeah. What you playing?" Griffy put his hand on her shoulder.

"Dolls. What does it look like?" Geri responded calmly.

"Nothing. You so dumb." He stood up and left

Geri was not sure what to make out of it. She put him out of her mind and went back to playing with her dolls.

Two days later, around the same time, Griffy found her playing under the tree with the trunk wide enough to hide them both.

"Hey little Geri. What you doing?" He bent down in front of her, this time close enough for her to smell the mustard that was caked in the corner of his mouth.

"Don't you want somebody to play with you out here?" Griffy saw that she was staring at his mouth. He wiped it with his thumb.

"No. I don't need anybody to play with me. I have my dolls and me." Geri answered back and tried to push him away.

Griffy's expression changed from the false smile to anger, but he quickly went back to the smile.

"Don't be so mean." He said now looking at her hands. He was already thinking about how he wanted her to touch his private parts.

"I'm not mean. I just don't want to play with you." Geri's answer was muffled by what now was an instinctual fear.

Griffy rubbed her shoulder and then her chest. He asked "What's that?" Clearly she had no breast, but he stopped his hand where they would have been.

She answered "What's what?" Still feeling afraid for reasons she could not understand, she was even more puzzled by his question. Looking at her in a way she thought was strange he did not answer, but moved his hand to her leg. At that moment Geri knew something was definitely wrong and pushed his hand away.

"You better leave me alone".

His response was "You so dumb. Ain't nobody doing nothing to you. You dumb and a scaredy cat!"

Geri considered his response and decided to just be prepared to ignore him the next time he came out. It was the next time, however, that he said nothing to her.

This time he bent down on his knees in front of her, grabbed her hand and held it between his legs. He used his other hand to press her shoulder against the tree so she could not move.

Geri's eyes grew wide as she tried to cry out, but nothing came from her mouth.

Griffy kept rubbing her hand against his privates and making little noises. He put his mouth on her neck and bit it. Tears ran down Geri's face, but still no words came out of her mouth.

Griffy pressed his head on her chest and let out a strange whimper. He let her hand go.

Geri could feel that his pants were wet. She thought he had peed on himself. Griffy smiled a devilish smile and said, "Don't you tell nobody about this or I will kill you and your family. You hear?" He looked dead into her eyes.

Geri shook her head. The tears were streaming heavily down her face as she put her hand over where he had bitten her. There was no mark. She then realized that it was his chapped lips that felt like teeth.

Griffy stood up and said, "You hear!" Then he ran off.

Around the same time Ms. Hayes began reprimanding her for daydreaming in class. How she wished it was just daydreaming about something good. Instead it was about how she could stop what was happening to her behind the big oak tree. Since promising her mother that she would be more attentive in school and feeling grateful that her teacher did not punish her for disrespectfully mumbling under her breadth, she tried to figure it out during lunchtime. She was a loner, sitting by herself, not talking with anyone was nothing out of the ordinary.

Again Geri wished Ms. Hayes had asked what she was daydreaming about. Then she may have felt like she had to tell the truth. But for now, she felt like she was on her own. If you are strong shouldn't you be able to do something about what is not right? After the third time it happened she decided she would never again go outside after school. She would stay in the house even if it meant looking at afternoon television shows with her grandmother.

Soon after making the decision to stay in the house, she noticed that Grandmother Ella would leave as soon as her father walked in the door. They didn't even speak. He would turn off the television when she left and the house would be silent except for her mother cooking in the kitchen. She would hear whispers between her mother and grandmother before he came in, but she could not make out what they were saying. Geri was not sure if it was always that way or if she just had not noticed before. Maybe because she was outside sometimes when the one came and the other left Maybe it had something to do with her. Maybe they even knew about Griffy and were whispering about the curse she asked her grandfather to place on him. Would she be the one to get in trouble instead of him? She was afraid to ask.

Geri also noticed that lately her parents were not talking to each other and because she herself was not much for talking, almost nothing was being said. Her mother was gaining weight in her stomach and Geri was smart enough to know that meant she was pregnant. But nobody said anything about it. She was living in a house where everybody was keeping secrets, including her.

The only talking was her parents' late night yelling. Sometimes she heard her mother crying in the kitchen in the middle of the night. She wanted to go to her and say, "Mommy, remember your strength." She knew, however, that her mother would shoo her away. Now she shooed her even when she wanted to talk about how she was trying to pay attention in class and all the good things the teacher said to her but never sent notes about. One night she had the unexpected resolve to tell her mother what Griffy had done to her.

The dark hallway benefited from the light coming from the living room. The only sound in the house was the humming of the refrigerator that she now heard as she sat at the top of the stairs. Imagining the comfort her mother would give after hearing about her problem, Geri made her way to the living room. The quiet movement of her daughter startled Victoria.

"What are you doing up? Do you know what time it is? Go back to bed, Geri." Victoria's reprimand was gentle, but Geri knew it was not to be challenged.

Her mother was holding something in her hand that dropped to the floor when she turned around. Instead of bending over to pick it up she pulled her daughter to her and gave her a hug. Unlike the scenario that Geri pictured, Victoria's hug ended with shooing her away.

"Go back to bed. School's tomorrow."

Geri wanted to tell her that it was Friday night, but like her resolve to share what was happening to her had left so had the desire to say anything but "Good night, mommy."

Tired of being confined to the house to avoid Griffy, the next day Geri decided to take things into her own hands. She put on her special "Dorothy" shoes and went out empty handed. No toys or books were necessary for her entertainment, she was on a mission.

She sat behind the big oak tree with her arms around her knees, looking around constantly and ready to jump to her feet when he came near. This time she would stand with her hand on her hip like Grandmother Ella and tell him that she would also burn his house down if he touched her again. And not only that, she would get her Grandfather to cast a spell on him from heaven so he could not walk or see ever again!

Weeks went by and no Griffy. Geri thought that her grandfather may have already put a spell on him to protect her. She felt safer each time she went out to play. But one day, seemingly out of nowhere Griffy appeared. Geri tried to gather up her dolls and her book to leave.

"You want some help?" He asked. "No." Geri spoke firmly.

"Okay. I'll leave you alone". Griffy responded nonchalantly. Thinking that he would leave Geri sat back down.

He did not leave. He squatted in front of her quickly and moved his hand to her inner thigh and squeezed it. Before she could say anything, he put his other hand over her mouth.

"Don't move." He said in a low threatening voice.

With one hand still over her mouth and now on his knees, he put his other hand down his pants and began rubbing himself, uttering groans that were now familiar to Geri. As the hand in his pants moved faster he pressed her mouth harder. It had begun to hurt, but still she could not move. Tears ran down her face. She wanted to close her eyes to see if she could wish herself to disappear. She thought he was doing the same thing with his eyes shut tightly as he groaned and bit at his lip. Suddenly it was over. He opened his eyes and released his hold on her. He stood up slowly with his hand still down his pants.

"If you tell I'm gonna burn down your house while everybody is sleeping."

Again fear suffocated any words that otherwise might have come out of Geri's mouth. She was stunned by the whole thing, particularly the fact that her grandfather had not protected her. And even more so because Griffy said he would burn down her house. That was what she had asked Grandfather Gerald to do to his house. She was confused. She asked herself why he had not protected her.

"Because he's dead!" Geri heard the words come out of her mouth. She almost did not recognize her own voice. It was anger. She sat quietly under the tree for what seemed like hours. No one called for her. And as usual no one had seen what happened.

Things changed. Everyone and everything around her was changing. If only Grandfather Gerald was still alive, he could make things better. Sometimes she wished his heart "As big as the ocean" would appear and swallow them all up, swish them around in that body of water, then spew them out onto dry land. They would come out happy.

They would dry themselves off and go about the day not even remembering what happened. But no bit of imagery could alter what eventually happened. Her parents separated. She and her mother moved in with Grandmother Ella who lived on the other side of town.

It was a confusing time. Geri was now just eight years old. So much had happened in one year. Moving meant they would be far enough away so that Griffy could not find her even if he wanted to. That was a good thing, and for once it seemed "better was good". It no longer mattered that her mother did not know her daydreaming began with trying to figure out how to get him to stop touching her or how to tell someone when he said if she did he would burn down her house. Still, once they moved every now and then Geri would stand on the sidewalk in front of the house and look both ways to see if she saw him.

Moving also meant Geri had to go to another school. It was the end of the school year so she would start fresh in another grade. To her surprise Ms. Hayes gave her a pretty journal as a going away present. She hugged her and said maybe this will help you with some of your thoughts.

Geri hugged her back and said, "Thank you, Ms. Geraldine." Ms. Hayes didn't know it, but calling her Ms. Geraldine was a compliment.

After moving Geri rarely saw her father. It was not until she was a teenager that she knew or thought she knew what caused the break between her parents. She was supposed to have left the house to go to the library when she overheard their telephone conversation and presumed they were talking about what happened. Apparently, he believed her mother had an affair. On her end she could hear her mother refuting the allegation and saying that even if he believed it, it was not an excuse for his being such a poor father.

Wishing she had not heard any of it, Geri remembers rolling her eyes and muttering, "Unh" under her breath. She left the house for the rest of the day and never asked about what she overheard or if what she thought she heard was right. To discover that her father had put them out made an imprint on her life. She would never, ever, ever place herself in a position to depend on a man to take care of her in any way.

Ella died when Geri was seventeen years old. They had lived with her for nine years. She could only imagine how hard it was for her mother to lose the one person who seemed to provide stability and certainty in her life. She never showed it, but every now and then Geri could tell how deeply her mother missed her. On occasion she would sing, "When you are strong, you can afford to have a good heart. Make sure one evens out the other."

Sometimes she would sing loudly. When that happened Geri would offer to help with the laundry or something. Geri smiles each time she finds herself humming the tune when under a lot of stress. She gives it her own melody, but each time she is conscious of the words silently repeating them over and over in her head.

In her reflections she thinks about how her childhood and teenage years helped to shape the way she saw things for years to come. She approached life in a way that took her places that were hard to stay in and even harder to leave. It was natural for her to respond to the needs of those who were crying out for help, and she was thankful for knowing how. Her grandmother and mother were her examples of doing what you can to make things work. She wished she had paid more attention to the way they handled letting go of what was unfixable or causing them to lose the balance between having a good heart and being strong.

Every now and then the memories including her parents' divorce and the telephone conversation between her mother and father about her younger sister, seemed to wipe out every good and perfect thought she had.

Geri was an adult before she told anyone about being sexually abused. She carried the silent shame and related feelings of guilt about it all in her heart for years.

The first time she spoke her abuser's name was when she was in therapy trying to make sense of her life. All of her past had served its purpose in helping to shape who she had become. Mostly she had been able to glean good lessons from bad situations. Every experience helped to strengthen her compassion for others, especially children.

Today, when she speaks in front of people on the issue of child abuse in any form, she begins with, "He was seventeen years old. I was seven."

She sometimes ends with saying, "At some point the hideous and hidden circumstances have to give light to the unadulterated truth, and that leads to recovery. We have to work on transforming what was ugly into God's purpose for our lives." It took her faith, therapy as a young adult, and finally feeling free to tell her family to heal the broken places that repeating Grandmother Ella's mantra about "strength, heart and balance" hadn't fixed. During the process she grew to understand that taking care of children would be one of her life's missions.

Though she had none of her own, she loved children and wished she could make sure that every child was safe and cared for. She was determined to make sure that her difficult childhood would not have been in vain. In her mind there was no greater aggression than that suffered against children. Her heart ached with the understanding that the violence of child abuse was universal and seemed to be taken for granted since it just did not stop. Helping to make it stop was part of her "splendid vision," a term that her mother used to describe it in one of their moments of sharing.

Geri read somewhere that "Inspiration has in it the key to our freedom." She added that, "If we are to fully live our lives, we have to embrace inspiration's fiery passion. And, if it is truly a passion, others will benefit from our embrace." At least this was the way she saw it. Children were her passion especially "tween" children. You know the ones who are stuck in the middle somewhere between ages 8 and 13 not knowing what to do about anything. They are too old to just whine and get positive attention, and too young to make decisions that make any sense to anybody not even to them. Somebody has got to look out for them in a special way. She believed that she had been chosen as one of those some-bodies.

Chapter 2

A *Haven for My Children* was a crown jewel in Geri Michaels' accomplishments. She opened the center in the winter of '99. Her marriage had ended and coming home to Baltimore meant beginning a brand new life. What better way than to start her own business, one that cradled her passion for children.

Geri sometimes had to remind herself about the saying "When one door closes another one opens." It was one that she added to the things her grandmother taught her. She also believed that things happened in threes and sevens as signs of completion. It was good that each completion opened to a new beginning. "Three years married. Maybe Haven will be at least seven." This was what she told herself when she moved back home.

The job as CEO of Haven for My Children turned out to be something she loved and hated. She loved it because of what it allowed her to do, but she hated it because of why she had to do it. Haven was a place of temporary respite for abused children who needed care and treatment before being placed in a more permanent environment. When they got to her, they were sometimes malnourished. Some had been beaten or sexually abused so badly that in the case of a couple of the youngest girls, they would never be able to have children of their own.

Along with being a stopover for abused children, Haven's services included child and family therapy and consultation to the family court system. Her choice of staff was done with tremendous thoughtfulness. The children needed to be loved and nurtured in a special way, from the care that was given to them to the space where they would be able to rest and feel safe.

Geri was meticulous about every ounce of detail in the center and made certain that her staff maintained the same standards. The night before the center opened its doors she wrote an entry in her journal. It was two days before Christmas, her favorite holiday. She had been given what she thought at the time was the ultimate gift.

The entry read:

12.23.99

Inside our place are yellow walls and in some rooms the ceilings are blue with puffs of white clouds painted with distinction. I like cumulous clouds. It all sounds corny I know, but each bright yellow wall and shiny desk cupped with fresh flowers generates hope, love, and warmth.

When you walk into our front door you'll see a mural on the wall above the receptionist's head. A beautifully bright butterfly perched on the stump of a tree – its wings symbolizing rebirth and the strength to fly. Written across the sky are the words "Fear not, only believe." – this passage undergirds my life. Love, Beauty, Strength and the Willingness to Change is scrolled across the base of the scene. All of that is what I want for the children

Chapter 3

The sky was clear and the glare from the sun almost blinding. She was on a bus. It was trying to climb a hill – at least that's how it seemed. 'It's stopping. Why is it stopping? Where is the driver? Who's driving?' Fear crept in. "Hello!" No answer. Just the sound of a winding engine.

A big yellow sign was flapping in the wind next to the bus. It looked like cloth. When the bus started up again, the sign went with it. It was trying to say something to her. It had black letters scrolled all over it. She couldn't read what was written, but thought she heard sounds coming from it. It whispered something that was inaudible. Each time the words moved around on the sign. The question "What? What do you want?" kept running through her head, but she was unable to speak.

She tried to call out for the bus to stop so she could get off, but no sound came out of her mouth. It started moving faster and faster. She clinched the sides of the stiff brown seats trying to steady herself. The yellow sign was now flapping wildly trying to keep up. She could finally hear herself yelling. "Who's there? Who's there?" The bus started to slide down the hill. "No! Stop!" Her scream was drowned out by the sound of children laughing. She saw them outside the window and started pounding to break the glass...

Geri awakened startled by the dream. She sat up in the bed and looked around to make sure she was alone. She thought the sound of someone calling her name woke her from the deep sleep. Her heart was beating fast and the neck of her T-shirt was wet with perspiration. Steadying herself with her hands planted flatly on the bed, she took a deep breath to try to slow her heart rate. She wiped her forehead and pulled the cotton away from her body. Clearly no one was in the room with her, but a sense of foreboding was still present.

"It was just a dream, Geri. Just a dream." She repeated the words as if to help convince herself. She tried to go back to sleep, but even with her eyes closed the numbers on the alarm clock were glaring in her face. Turning away from the clock with the cover pulled over her head did not help. Now wide awake all she could think about was the alarm going off in an hour. "Okay. You win." With a sigh of resignation she rose up on her elbows and scanned the room again.

Barely the crack of dawn, the quiet in the house was interrupted by coffee beans grinding and a single bird outside her window calling for the sun to fully rise. The aromatic scent of coffee permeated the house reminding her of the mornings she woke up to the smell percolating in the electric pot in her grandmother's kitchen. It was always intoxicatingly inviting. Starbuck's had taken on the tradition in her house and it was comforting after the strange dream. As she made her way to the kitchen, she thanked herself for buying the automatic coffee maker. It was not close to how she felt being greeted by Grandmother Ella on those very early mornings, but it would do. The coffee wasn't bad either. Walking into the kitchen Geri saw the reflection of car headlights bouncing through the window. They were coming from her neighbor's driveway.

"Where could Sam Townsend be going this early in the morning?" Geri wondered.

"Humph, I bet that isn't even him." She was slightly amused. She had not turned on her kitchen light and considered that whoever it was could not see her peering nosily through the window. Raised up on her tiptoes to get a better look she thought it was probably some woman rushing home to get dressed for work with her tired happy self.

"Ms. Busybody." Geri laughed and closed the curtain.

"You're just jealous, Geri Michaels." This came out of her mouth as an afterthought, but it certainly was the truth.

She turned on the kitchen light and mused about how long it had been since she left anybody's house in the wee hours of the morning happy or not.

The night had not been restful and a hectic day was awaiting her. She wished she could just go back to bed, but when the coffee pot beeped it was the sign that her day had begun. She poured a cup of the hot liquid and inhaled its fragrance appreciatively before lifting it to her mouth. She turned on the local morning news.

"Let's see what's happening this morning." She spoke to the television.

Deana Sanchez, a bright and beautiful reporter recently hired to the station, was pointing to an ambulance.

"A young child was just placed in the ambulance. I was told that she had burns on her body, but just how badly burned they didn't say. The child's mother was pulled from the fire and they're saying that she suffered from smoke inhalation, but was not burned. The cause of the fire will be determined..."

The story was one being told too often lately particularly because the cause was almost always related to the use of space heaters. Geri turned the volume up when she saw the Fire Captain standing next to the reporter. He was stating how dangerous it is to go to sleep with heaters on.

"I certainly agree, sir. But since it's the only form of heat that some have, wouldn't it also be helpful if families knew which were the safest heaters to use and how to use them? Can the Fire Department educate the public on that, even if that means naming the companies whose heaters are not as safe as others?"

Geri liked her style. Sanchez always asked the next question. Seeing the news coverage made her think about how many children had fallen to tragedy in her town that year. She rattled off the incidences in her head and shuttered to think what would greet her that morning at work. Shifting gears she wondered why she had not heard the fire engine sirens when the Fire Station was right up the street. Was it because she was so deep into her dream that she did not hear them? Or maybe it was the siren that turned into the voice she heard calling her name. You know how dreams go. Turning the volume down on the television, she sat at the table trying to recall the rest of the dream. There was a bus that looked like one of those yellow school buses. She was alone on the bus and now that she thought about it, there was no driver. Trying to apply some logic to the scenario, she considered that it must have been on autopilot and being manipulated by something or someone someplace else. She remembered passing a lot of fields where what looked like hundreds of children were playing. She could tell that they were laughing and screaming happily, but she could not hear any of it.

Chapter 4

Still thinking about the dream Geri wondered why she could not have had one of those dreams that let you wake up with a smile on your face. The lightheartedness of a sweet dream thought was replaced by a sinking feeling inside her stomach. She remembered trying to call out for the bus to stop so she could get off, but no sound came out of her mouth. Remembering more she sat the cup on the table and said aloud, "It stopped. It stopped on a hill."

The sound of the alarm clock going off surprised her. Grateful she'd forgotten to reset it when she got up, she turned everything off in the kitchen and headed for the bathroom. She had been so focused on the dream that the time had gotten away from her. Waking up too early after a restless night was not a good way to start anyone's day, but at least she was not running late. A long hot shower might compensate for the tiredness.

Finally out the front door and checking to make sure she locked it from the inside she heard her neighbor's voice.

"Hey Ms. Geri." Sam said as he was getting into his car.

"Hi Sam. How are you?" Geri replied.

"I'm good. Just wish I could take the day off. Feels like one of those days you'd like to be outside playing." Sam said whimsically. He waited for her to respond before shutting his car door.

"I know what you mean." Geri said.

She thought about saying, "Seems like you already played, Mister. I saw that car leaving your house early this morning. But it ain't my business."

Instead she smiled and said, "Have a good day neighbor." She tried not to watch his car as he drove out of the driveway, but could not help herself.

Catching a subtle whiff of his cologne, the idea that perhaps she had not taken a good enough look at him since he moved next door loomed across her mind. She decided the next time she saw him she would ask him over for dinner. Maybe. Even if he was serious about the woman who spent the night, it would be nice to invite him over just to be neighborly. Whatever happened to that concept anyway? Conceding that it was really a strange morning, she waved again as he backed out of the driveway.

Traffic on the main road was more congested than usual. It was probably because of the sun glare. Feeling unsuccessfully for her sunglasses in the front part of her bag, she let down the visor. The cars in front of her started picking up speed and she adjusted hers. It would be a good half mile before the next stop light so she pressed her foot on the gas. The weather forecast called for a warm balmy day, but it was still cool enough to enjoy the morning breeze. Welcoming the fresh air, she let her window down half way.

"Stupid light!" She slammed on the brake. Fortunately there was no one behind her. She looked in the rearview mirror and moved back. Tired as all get out, she knew she should have taken the day off to get some much needed rest. Still that was no excuse. The light was not stupid, but her decision to go in might have been.

Fidgeting with her seatbelt made her think about the bus in her dream. There were no seatbelts. That was interesting. Wasn't it a school bus? "An empty school bus. Like my life." As if responding to someone with indignity, "My life is not empty" came unexpectedly out of her mouth. Her life was not empty. Maybe the dream was her subconscious telling her that she was not in the driver's seat of her life. Geri could feel a headache coming on. She had lots of them lately, but just popped a couple of aspirin and went about her day.

Honk, honk, honk. "Hey lady, any day now!" The light had turned green. A car was now behind her and the driver was yelling out the window and honking his horn.

"Maniac!" she muttered irrationally, but gestured with a friendly wave and moved on. "Why are people so impatient?" Her alter ego responded with "No, why are you over reacting?"

The turn on Water Street gave her a clear view of *A Haven for My Children*. It was 8:15 a.m. Just in time for her to do her 8:30 a.m. rounds.

She pulled into the parking lot and pulled the visor down again. She looked in the mirror and shook her head. The tiredness showed on her face. Deciding not to apply another coat of anything to her face, she flipped it back up. "It is what it is" came out of her mouth automatically. That statement often helped get her from point 'A' to whatever point she needed to be in the moment, but she never thought about the attitude that went along with it. Today she heard herself and frowned.

The sound of a plane flying lower than usual made her look up as she got out of the car. The sky was almost effervescent. It seemed bluer and the clouds puffier than she'd seen in a while.

"You sure are looking pretty good today!" The words moved from her mouth as if she expected a reply.

Geri looked around to see if anyone had heard her talking to the sky. Sure enough someone did. Carlton, the UPS delivery guy was just a few feet away. She could tell by his grin that he thought she was talking to him. Her immediate thought was,

"How could he think I was talking to him if I was looking up? Silly man."

Geri smiled as the thought ran through her mind.

"Hey Ms. Michaels. You looking good too! How you doing?" His greeting came with a little flirtatious slur.

"I'm fine, Carlton. How are you?" Still amused, she answered him with a polite smile.

Carlton had been the center's UPS man for a few months. She caught him looking at her a couple of times. Once she thought to say something, but considered that he might get embarrassed or even think she was flirting. Did he really think I was talking to him when I said, "Looking good?"

Geri walked into her building laughing to herself. He was really a nice guy. But really? Did he think she would say that to him?

The receptionist smiled quizzically at her when she approached the desk. She wanted to ask, "What's so funny, Ms. Michaels?" Instead she just greeted her with the usual,

"Good morning, Ms. Michaels."

Seeing the questioning expression on the receptionist's face, Geri responded,

"Good morning, Mai. You don't even want to know!"

"Okay." Mai responded with a chuckle.

Without looking back, Geri proceeded down the hall.

The children who were sent to Haven were there because something had gone horribly wrong in their homes. They were now in a strange place surrounded by people they did not know. They had to be confused and afraid even the ones who pretended to be tough. Their short stay was often set in confusion and fear that manifested as anger or withdrawal. To be honest, they all had something to be angry about.

There were eight beds that were often filled most of the week with children waiting for placement in foster homes. This week there were six children, four from one family who had been there for three days. Each morning Geri's rounds began with a visit to the cafeteria. When she got there today the children were sitting at the big round table eating breakfast with Tristan, one of the counselors. She went over to say good morning. One of the girls looked up and responded "Good morning", but the others kept their heads down or just looked at her with questions covering their faces. Geri pulled up a chair to join them and introduced herself with a smile and looked around the table asking their names.

Most of them responded so quietly they could barely be heard. In contrast one of the younger girls sat up straight in her chair and replied proudly.

"I'm Angela." The boy sitting next to her rolled his eyes.

"What a beautiful name, Angela." There was a resemblance between Angela and the boy who rolled his eyes. He looked like he was her older brother.

"And yours?" She looked at him directly and asked in an inviting tone. "My name is Juan. Juan Chaves." The anger in his voice was bated only by a hint of fear. Geri could see it in his eyes.

"Well, good morning Juan." Before she could say more, little Angela leaned over to touch her arm and spoke.

"What do you do here?" Angela gave her a big smile and waited for an answer.

"I see to it that you're taken good care of while you're here. Are you being taken good care of?" Geri responded to the child's infectious smile with a big grin and teasing wink.

Angela tried to wink back. She closed and opened both eyes quickly and started to giggle before answering "Yep!" Right before she was about to say something else Juan nudged her and said, "Be quiet. You talk too much."

Angela began to cry as easily as she had smiled. Juan poked out his lips as he folded his arms and placed them with his head on the table.

"It's okay Angela. Juan, its okay. But you shouldn't push your sister. How about a little apology to her."

Juan looked up at her and then to Angela. "I'm sorry."

It was not the most convincing apology, but then he put his arm around his little sister. Nodding her head and wiping her eyes Angela looked at Geri and gave her a much smaller smile this time. Geri winked again and turned to Juan. "That was nice that you apologized, Juan." Purposely lingering in her attention to him, she gave him a big smile.

Looking around the table she saw that most of the children were looking at her. Almost whispering she leaned over and said, "You guys have a wonderful day. I'll check in on you later."

"Take good care of these beautiful children, Tristan." Geri touched Tristan's shoulder before walking away. It was her way of saying "good job" without the spoken word.

With that pleasantry, she left the table and headed for the food counter. Tom Wade, the food prep supervisor, was sitting at a nearby table looking at the report he had prepared. She needed to meet with him about his budget.

It seemed a little high and she wanted a more detailed explanation about a couple of line items. The Budget Director was on medical leave which meant that some of the intercessory work that the staff member would have done was left up to her. She gestured to Tom to let him know that she was going to the kitchen to get a cup of coffee.

"Good morning, Sir." After getting her second and much needed cup, she sat at the table with him.

"What do you have for me?"

The meeting with Tom went well and once again she was thankful for being surrounded by such competent and loyal people. It was a blessing for the children and for her. She left the meeting knowing that everything was under control.

Mid-afternoon crept up on her before she knew it. Her rounds, the meeting with Tom, the phone calls made and returned along with the last meeting with her counseling staff required seamless attention. Finally back in her office the growling in her stomach was evidence that she had not eaten all day.

"It's lunch time." Remembering the promise she'd made to herself to start eating right, Geri shook her head as she said the words. She took a few M&M's out of the silver container on her desk and leaned back in her chair.

"Bon appétit!" She mimicked herself with a grand gesture and took another handful.

It was an unusually peaceful and quiet moment. Geri swiveled her chair to face the window. Surprisingly there was no activity on the street. Not even at the bus stop.

"Humph." She said quizzically.

It was almost as if the moment was giving her a blank canvas on which to paint her thoughts. Through her peripheral vision she could see the lights blinking on her telephone, but pretended that they were also a part of her blank canvas.

She concentrated on her breathing long enough to feel her body fully relax and her mind stream with it. The dream about the bus tried to intrude, but she pushed it away. Still the thoughts that may have even caused the dream crept through.

Geri was feeling the gentle press for her to face the need for change in her life. She had filled the lonely spaces with work for as long as she could and recently she had become restless and wanting. She could not remember the last time she had even dated, but could certainly remember that she had not been involved with anyone since her divorce. Was the empty bus a sign of her life? Sure, her life was busy, but was it full?

The quietness in the office and outside was still lingering. Geri walked over to the window and opened the blinds completely. There was a man standing on the corner apparently waiting for the light to change so he could cross the street. She could see him pushing the button on the post for the light to change over and over again.

"Why is he waiting? Nothing's coming." Geri almost grumbled the words.

The idea that he was waiting for the light to turn green when there were no cars coming made little sense to her. She closed the blinds slightly and walked back towards her desk with the thought of him standing on the corner waiting unnecessarily rummaging through her mind. The observation made her ask herself why she was waiting and what she was waiting for.

Suddenly the conversation she had with her friend Kyra a few weeks ago surfaced in her mind. Instead of sitting at her desk, she pulled out one of the chairs at the small table she used for meetings and sat down. With her arms folded on the table, she leaned forward as if to lean into the conversation that had already taken place. She and Kyra had met for dinner at "Divine Chocolat", a new restaurant on the wharf that promised to be one of her favorites. They served great seafood which was a staple in Baltimore. They also made outstanding chocolate mousse and the best chocolate chip cookies she had since her grandmother's Toll House cookies. They called the cookies something else, but they were the same and she was happy about it. She suggested to Kyra that they meet there and Kyra agreed.

"Hey, how about getting together Monday night for dinner?" Geri left the message on Kyra's cell phone.

It was the Thursday night before and although she would have wanted to get together over the weekend, she was already committed to go to a conference in Washington, DC. Even if it had to be delayed a few days, she was feeling the need to not only talk with her friend, but take a break from her boring routine as well.

Kyra called back the next morning.

"That sounds good. Where do you want to meet?" Kyra was glad that Geri had called.

Divine Chocolat. The new place on the pier. It's great. I think you'll like it." Geri's tone was light and airy now that she could look forward to their dinner.

"But we have to get there by 6:30 to make sure we get a good table. They don't take reservations." Geri accentuated the point about getting there early.

"Sounds good, love. See you then."

Kyra responded, "Gotta go. Got a patient waiting."

"Go on. Looking forward to it." Geri's response was almost cryptic, but that's how busy people sometimes communicate.

Geri had not seen Kyra in a while, so getting together would be a treat. Ms. Kyra, as Geri used to call her, was one of her best girlfriends at Baltimore's Dunbar High School. They met a couple years after Geri and her mother moved to Grandmother Ella's. Victoria enrolled Geri in an after- school program at a neighboring community center. Concerned that after two years Geri had not made any friends since their move, she thought an afterschool setting might lead to getting to know some of the neighborhood children. Victoria still had no idea that Geri had adopted Dorothy from the Wiz with all her friends whom she named her dolls after, as friends. Well, she did have some idea, but did not know what was behind it.

Kyra Andrews was one of the kids attending the afterschool program Geri remembers her being sassy with boys who liked to pull her hair. She was always threatening to "beat them up" in the park outside the building. Other than that, Kyra didn't have a lot to say until one day she approached Geri.

"So what's your name? And why are you here?" Kyra asked precociously...

"I guess the same reason you're here." Geri answered in kind.

Their stilted conversation sparked the beginning of a great friendship.

The now Doctor Kyra Andrews-Mason was a prominent OBGYN in private practice and on staff at Baltimore University Hospital. From the ninth grade on Kyra was the girl labeled too smart to be so pretty. She took every biology course available and was on the honor roll every marking period. With skin like caramel and sandy colored curly hair that she wore short, she looked like butter wouldn't melt in her mouth. With brains and beauty she was also fearless and had no problem telling anyone "I will beat you up in the park if you bother me." The other girls hated her and the boys were intimidated by her. Not knowing how to take her, almost everybody shunned her.

Geri, on the other hand, had grown into a little social butterfly. She was pretty in her own right with high cheek bones she'd inherited from her grandmother. Her hair was so long and thick that as soon as she was ten her mother cut it to shoulder length and gave her a mild perm. Geri did not like losing her hair, but she was happy not to go through the pain of having it washed and braided so tightly that it felt like her scalp would burst. Somewhere along the way, she adopted an "I don't care what anybody thinks" attitude mostly to cover up the low self-esteem that haunted her for years. Academically talented, Geri's gift for writing and drawing was developing. She had an entrepreneurial spirit. She didn't just write and draw. She sold her poetry in a book with a cover she illustrated to family and other classmates. At least she did this until she got bored and decided to join the drama club and student council for which she became president in the tenth grade.

When Geri and Kyra graduated from Dunbar High School, Geri went off to Howard and Kyra left for Michigan State. They vowed to keep in touch but after a few years, they lost track of each other. Who would have thought their first reunion would be in Chicago? Back then Kyra was doing her residency at University of Illinois and Geri was working while finishing her graduate studies at Northwestern. They ran into each other one afternoon at Marshall Fields on State Street. When they saw each other, both screamed. "Geri?" Kyra saw her first.

"Kyra? Get out of here!" Geri could not remember the last time she'd been so happy to see anyone.

That moment of reconnection would prove to be the rekindling of their friendship. They needed to catch up on their lives. Still standing in the middle of the store aisle, Geri asked,

"Where are you?"

"I'm at U of I doing my residency." Kyra was still beaming from their chance meeting.

"What about you?" Kyra asked.

"I'm working at an agency on the South Side and finishing my MSW." Geri responded.

"I can't even believe this. We have got to get together. How's your week?" Kyra was pulling out her business card as she spoke. She wrote her home phone number on the back before giving it to Geri.

"This week is crazy." Geri responded. They were doing an audit at her agency. It required all hands on deck.

"But what about Sunday afternoon? Mark and I go to church on 95th, but I can meet you on Michigan…what about at Ruby's? Do you know that restaurant?" Geri asked the questions while taking Kyra's card and giving her card to her long lost friend.

Both were married when they reconnected, but within a year each was seeking a divorce. They wondered if their finding each other after years of going to school and working in different places was so they would have someone to help them get through their personal problems.

Kyra ended up divorcing her husband Jim after finding him sprawled out on the floor with his nurse after they had apparently finished "doing it" – as Kyra would say.

"I will never date another doctor and I certainly won't marry one!" Kyra was now ranting. "They have this God complex thing going on. It makes them feel entitled to anything and to do anybody!" Kyra said still ranting.

Geri asked her, "So what's the difference between you being a doctor and him being a doctor?"

She knew that Kyra would just suck her teeth and roll her eyes, but she could not let the moment pass.

"It's the difference between good and evil. You didn't know that?" Kyra laughed, lightening the mood with her reply.

Geri was now remembering telling Kyra that her husband, Mark was even worst than Jim.

"Mark is the epitome of a man who constantly and carelessly fools around because he thought he should and could get away with it. And he's not a doctor!" She went further to say,

"Girl, if you opened the dictionary you just might find his face next to the word hoe and I do not mean a garden instrument." They both laughed but Kyra could feel Geri's pain.

"Not only that," Geri continued. "His face would be there next to the word and definition just grinning with pride!"

It was almost nine years later. Remembering her words about Mark, Geri laughed and said out loud, "It's the truth. Where's my dictionary?"

The two women were now living in Baltimore with little in their lives except work. After a long hiatus without being in a serious relationship, it seemed that both were ready to step back into the game. Sitting in her office thinking about the last time they got together, Geri couldn't help but compare the conversations they used to have in high school about their future goals, the conversations they had in Chicago after their divorces and the one they had a few weeks ago. It was abundantly clear that they needed a change.

Once they settled at their table Geri asked Kyra, "So, what's up my friend?"

"Girl, I am so tired of spilling myself out every day and then coming home to nothing but an empty bed that promises to lull me to sleep so I can wake up the next morning and do the same doggoned thing." Kyra was blunt and to the point.

The words were unexpected. Geri sat up and laughed. "Spilling? I never heard that before." Geri responded teasingly.

Kyra rolled her eyes. "I am, Geri. For some reason it's starting to take its toll." She replied.

The seriousness in Kyra's voice made Geri lean back in her chair and give pause to what she herself had been feeling for months.

"Look, I know just what you mean." Geri responded but looked down at the table to avoid Kyra's eyes.

Looking at Geri with probing eyes, Kyra folded her arms and said, "Well let me speak for me! I haven't spoken with you in a while, Ms. Girl. What's up with you? You seeing somebody?"

Kyra was all too familiar with how Geri would cast down her eyes when she was hiding something.

"Please!" Geri laughed unwittingly.

"You know that all I do is work, sleep and go back to work, just like you! I can't even remember what it means to see anyone." Geri continued. The conversation and the reason they needed to get together was now unfolding.

"Listen, I have been praying about it and everything else in my life." Geri could feel herself getting a little upset.

"You know what..." Before Geri could finish her sentence, her friend cut her off.

"I am at the point that I don't believe it's ever gonna happen." Kyra spoke in a matter of fact tone.

Kyra sat up straighter in the chair. "I'm sorry, Geri. I just had to get that out before you started with a pep talk that I can't hear right now. You know how you do."

Geri was a little annoyed by the interruption, but came back with, "You know what? As I was about to say, I've been thinking a lot about my life lately too. I am not ashamed to admit that it's getting kinda lonely around here." She did a sweeping motion around her body.

Kyra laughed. When she saw that Geri was not laughing with her, she touched her arm with the best sincerity she could muster and tried to say something encouraging. It did not work. She thought her friend's sweeping hand motion was hilarious and burst out laughing.

"Okay. See? I'm trying to be serious." Geri could not hold back her laughter either.

That evening Geri had wanted to share how making a change in her life had been nagging her for weeks. She decided to wait. Maybe it was not time for her to reveal what was on her mind with her friend. She had not processed it herself. It was good just having a night out to relax a little and laugh.

After the good meal that included the chocolate chip cookies for dessert Geri started feeling the familiar end of the day exhaustion. She said with a sigh,

"I'm fading, my friend. I think I'm gonna have to call it a night."

"It's that time for me also." Kyra said in agreement.

"I can't believe it's only 8:45. We really can't hang anymore." Geri was looking at her watch and at the same time taking her wallet out of her bag.

"I know, right?" Kyra answered.

"I promise not to let so much time go by." Geri said to her friend.

Seeing that the two women were winding down their evening, the waiter came over with the check. He placed it in the middle of the table.

"I've got this one sweetie." Geri spoke softly. She did not want the evening to end because it had been so good for her to spend time with who was now probably the closest person in her life.

"Okay. The next ones on me."

Geri put cash in the check folder and gestured to the waiter. She handed the folder to him and said "Thank you".

"Thank you. Do you need change?" The waiter asked.

"No, it's good. And the meal was great as always." Geri responded to the waiter.

"Are you ready?" She asked Kyra.

Kyra responded with a positive nod. The two friends walked out of the restaurant in silence. Kyra had parked in the lot across the street. Geri parked next door to the restaurant.

"I'm right here." Geri pointed to the restaurant parking area.

"Oh. I didn't even see that when I came in." Kyra said as she raised her arms to give Geri a hug.

"See you soon, girlfriend." Geri returned her friend's hug with a squeeze of encouragement.

They went their separate ways.

When she got home that night Geri thought about their dinner conversation and wished she had shared more with Kyra. Specifically she remembered the prayer she had planned to share with her. She said she would be happy even if she met someone who was not completely available to her. If she couldn't have it all, she'd settle for just a little. She recalled ending with, "As long as he isn't married, an ax murderer or crazy we can work something out." The concern was that he be able to fit into her current schedule. When she prayed the prayer she knew there was some foolishness in the request, but maybe foolishness was what she needed.

The next day Geri was convinced that she needed to do something to satisfy the compelling urgency she felt to change the way her life had glided along.

It was Tuesday, the day she always declared was her favorite day of the week at work. Walking into Tuesday feeling okay meant she had survived Monday and was prepared to press productively through the rest of the week. Seeing Kyra the night before was a bonus that would make this Tuesday even better.

Recalling the prayer she neglected to share with Kyra the night before caused her to look up at the ceiling and say, "God, I know that was crazy." It was so contrary to her belief that "every good and perfect gift" was available to her if she asked. She thought in response, "So why ask for so little?" Her next thought was one she had not been ready to receive. The disquieting truth was she was not sure she could handle it or moreover was not sure she had done enough to deserve it.

Realizing that she'd been lost in her thoughts for several minutes, Geri went back to her desk. She absentmindedly shuffled some papers from one side of her desk to the next. Blocking out the thought of handling and deserving something better, she murmured, "What shall I do?" For some strange reason the famous line from "Gone With The Wind" popped into her mind. The truth was, doing something different meant giving birth to something unfamiliar in her life. For a moment it scared her to death. Her eyes were suddenly directed to the paper weight on her desk inscribed with, "Fear not…" She lifted the paper weight and laid the palms of her hands on the papers as if there was a hidden answer in the stack.

Nothing came except her own words, "I'll go through and sign the things that need signing. That's what I'll do." With that she searched for her favorite pen and went back to work.

By the end of the day Geri had forgotten about the questions she asked herself about her life. She'd even forgotten about the "bus dream." Exhausted, all she could do was drive herself home, scramble some eggs for dinner, eat while loading the dishwasher and eventually crawl into bed. Another day had ended the same as the one before. She drifted off to sleep again while saying her prayers.

Chapter 5

Rest had become trivialized by the intrusion of the dream. Days of routine responses to the needs of children and the supervision of staff were now accompanied by fitful nights and mornings that came too soon. Exhaustion became the prevalent and common thread from the light of day through its return the following day. Sheer irony was becoming evident as Geri understood the purpose of the dream. It was time to turn her fatigue into the excitement she no longer experienced in anything she did. She was reminded of the movie "Get on the Bus" when a group of black men from the community headed to the Million Man March. She was in graduate school and studying for finals when the event occurred. How she wished she could have experienced such a plight to make a difference. The movie provided a powerful insight into how things can change even in route to a life changing event. Was she in that space and time in her own life? Were things changing for her, introducing her to newness that she had denied was necessary? Was it time for her to "get on the bus"?

With her eyes half closed Geri reached over to turn off the alarm clock. Unwelcomed sunlight streamed through the window. Yet another morning began with her heart pounding and perspiration covering her forehead. She put her arm over her eyes to block out the light that chided her state of mind. She had the dream about the bus again. The bus was moving faster this time. She woke up just as she was about to cry out for the bus to stop. A couple of days earlier she knew that her fatigue had turned into mild depression. The glimmers of light that imbued her life, especially the joy she got out of caring for the children and the mini respites she experienced in the company of her friends, were no longer enough.

Thoughts about the dream offered a different perspective this morning. At least she was not as tired as the morning before. In fact, she actually felt a strange sense of exhilaration.

After her usual conversation in prayer she got up and headed for the shower. There was a noticeable lightness in the short walk to the bathroom. She commented on it quietly simply by saying "Humph".

Geri did not know why the change occurred, but she welcomed it with open arms. Now standing in front of the bathroom mirror she gave her face a once over. She smiled and thought about what an elderly woman said to her one day standing in the checkout line at the super market.

"You sure is a pretty little thing. But you look tired. Aren't you getting enough sleep?"

Geri's reply was, "Yes Ma'am, I am tired. I'm just starting to look as old as I feel." She regretted the words to the older woman as soon as they came out of her mouth. As if she sensed it, mother quipped back with a cynical laugh, "No honey. It ain't sags, its bags you got!" They both laughed. Mother turned back before walking away and said to Geri "You too young to be so tired. Take care of yourself. I can tell God's got something for you to do." Remembering the conversation made her smile as she looked closer at herself in the mirror. "Yep! Still got them bags!"

Just as she was about to step in the shower the phone rang. "Who could this possibly be?" She hurried to answer but whoever it was hung up. Between the hang up and the dream, the exhilaration she felt earlier was beginning to feel more like anxiety. She stepped back into the shower trying to fight off the feeling. The soft lavender and vanilla smell of the body wash was helping. But as the water splashed across her face, the calming effect of the scents started to wane. She began thinking about the dream.

For as long as she could remember her dreams were in some way telling her about what was going on in her life. Sometimes they helped her make major decisions or put challenging concerns to rest. Other times they were about simple things like the time she spent too much money on a dress knowing she really couldn't afford it. She convinced herself it was an investment in her future. That night she dreamed that Grandmother Ella, standing before her with hand on hip said "Return that dress! Your success is not outside you. It's inside you." The next day she returned the dress. The same week she attended a function where she would have worn the dress and two other women showed up in it. So much for her dress for success theory! Ruminating over the simplicity of that experience made her ask herself why she was making the bus dream so complicated. It was a rhetorical question. Was it that she just didn't want to see what the dream was revealing?

Like the shopping list Geri kept on the refrigerator door, her schedule was written in her mind. First on the list was a meeting with one of the center's funders. The foundation officer was a serious acting guy who seldom smiled, but was always very polite. Today she needed to request an increase in their funding. The interaction would be like a dance between the two of them. Everything was in order from a report and discussion perspective, but she also needed to wear something suitable for the occasion. Choosing one of her most striking black suits, she dressed and headed for the office. .

Luther Vandross' *Never Too Much* was playing on the radio when she got in the car. Without hesitation she started singing with him. Her cell phone rang in the middle of her duet. Trying to keep her eyes on the road, she reached in her pocketbook to get it. She glanced at the Caller ID and saw that it was her girlfriend Candace.

"Hey girl, what's up?" Singing loudly and laughing at the same time she answered the phone. She was amused by the expression she knew was on her friend's face.

"Well, hey back. I called your house earlier from my cell, but I lost the signal. And then I got another call. Sorry 'bout that. Anyway, you sound happy!"

33 Sometimes In December

"Might as well be! How are you?"

Something was up because Candace didn't have anything sarcastic to say about her singing instead of answering the phone like normal people. She usually teased Geri about not being like 'normal' people. Sensing the serious tone in her voice, she turned down the radio.

"I'm okay. I'm glad I caught you. What are you doing after work?"

"Hey girl, I got a hot date!" She smiled when she heard herself respond and tried to lighten her tone even more for her friend's sake.

"Girl, I just need to do something different. If I don't do something tonight, no telling what I'll do tomorrow." Candace was clearly in need of a girls' night out.

"Okay. Let's hang on that last thought for a minute. What's going on, sis?" Now Geri was really concerned.

"Girl, life." Candace quipped. "I'm just bored, girl."

"When's the last time you went out to dinner or a movie? I know that's not like going on a vacation, but it's a start." Geri coached her friend.

"Enough about me. How are you Ms. Haven for My Children?"

Geri shared a little about her dream and asked Candace what she thought.

Candace responded with, "Pay attention to the things happening to and around you. The dream could very well be pointing to something that's about to happen without you doing anything but receiving it."

"Well, as long as it's a blessing!" Geri quipped back.

"Sometimes we don't recognize our blessings!" Candace laughed as she responded. She knew that would be Geri's response.

Before hanging up they agreed to catch a movie Saturday afternoon. That way neither of them would be too tired from their work day.

"Since you have such sage advice, you can choose the dinner and the movie!" Geri knew why Candace was laughing.

"Call me later." Geri laughed.

"Done." Candace replied.

Geri and Candace met at a conference in Boulder, Colorado three years ago. They were surprised that they lived and worked so close in proximity, but their paths had not crossed until they met in Boulder. They decided to skip one of the conference sessions one afternoon to go mountain climbing. After all, how could you be in Boulder and not at least climb a little? It did not matter that neither of them had ever climbed a mountain. They were two adventuring spirits with determination. The story goes that they climbed to a cabin resort about a mile up a mountain and called a taxi to get back down. Each time they talk about it, the mountain gets higher and the story more hilarious. It was a moment that would seal their friendship forever.

After the conversation with Candace, Geri mused about how free spirited she was back then. It wasn't even that long ago. Laughing to herself she thought about picking up a pair of climbing shoes to give to Candace as a joke that night. As soon as the idea came it left. "Right, like I will have time to do that."

Driving into the parking lot Geri noticed that the security guard from the building next to hers was in the lot. He was looking right at her. All thoughts of Candace and their get together vanished.

"Oh shoot, he's walking towards my car." She bent her head down so he could not see her talking to herself.

Trying not to look directly at him, she lifted her head slightly. She could feel her heart racing like earlier that morning. The sun was bouncing off his face as he glided across the lot. The glare of the sun made his image seem almost surreal resembling one of those commercials about romance and imitation butter. She always wondered how the advertisers for the product thought something you ate on a baked potato had anything to do with romance. She found herself comparing its foolishness to the moment.

Over the past several weeks her intermittent glances at him when he was not looking were now culminating into a little frenzy. It was one thing to sneak a peek, but this…

Geri's mind traveled back to the first time she caught sight of him. It was September, in the midst of an unseasonably warm Indian summer. The sun shone on his chocolate brown skin like it would melt at any moment. She wasn't much for uniforms, but his fit perfectly accentuating his lean yet muscular frame. His sleeves came just below his biceps and with every move of his arm she could see his strength. Geri chided herself for the thoughts and how sexist they were, but they sure would serve as a good way to describe him to her girlfriends. The description also allowed her to make light of what he did to her. Each time she saw him, she felt a quiet quacking.

It was a surprising reaction because she was also aware that it wasn't just about how fine she thought he was, though he was fine enough. No. There was something mysterious about him that she was attracted to and almost intimidated by. All of it was running through her mind as she watched him coming towards her. Chocolate. Her favorite indulgence. "Get a grip." She whispered to herself.

As he got closer his mouth opened to an enormous smile. She found herself really exploring his shoulders and the movement of the arms she had only seen from a distance before today. Her eyes stopped briefly at his hand to see if he was wearing a ring.

Feeling a little embarrassed by her stare and private thoughts, she leaned over the middle console of the car pretending to look for something on the back seat. It only made things worst. As she moved her hand across it she quickly realized that feeling the smoothness of the dark leather made her blush. She suddenly remembered a few weeks ago when she saw him standing in front of the building where he worked. She was sitting in her colleague Dan's car talking about the meeting they just attended. Watching him that day, Geri was reminded of the calm and tranquil motions of a midnight sea – mysterious and revealing at the same time. On that particular day she was more intrigued about who he was than what he looked like. She laughed to herself when she realized that she was really checking him out and turned back to her colleague to see him looking at her with an indignant expression on his face.

"What?" Was Geri's immediate response.

"Did you hear anything I just said?" Dan asked. "Yes, I heard you." Geri responded incredulously.

The truth was she had not heard a thing Dan had said. All she heard was what was going on in her head.

And now here he was…

"Good morning." Mr. Security Guard spoke.

With the smile still beaming, he was now leaning forward. He smelled like autumn air but Geri could not make out the real scent. Afraid of what would come out of her mouth if she opened it, Geri smiled, nodded her head and gestured that she was rolling up her window. She picked up her bag and briefcase from the passenger's seat, pulled the key out of the ignition, and pulled the handle out to open the door. She moved fluidly in a way that seemed to be normal, but was strange as hell.

He stepped back to give her room to get out of the car, but did not retreat from her space. She could almost feel his breath as he maintained his alluring smile. For some odd reason it was not at all intrusive to her. She wondered if it was a cultural thing for him to stand so close. His accent was kind of French-Caribbean. She wasn't sure. She was sure that standing that close to him gave her an unexpected rush of anxiety while at the same time a flushing excitement.

"Good morning." He repeated his greeting when she got out of the car as if his first was not heard.

His accent caught her breath as an early morning songbird catches the wind. His gaze was now seeking her eyes. She felt herself being immersed in that deep sea she saw in him that day while sitting in Dan's car. 'Unh, he is too fine.'

He had no idea that at that moment her thoughts were as close to his as anyone's could be. He did know that the rush he was feeling needed to be settled a bit and a brief retreat might help to accomplish just that.

Geri hesitated as she considered a clever way to respond. Nothing came except "Good morning." Her tongue was all tied up in the thoughts that were quickening through her mind.

"Do you know why it's such a good morning?" His smile broadened. Her immediate reaction was to answer sarcastically by saying, "No, so why don't you tell me?" Before she could answer, he asked again.

"Do you know why it's such a good morning?"

She thought 'Why is he repeating everything he says? I can hear.' Her response, however, was "There are a lot of reasons for it being a very good morning. But I guess you want to tell me your reason."

"My birthday is today and I'm having a party tonight. Will you come?" He chose his words carefully, pronouncing each almost too slowly to make sure he was saying exactly what he wanted to say.

Although he spoke pretty good English, at that moment he wished she spoke his native language so he could be freer in his expressions. He had the feeling that this would be his only chance to get her attention.

Geri leaned her head back in amusement at his audacity. Looking at him those part smile part frowns on her face she thought 'No he didn't just ask me to go to his birthday party tonight.' His saying each word like he was reading or had memorized the lines didn't help the situation.

"First of all, I don't even know you. In fact, I don't even know your name." She finally responded.

She reflexively wiped the perspiration from her forehead as she spoke. It was "hot as Hades" as her grandmother use to say. Ordinarily she might have been embarrassed that she was sweating so much, but now she was more focused on the conversation. He was impressed by her calling him out and decided that the best way for him to continue was to start over by introducing himself.

"Hi, my name is Nathan Muafumba." He smiled after the words came out. He saw that she was now reading his name badge. It read Ntheba as the first name and not Nathan. He ignored her obvious curiosity.

When she still didn't respond he kept talking. "Okay, I understand you might want to say 'No', but will you think about it?" The way she was looking at him almost made him apologize for even asking. He thought maybe it was a good time to say "I'm sorry. Never mind". His instinct told him to just be silent and wait a minute.

"Okay, Nathan. And I don't mean 'Okay, yes I'll come'. My name is Geri, Geri Michaels."

His smile came back. He was about to say something when she cut him off.

"But I still don't know you." She was beginning to enjoy the banter.

"I'm sorry. I don't mean to offend you. It's just that I have wanted to meet you and thought today was the right day. Especially since it's my birthday."

Looking directly into her eyes, he hoped that she saw his sincerity. This time his smile was a bit sheepish. Geri's eyes inadvertently explored his mouth. It was about the most beautiful mouth she had ever seen. His lips were the perfect fullness and accented the tone of his skin as if they were part of a painted portrait. It didn't help that she had not kissed anyone in so long that all she could think about was kissing him at that very moment.

Surprised at herself, Geri stepped back a little and readjusted her attention to his whole face. As she was about to tell him "No" she saw that sweat had beaded up on his forehead. She thought, 'Look at him. He's not so cool after all. In fact he's a little nervous.' It was not that warm, so the sweat seemed to come out of nowhere.

"I'll think about it." Now, that was actually a lie. But for some reason, at the moment you could not have paid her to turn him down outright. Suddenly she could feel the heat of the morning rushing over her. The truth be told, their exchange was now clearly the cause for both of their little outbreaks. She felt embarrassed and wondered if it was obvious to him.

"That's good! Let me know. I'll be here all day." Nathan smiled as he pulled a white handkerchief from his back pocket and wiped his forehead. Geri again noticed that he was not wearing a wedding band.

With the conversation seemingly over, and feeling encouraged by her response, Nathan started backing away now looking purposefully into her eyes. He repeated, "Let me know."

"I will do that, Ntheba Nathan. I will let you know." She stumbled over the pronunciation of "Ntheba" knowing that she was not going to his party.

As she walked away, she laughed and quietly started singing "Never Too Much" to herself. She couldn't remember the last time when someone she was really attracted to approached her. She walked towards her building ruminating about how much he reminded her of bittersweet dark chocolate the first day she noticed him. She laughed aloud about the conversation they just had. Her amusement halted when she almost tripped over an open bag of trash on the pavement.

"You would think that people would stop being so trifling!" She said with disgust.

Feeling foolishly hopeful, Nathan had watched her walk away. He thought about how for weeks he had wanted to say something to her, but was afraid that she might take offense. She walked in and out of her building with an aloofness that could have been construed as self-absorption. All he would ever say was good morning or good afternoon. Until that morning he had not brought himself to look in her face with more than a glance. He knew her name because he had asked one of his coworkers.

"Who is that woman?"

"What woman?"

"You know the one who always seems so serious. I see her almost every day and she just walks by like nobody's on the street but her." He laughed as he realized what he was about to say. "I like her."

"Nathan, man you talking 'bout Geri Michaels? She is serious, but she's also fine. I've seen you looking at her." Paul chuckled to himself, then continued,

"They moved into that building a few months after I started working here. She came over the first week to introduce herself to the guys at the desk. She's nice enough man. But hell! She out of your league!" Still laughing he headed off to his station. He turned around and said, "What you think you can do with that?" Paul shook his head. Nathan ignored his question.

Now muttering to himself, Paul said, "Just cause you were an engineer in your country, you're still a security guard in Baltimore."

Nathan heard his colleague's remark and smiled to himself. He knew exactly what he wanted to "do with that". There was something about her that touched him in a place where he thought was tied up and put away. Sure, he had looked at other women and on a couple of occasions asked a woman out. But those encounters lasted for a few weeks at best. No. Something was different this time. What that difference was, he didn't know. He decided to wait until another time to try to figure it out.

As much as Nathan tried to shake off the thought of Geri, she stayed on his mind all morning. The more he thought about her, the more fascinated he was with how she went back and forth with him. To tell the truth, he saw something of himself in her. He thought about it incessantly as he waited for her answer about his party.

Chapter 6

Now sitting at her desk, Geri called Diana to come down. Diana Lopez-Delgado was the Director of Operations at Haven. They had gone through a lot together over the years and had become friends as well as colleagues. She reminded Geri a lot of her friend Kyra. They had the same feistiness. Diana was Ecuadorian and had come to the United States to attend graduate school. She was the first person Geri hired to work at Haven. She was bright, dedicated and loyal. She never hesitated to go the extra mile when Geri needed her to step to the plate. She was there when the pipes burst a couple days before the agency opened. She was there when Geri cried over the little boy whose father had sodomized him and beat him before dropping him off at his grandmother's. Diana was there when Geri was tested for ovarian cancer and celebrated life when she was diagnosed otherwise.

"LoDe," as Geri called her in private, was one of the most compassionate people she knew. She took life as it came and dealt with it accordingly. For years Geri was a witness to the changes in her life. She was there when Diana miscarried and was afraid her husband was cheating. She was there when she got pregnant again and decided to stay with her husband even though he had cheated. She was there when they bought their first house and christened their new son. Geri could always tell when something was changing in Diana's life by the length of her curly brown hair. She would let it grow, then cut it so short that the curls seemed to disappear. Through the joy and the pain she would say that cutting her hair was one of the only things in life she had some control over.

Geri believed that sometimes God just placed you with the right people no matter what the circumstances. And like Candace and Kyra, Diana was as special to her as family. She had not shared about the dream in any detail with anyone, but today she just might. Certainly Diana could be affected by any decision she made regarding a change in her life.

"Good morning, Mrs. Delgado." A staff person spoke as Diana walked down the hall to Geri's office. Two children were with the staff person heading for the cafeteria.

"Good morning. How are you today?" Diana responded with her normal upbeat tone.

Everybody answered in unison. "Fine."

It was unlike her to meet with Diana before she made her rounds. But then again Diana considered that Geri seemed so tired lately that maybe she needed some time in her office before doing anything. The look on Geri's face when she walked into the office was not expected. Her boss was leaning back in the chair smiling.

"Good morning, my friend." Geri leaned over and with a mischievous whisper said "Shut the door."

"Good morning to you, jefe. What's up?" Diana used the Spanish word "jefe" in place of the word boss because she knew it annoyed her. The first time she used it Geri thought she was calling her a heifer.

Geri gave her the 'Yes, you are annoying me' look. Diana laughed.

"Okay, what's up?"

"You won't believe what just happened." As if to share a top secret Geri leaned forward. Just as she was getting ready to fill her in the intercom buzzed.

"Ms. Michaels, you have a phone call on line one." The voice on the speaker broke into the moment.

"Who is it, Gina?" She pressed the intercom button then picked up the receiver incase privacy was necessary.

"It's the Department of Child Protective Services." Gina was too familiar with the first thing in the morning phone calls from DCPS, especially when they asked to speak with Ms. Michaels directly. Her tone reflected how hurtful it was to think of what might have happened to the children they were bringing to them.

"Okay, I'll be right with them."

The fleeting pleasure of her exchange with Nathan was erased by having to respond to what she knew would be the latest crisis. Diana saw the changed expression on her bosses face and took the cue to leave. She mouthed, "Let me know when you're done" and left the office.

Refocusing, she reached for her notebook and a pen to take notes during the phone call. Now that she was alone she put the phone on speaker and pushed the blinking button.

"Good morning, this is Geri Michaels."

"Good morning Ms. Michaels. This is Natalie Collins from DCPS. We're sending two children to the center this morning."

Natalie Collins continued sharing that the children had been locked in a basement by their parents.

"How long were they locked in the basement?" Geri asked knowing that the length of time might determine how fragile they were.

"Have they been examined by a doctor?" She continued with the normal line of questions.

Getting as much information as possible would help Haven prepare to receive them.

"All I was told was that the children were picked up this morning. A neighbor reported hearing cries coming from the basement. They said there is a crack in the window so they could tell the crying was coming from more than one child." Natalie tried to answer Geri's questions, but felt frustrated even by her lack of information. She ended with,

"I am sorry Ms. Michaels, but that's all the information I have. I believe Ms. Torres will have more for you in her report."

"Thank you. We will do what we can to take it from here."
Geri responded with obvious dissatisfaction in her voice.

Under the circumstances Natalie described, children were generally taken to the hospital before they arrived at Haven. It appeared that step had not been taken this time. Geri tried not to express her frustration to the person on the phone, but was sure some of it came out. It would be helpful to know more so the center could better prepare. Shaking her head, she pushed the button to end the call.

Fortunately it was the morning that her doctor was there. Dr. Jay Connors would be able to examine the children as part of the intake process. Everything else would be discussed with the social worker when they arrived. After speaking with the doctor and other staff, she went to the lobby to wait for their arrival.

As soon as they got there Geri had staff attend to the children, then invited the social worker and police officer to her office. Angela Torres was the social worker who often accompanied children to the center. She was nice and seemed genuinely concerned about those assigned to her.

"Hi." Geri greeted her and turned to the officer.

"Hi, I'm Geri Michaels."

"Officer Singleton. Pleased to meet you." He extended his hand.

"What do we have today?" Geri asked looking at both of them.

"The neighbors reported hearing cries from the basement and upon investigation the children were found tied to a pipe against the wall." Angela replied.

She went on to say, "They had bowls of water and cereal in soured milk sitting next to them. And this was a foster care home."

"When will this stop?" Geri shook her head and repeated Angela's words. "And this was a foster care home."

Angela gave Geri an overview of the written report, then handed it to her to sign and get a copy taken. Knowing the drill, Mai was standing by to make the copy.

"Thanks Ms. Torres." Geri shook Angela's and the police officer's hands.

"And thank you for doing the work you do." Angela responded while the police officer nodded in agreement.

As they walked out the front door, Geri stood for a moment at the front desk with Mai.

"All we can do is what we can do, Ms. Michaels." Mai said softly.

After meeting with Angela and the police officer, Geri wondered what else she would encounter during the day. Often she would leave the job with the residue of issues that were not settled and thoughts that were unsettling. In the midst of the conjecture, Nathan's face came to her. She almost asked the receptionist "Did you see that?" Instead, she walked back to her office. Before tackling the return phone calls from the stack of messages handed to her, she called Information and asked for the number to the building next door.

"Hi, may I speak with Nathan…" Geri was surprised that before she finished the question, he responded.

"I was wondering if you were going to call." It was Nathan.

"How did you know who I was?" Geri asked surprised.

"Are you kidding me? I'd know your voice anywhere." There was a hint of playfulness in his voice.

"Okay. So, I'm calling to let you know that I won't be able to make your birthday party." Geri said in a matter of fact tone, not feeling in the mood to banter.

"No problem. Maybe next year." Nathan had discerned her tone and responded accordingly.

"Sorry. Have a good day." Geri did not wait for him to say anything else. She hung up the phone and started prioritizing her return calls.

"Good…" Nathan was just about to say good bye when she hung up. The idea that he was disappointed gave pause for him to do a reality check. He hung up wondering if there was really any possibility for them to get to know each other.

Geri watched the clock all day and ate almost the whole dish of M&M's on her desk. She made a mental note to pick up another bag over the weekend. Today was another one of those days when the little chocolate morsels were her only meal until she left work. She was glad that she was meeting Candace for dinner. It was something to look forward to after the day she was having.

Off and on during the day she thought about Nathan and had to stop herself from fantasizing about how it would be to hold him. 'I bet he kisses good' was one of the thoughts.

'Who is this man and why has he stepped in front of me? Especially now.' She wanted to just walk next door and ask him,

"Okay. What do you want?" She realized, however, that it was her anxiety and her problem, not his. If she pressed him, she could scare him away. And to be honest, she did not want to do that.

Finally, it was 6:30 p.m. Diana poked her head in her door. "Hey, I'm heading out. See you tomorrow."

Geri nodded at her, but didn't say any thing.

"Okay. Now are you going to tell me what's going on?" Diana came in the office.

"Diana, I don't know. I'm just tired. I'm just tired of so many things." She started stacking the papers on her desk while considering how much she could share with her. Geri looked up and continued.

"There's got to be something better than this. I mean, I love what I do. At least I think I do. No, I know I do. It's not the job. It's having nothing but the job!"

"Geri, how long have I been telling you that you need some balance in your life? You give and give. Girl, when's the last time you did something just for you? I'm not talking about going to get your nails done either. You do that all the time, but it's just as much for the image you want to project for the job than it is for anything." Diana paused and finised with, "I'm talking about something that's just for you?"

"You know what, LoDe? Sometimes I think that if I ever started doing things for myself, I might get carried away literally! I mean, I might not be able to stop. I might get in my car one morning and just keep on going." Surprised by her own statement, Geri took a deep breath.

"Okay. I'm not talking 'bout all that." Diana laughed lovingly at her friend. But she knew that she was telling the truth. She was one of the people that felt so lucky to have Geri in her life because she knew she could be just who she was with her. She and her husband had recently gone through some new things, and Geri had helped her keep it together. Diana tried to do as much as she could for her on the job to help take up some of the slack, but she knew that she could only do so much. Geri was one of those women who thought that it was her plight to take on the world one child at a time. She sometimes gave the impression that anyone trying to help her would just be in the way.

"So what was so good that you didn't get a chance to tell me this morning? Whatever it was you should have held on to it." Diana could also see that Geri had gone to an entirely different place since then and wanted to try to get her back to before they were interrupted by the phone call. Geri told her what happened in the parking lot. Diana was all ears and trying hard to wait to ask her questions. She could tell that there was something about it that made Geri a little uncomfortable. There was also a tone of excitement that she had not heard come from her in a while.

"You know I've been thinking about him all day. I keep seeing his face. I don't know, something tells me that getting together with him is going to be more than I can handle." Geri raised her right hand as if to pledge to the idea of "more than I can handle."

Diana leaned over and placed Geri's hand on the desk. Smiling dramatically she said, "Girl, you handle big stuff that don't do a thing for you every day. Go on and handle that man however big his stuff is and let it be good for you. That's all I got to say about it."

She then stood up and went around the desk to give her a hug.

"Now, get out of here."

Diana stopped at the door and laughed at the irony of Ms. Geri Michaels falling for the unlikely.

"The security guard, Geri? Hey, one never knows…" With that, she left yelling back as she walked down the hall, "Goodnight, jefe! Get out of here!"

"See you tomorrow." Geri smiled and said in a singsong way. Putting her belongings together, she thought about calling Candace to make just to see how her day had gone. As she reached for the phone, one of the lines lit up.

'It's almost 7. I'm going to let that call go upstairs to the office.' With that thought she threw her bag over her shoulder, pulled her office door shut and locked it. She felt a little strange as she walked down the hallway to the front door of the center. The first floor staff had gone for the day, but someone had picked up. Staring briefly at the yellow light, she felt the strangeness again, but walked out the front door after glancing at the photo of Mai's family in the small silver frame she gave her for Christmas. She smiled thinking about her caring staff.

Chapter 7

It could be said that the universe creates situations to see what we do with and in them. Geri considered that meeting Nathan was one of those universe driven things poised to see what she would do. After their first conversation, they seemed to run into each other every day. Each time their conversation was longer. Initially she thought he planned it and teasingly asked him if that's what he was doing. His response was, "No. Not at all. They changed my shift. Maybe it's just a coincidence."

"But did you ask them to change your shift?" Not being a woman who believed in coincidence, she thought that the all of a sudden constant meeting was something he set up.

"No. I just told them I wouldn't mind. Seriously." He laughed as he saw the suspicion on her face. "Really, I didn't. But it still seems like a good thing to me."

"Alright good thing to me." Geri shook her head from side to side as she responded.

"Geri, do you mind if I have your telephone number? Sometimes I'm thinking about you or something I want to tell you when I'm at home. Do you mind?" Nathan asked.

"Sure. Just don't call me in the middle of the night." She was surprised it had taken him so long to ask.

Writing the number on a piece of paper he pulled from his wallet, she decided to give him her direct work line as well. When he wrote his numbers on a piece of the same paper, she accepted with a bit of relief. She still wasn't too sure about what his situation was. Giving her his home phone number was a clue. She had taken his word about being free. Still, as he was writing she felt a little anxious about what their communication after work hours might create.

"This is good." He kissed her on the cheek. The kiss was unexpected, but she had to acknowledge that it was sweet and to be honest, somewhat recognizable as if he had done it before. It did make her a little uncomfortable, however, since they were just outside her office She looked around to see that no one had seen them. The biggest surprise came when surprisingly she realized that she didn't really care.

All the familiarity that she felt when she was near him was beginning to scare her. What was it that made her respond to him as if she had known him all her life? Was she just missing what he was offering? She could not get him off her mind, and that night was no exception. She thought about him until she fell asleep.

The next day Geri was excited about the possibility of seeing Nathan before she went into her building. When she thought of him, she found herself being moved by the sound of the name Ntheba.

She decided that she would call him Nathan and reserve Ntheba for special moments. Why she thought there would even be 'special moments' was something she could not explain. The thoughts were causing a weird and wonderful feeling in her. Preoccupied by the sensation, she did not see the two people approaching her car. When she finally noticed them, they were very close.

"Lady, can you give us some money to get our baby some milk?" The young woman spoke as she reached her hand out to Geri. Getting her full attention now, Geri recognized the scam from one that she'd witnessed so often on the bus and at bus stops while living in Chicago.

"No. I'm sorry I can't." She started walking quickly to get pass them and out of the parking lot.

Seeing that she was trying to move away the young man went around his companion to the back of Geri to try to take her bag. He could not really tell the difference between her bags. He pulled at both of them. In her panic and stubbornness, she held both tightly under her arms with her hands. With the woman standing in front and her partner in the back, they boxed her in. When he began pulling harder at one bag, she yelled, "Hey! Stop! Stop!"

The woman moved closer and said, "Shut up, bitch." She stopped yelling fearing that the woman might pull out a weapon. She lost her grip on one of the bags when the woman pushed her. Geri yelled again.

"Help! Somebody help!" Just as she was beginning to weaken by their pushing and pulling at her, she heard Nathan shouting as he ran towards them. Even though she didn't know what he was saying, she understood the meaning of the force of his voice. After knocking her on the ground, the two assailants ran off. They split up at the end of the parking lot.

"Are you alright? Are you hurt?" He helped her get up and held her long enough to hear her say "I'm alright. Ntheba, I'm so glad you were nearby."

"Bastards! Give me your keys." He took the keys that she still held tightly in her hand. Holding her by the waist, he opened her car door and helped her in. He went to pick up her bags. She had dropped both when they knocked her to the ground. They didn't stop to pick them up after Nathan shouted. He came back to the car and tossed them on the back seat. With one hand on her shoulder he pulled his cell phone from his pocket with the other and called the security guard on duty in his building.

"Marco, this is Nathan. Call the police to come to Haven's parking lot. Ms. Michaels was just attacked. No, the two bastards ran away. We're still in the parking lot. Just call them to get here right away." His accent was heavy.

"Maybe we should go into the building." Her voice was low, but steady.

"No, it's alright. Just sit here for a few minutes until the police come. They will probably want to see where it happened. It's alright. I'll stay here with you." Nathan's tone had changed from angry to consoling.

His words had a calming effect on her. Oddly enough, it was his comfort that made her start to cry. While they were trying to mug her, she felt strong and foolishly determined not to give them their way. She was just pissed! His touch and voice made her feel like she could let down her guard.

He made her feel safe in a strange and powerful way.

"I guess I should have just given them the damn bag." She laughed quietly as she reached for a tissue from the passenger's side of the car.

"Well. Well, yes. But you're alright and that's all that matters." He took the tissue from her hand and wiped the tears from her face. Seeing that she was laughing at herself, he smiled and said, "What's so important in those bags?" He brushed her hair and smiled jokingly.

"Nothing that could not be replaced. It was just my reaction to their nerve. I guess their nerve revved up my nerve." She continued to laugh almost out of embarrassment.

"The police have arrived. Stay here." Nathan saw them as they came around the corner.

He touched her face as if to assure her that he would be right back and did not intend to leave her. At least that's what she sensed. Watching him walk over towards the police car, she felt as if she was part of a bad movie. Nothing and nowhere were safe anymore. She suddenly felt some of what she thought her children were feeling when they were brought to the center. This time Nathan was the caregiver and she received his caring without hesitation.

Nathan met the police midway into the parking lot. He started telling them what happened. She got out of the car when she recognized one of the police officers as the one who brought the children in with Angela a few weeks ago.

"Hi Ms. Michaels. Are you okay? Do you need to go to the hospital?"

"No. I think I'm okay. They knocked me down, but fortunately I fell on my briefcase and it broke my fall." As she said that, Geri thought 'God that was stupid. Why didn't I just give them the bag?'

"Are you sure? You may not feel it now, but you might later." The other officer spoke like he was basing it on experience not just protocol. "We can take your statement at the hospital."

"Geri, I'll go with you." Nathan was standing at her side.

"Okay, maybe." As she took his hand, she saw Diana walking towards them and released it. Shortly after phoning the police, Marco called Geri's office to make sure they knew what was going on. Nathan had taped her business card to the blotter on the front desk.

The drama of the morning, including going to the emergency

room to find out that it wasn't her bag that broke her fall, but her wrist, gave her a good enough reason to take it easy for the rest of the day.

That did not happen. As soon as she got back, she prepared for the meeting she had scheduled for that afternoon with one of her board members.

Nathan had been on his way home when he heard Geri yelling out in the parking lot. After he took her back to work, he left to get some sleep before having to come back that evening. She was so grateful to him that she could not find the appropriate words to express how she felt. It wasn't just that she was thankful for his coming to her aide, but she was moved by how protected he made her feel. It was safe in a way that allowed her to be who she was in that moment as much as she was in the moment she was attacked. She was reminded of how she once prayed as a child that her grandfather would come like a wave and wash away everything that was bad in her life. Could that be the connection that she made in sensing the depth of the sea in Nathan?

After the mugging experience, Geri and Nathan talked almost every night. It began that evening when he called her from work to see how she was doing. She was happy to hear his voice as she sank into her pillow.

"Hi, how are you?" His tone was low and caring.

"I'm okay. I got home earlier than I thought. My meeting was cancelled." Geri was relieved knowing that his caring was not just an in the moment of a crisis expression.

In the midst of everything that happened that day, a bond was created between the two of them. That night she could hear a freedom in the tone of his voice that had not been there before. His accent was more apparent than ever as he spoke of his concern for her. She knew she already liked him a lot, but experiencing how caring he was made her like him even more.

Geri felt comfortable telling him about who she was and what she wanted out of life. He wanted to tell her everything that happened to him to get him to the point of how he was feeling about her, but decided to wait until they were in each other's presence. He committed himself to the discussion.

"As soon as we can sit together I want to tell you everything about me and how I even came to this country."

"Why can't you tell me over the phone? Maybe if you tell me over the phone, there won't be a need for us to sit together". Only half joking she responded to what seemed to be a little mystery in his voice.

"It's just because there are some things that are hard to talk about. I promise you'll understand when I tell you." There was a reserve in his voice that she had not heard since that awkward day that he invited her to his birthday party.

"Okay." Her response was prudent. Still, she wondered what he was holding back.

Hearing the question in her voice, he knew that when he shared his story with her she might not want to see him or talk with him again. It was perplexing to him to think about losing her when he didn't really have her. No matter what, though, he knew he needed to be honest. He also knew that honesty came with risking how she would react. Her exhaustion setting in, Geri found herself moving into a soft sleep. At one point she thought she had fallen asleep while he was talking.

"Oh, God, I'm sorry. Was I snoring?" she asked embarrassed.

"No, you weren't." He laughed quietly to himself thinking that he may have dozed off himself. "I'll let you go."

With a soft "Good night" on her lips she was about to hang up when she heard him.

"Geri…" There was a pause and then he said, "Good night. I'll talk with you tomorrow. Have a good rest."

She drifted off to sleep in a surprisingly peaceful state. Knowing that she would not get through it, she didn't even attempt to say her prayer. Talking with Nathan had taken the sting out of her day. And for the first time in a long time, she slept through the night without any disturbing dreams.

Chapter 8

Nathan. Her soul mate? What did that really mean? The intensity of what she felt for him was certainly causing her to dig way down in places she did not even know existed. It was happening so quickly. Was there a real bond between them or was it merely a physical attraction?

Geri had to consider that it was not what she was making it out to be. When you are lonely or longing for someone to be in your life, you can make even the strangest situations seem right. She knew that everything that glittered was not gold and everything that felt good was not necessarily good for you. What she was feeling about Nathan was unnerving, yet strangely welcomed. The more they shared, the more they discovered how much they had in common. They had both sat at the feet of their grandmothers gaining wisdom from their words and how they lived their lives.

Nathan's mother died giving birth to him. Her mother raised him. In the village where he was born children were named with meaning. He talked about the connection between his name, his mother's death and his survival through the trauma of birth. He was given the name Ntheba, meaning 'mercy and peace' to express that although God had taken his mother, he lived as a blessing to the family. At least that's what his grandmother told him. Although he was born and raised in Angola, his father's homeland, the word 'ntheba' was from his grandmother's native language of Mali. His Christian name, Nathan, signified that he was a gift. His grandmother believed that even in the sorrow of death, life surfaces as a gift.

When his grandmother passed away he was sent to live with an aunt. Per her request, he called her "mom". She wanted him to feel that he was truly one of hers, like his new sister and two brothers. It was a powerful story. Geri suggested that he write about it someday. Nathan responded unknowingly with, "Or, maybe you can write about it someday."

There was nothing boring about their conversations. They could go on for hours, often leaving Geri tired in the morning but able to sleep soundly through the night. One night Nathan shared how his grandmother taught him to have respect for himself and others. She told him how brave his mother was in the last moments of her life. She taught him to revere women out of a love and appreciation for life itself. His grandmother also cautioned him to listen to life's lessons and learn from the hearing.

"Little one," Meme would say, "listen carefully to the ground so that you won't step on the wisdom of the earth. Always remember that you are not Him who created you, but the one who is the gift of His creation."

He shared the loose translations of what she said. From his grandmother's teaching, he grew up having utter respect for older women. Finding out that Geri was a few years older than him was not surprising. They marveled at how they both thought the other was younger or older than they were.

Geri remembered and shared that her grandmother demonstrated how to be smooth, and when necessary bold and bodacious in a womanly kind of way. That did not mean coy or crazy, but certain about herself and her actions and sometimes even a little aloof. "Geri," Grandmother Ella would say, "You have to stand strong inside yourself and don't ever let nobody pull you down no matter how hard they try."

Geri spoke lyrically when she repeated the words for Nathan. As a little girl she didn't know exactly what it meant, but now she knew quite well.

Geri had not thought about where she'd gotten the aloofness that she had been accused of all her life until she began talking with Nathan. She thought about how her Ella would walk into a room head high and arms slightly swinging. Her presence seemed to take away the air until she smiled and acknowledged whoever else was there. In her smile was the exhale that Geri had inherited and grown into with each life experience.

"So that's what it was. I saw you and…" Nathan teasingly exhaled.

"Hey! What can I say? When you got it, you got it!"

She mocked back, but believed exactly what she was saying. She wondered what Ella would think about this new man in her life. She wondered too if there were any secrets that her grandmother would have revealed about him. Ella was good at reading people.

They were amazed by how their grandmothers were so much alike. Some of their sayings meant the same thing even if the examples were different.

One that they both used was. You can't catch a running slippery pig except by its tail".

They fell out laughing after he repeated the saying and she explained how her grandmother would put her hand on her hip when she said it. After thinking about it for a minute, they asked in sync.

"What does that mean?"

In a moment of seriousness Geri shared about her grandfather Gerald Reynard and that his name meant a "mighty spear." She could hear her grandmother's voice describing him and then cautioning her to have a good heart and be strong like him. She also remembered the last part of her grandmother's mantra, "Make sure one doesn't cancel out the other". Believing that it was for her ears only, she did not share any of that with him.

"What else should I know about you, Ntheba Nathan Muafumba?" His name flowed like velvet off her tongue.

"What else, you say? You like knowing about me, eh?"

Nathan always got excited when he talked with her about his upbringing. It was as if he wanted to pour all of himself into her or at least before her in their ritual of sharing.

"Yes. What else?" When he finally answered, Geri was surprised by his disclosure.

"Not many people know this, but I sing." Nathan could imagine her surprised expression.

"Seriously?" Geri asked.

"Yes, seriously. And I write music." Nathan responded amused by her response.

"So, do you have a song that you can sing for me right now?" She was now excited about the possibility of sharing that part of him.

"Soon. Soon. But, what about you?" Nathan changed the subject.

"Mostly I love to write. I like to write poetry. And some day I will write a novel."

Well, who had she ever shared that with? She shook her head nervously. She realized that she was really opening up to him. True, they were simple things, but they were the things she'd been holding on to so privately that she'd almost misplaced them. Feeling that she'd already let the 'cat out of the bag' she continued.

"Someday I'm going to write a best seller. Maybe it will have something to do with your story. Who knows? I can see it now 'Best Selling Author Geri Michaels has taken the country by storm with her latest novel about this fine African brother…'"

She spoke the words with an exaggerated tone. They both laughed.

"Oh. About me? No. But, I think you'll write someday. I'll buy hundreds of your books and send them to my family. So the notice will read, "Bestselling beautiful and magnificent author Ms. Geri Michaels has taken the continents by storm…"

She laughed, but stopped quickly to ask the question. "You've got hundreds of family members? A whole village or two."

"I'll tell you about it someday."

"Can't wait to hear that story." She laughed thinking about how many relatives she has. They laughed and talked a while longer. Realizing how tired she was beginning to feel, Geri looked at the clock.

"Do you know we have been talking for over an hour?" She asked Nathan.

"I think it's time for me to say good night, pleasant dreams and all of that." Geri spoke softly hoping that Nathan would not be offended.

"You're right. I'll talk to you tomorrow. Have a good sleep." Nathan closed his eyes to try to envision her face as he said the last words. He needed to take her with him as he slept through the night.

"You too." She gently pressed the button on the phone and held it to her chest. She closed her eyes trying to feel his lips on hers.

For years she had filled her life with her work. She convinced herself that her work was for a cause more worthy than any personal desires she may have had. Maybe it was because she'd been hurt deeply in her past efforts to love and receive love. Taking another chance on love didn't seem worth her while. Her willingness to give him the benefit of the doubt was now breaking through the tight space in which she had been living. She could feel it stretching every day and it felt good. She was experiencing a new kind of conversation, a new kind of attention, and a new kind of freedom to be more of who she really was. She was standing in the freedom to share her own thoughts while appreciating listening to his.

If there was ever a challenge in their conversations, it was to consider that all things were possible. He did not try to bate her or challenge her intellect, and he did not try to impress her with his. No. It was fresh. Their words spoke into the deepest crevices of their communication as if they sprang from the ground. She received them, caressed them, and then sent them back with gentle whispers that almost eluded human ears. So, was it time to invite him into her physical space?

Chapter 9

Nathan accepted her invitation to come for dinner. She couldn't remember the last time she cooked a complete meal. Between take out and frozen dinners, her time in the kitchen was generally for doing paperwork. Even though she had a home office, for some reason she was more inspired when working in her kitchen. She laughed at how long it had been since she even turned on her oven.

"Nathan, you have no idea what this means." Speaking aloud Geri shook her head with hilarity and reached on the shelf to get a box of rice. She suddenly remembered how she used to cook almost every night when she was married. She chuckled to herself when she realized how she rarely thought about the fact that she had even been married. It was as if she had been reincarnated as a single woman with no memory of anything in her first life.

"What was his name?" A burst of laughter came out of her mouth as she poured the rice into the pot of boiling water. Some of the water popped out of the pot onto her hand. She jumped back and said jokingly, "See, even thinking about it is painful!"

When the telephone rang she thought it might be Nathan, but it was her girlfriend Candace.

"Hey girlfriend. What you doing?" Candace's voice was light and happy. "Cooking." Geri did not want to say why she was cooking. She knew it would lead to a conversation that she was not ready to have with Candace and didn't have time to have it even if she was ready.

"Get out of here! What? Is your boss coming to dinner?" Candace laughed at the idea that Geri, the 'take out queen', was actually cooking.

"First of all, I'm the boss, and second of all you are not funny. I keep telling you that, but you just won't listen."

"Geri Renee Michaels. What are you up to?" Candace knew her well and could sense that something was different in the tone of her voice. It was a nervous excitement that seldom came from her friend's mouth.

"I knew I should'a never told you my middle name! Man! Can't I do something for myself? Anyway, to what do I owe this rare occasion of a weeknight call from you?" She said trying to change the subject.

"I was just thinking about you. You crossed my mind, so I stopped what I was doing and gave you a call. Is that alright?" Candace still knew that something was up, but decided not to press. Her concern was that something might have been wrong. She could tell by Geri's responses that nothing was wrong. Whatever was going on, Candace knew that she wasn't going to share it at that moment. She knew her friend all too well.

Feeling the burn from the boiling rice pot beginning to blister, she used it as an excuse to get off the phone.

"Girl, I just burned my hand. Let me go so I can do something with it. I'll call you tomorrow." Geri was so caught up in her own drama that she hadn't really considered that something might be wrong on Candace's end.

"Wait. Are you okay?"

"I'm okay, if you're okay." Candace responded.

"I am. Talk tomorrow. Love you!"

Geri blew a kiss through the phone. "Love you too." Candace hung up thinking, "I know she's not cooking for some man." She laughed to herself and said, "Na".

Geri did not know exactly what would happen that evening, but she was ready to spend time with him. They talked over the phone for weeks now. She finished cooking and started lighting her favorite scented candles. A mixed tape of music was already playing softly in the background. She wasn't sure what kind of music he liked, especially since he said he was a musician, but that particular tape always calmed her down. It was just what she needed.

The phone rang and she knew this time it was him. Everything about her seemed to smile as she answered.

"Hi. I'm on my way. Do you want me to pick something up?"

"No, everything's here but you."

"Okay. Can't wait to see you."

"Me too."

He was not sure whether he should tell her how excited he was about finally being able to spend time with her. Tired from the long day of work, he stopped home to shower and dress for the evening. He thought the shower might give him more energy, but he was still feeling sluggish. He also thought about how long it had been since he had spent an evening with anyone except the occasional after work stop with his co-workers for a beer. He had dreamed about holding her, but was trying not to make any assumptions about the night. Still it would be nice. Concentrating on the possibilities he almost drove past the exit to her house.

"Pay attention to the ground, Nathan." He grimaced slightly as his grandmother's words rang in his ears.

"What is it that the ground is saying to me?" After almost missing the exit he considered that it might be a mistake for him to visit while he was so exhausted. But more than anything he wanted to see her.

Chapter 10

The doorbell rang. Geri looked around the living room to see if everything was in place. She turned on another light so it didn't appear that she was trying to seduce him. 'Or am I?' she thought nervously. "Okay, pull it together. The man's waiting for you to let him in."

"Hi." His voice was soft, his smile charming as ever.

"Hi, back. Come on in."

She gestured for him to sit on the sofa. He noticed the Band-Aid on her hand and asked, "What happened?"

She stated that it was just a minor burn. He took her hand to his mouth and kissed it gently. He moved closer and kissed her mouth. How wonderful it felt as their lips met. It was soft yet intense like a slow bolt of lightning.

"Hello." He spoke softly into her ear while still holding her.

"Hello to you. Are you ready to sit down now?" She spoke teasingly.

"Yes I am. Are you going to sit with me?" He took her hand as they walked to the sofa. They sat just far enough apart to be able to turn comfortably to face each other. Nathan brushed her face with his hand and slowly exhaled.

"What was that?" She asked concerning the exhale.

"I am so happy to see you, to be here. I just feel so comfortable."

As he spoke the words, he realized that his comfort in her space relaxed him a little too much. He could feel his exhaustion begin to settle in. Her romantic mood setting was backfiring already. "Are you okay?" she asked.

"Just tired." He kissed the burn on her hand again, then laid his head back on the sofa.

"Do you mind if I close my eyes just for a few minutes?" She was surprised by his request.

"No, go ahead."

Almost as soon as she said it she could see him sinking into the sofa. He closed his eyes. She watched him silently for a few minutes, he was actually falling asleep. Her immediate thought was to nudge him. In her estimation, closing your eyes didn't mean going to sleep.

Fighting the desire to kiss him, she removed her hand from his, moved down and bent forward to get the remote off the coffee table. He did not move. She switched on the TV. Speaking softly to herself she said, "So much for romance and mood setting".

His upper body leaned sideways towards her and before she knew it, his head found her lap. He was half on and half off the sofa. Thinking he might be uncomfortable she thought about whispering to him to stretch out. But then he might end up sleeping through the night. No way was she going to let that happen. As it was, part of her wanted to wake him to let him know that this was not the way she'd planned to spend her evening. Another part felt a sense calm.

Something she hadn't experienced in a long while. Maybe she was more disappointed than surprised that he felt comfortable enough with her to fall asleep. With all the grace she could muster, she stroked his head tenderly deciding to let him rest. Still, watching him actually go to sleep her mind kept reverberating with the question, "Who does this?"

The sensuous smell of the candle moved through the air. It felt like they had shared a moment like this before. It was nice. Her shoulders released the tension of the day. She rested her head on the back of the sofa as she fought the idea of sleep herself.

He slept quietly, stirring when he realized that his head was on her lap. Embarrassed, he sat up. He had arrived at her home, sat on the couch and made himself too much at home. No telling what she might be thinking.

"Thank you." The words were muffled as he sat up trying to pull himself together. Saying "thank you" may have sounded lame, but he didn't know what else to say.

"Thank you for what?" Geri answered politely.

"For letting me rest. I don't usually go out after working so many hours, but I really wanted to see you."

"Do you feel better?"

There was a trace of sarcasm in her voice. She couldn't help it. As pleasant as the last few minutes had been, he still came to her house and went to sleep. He should have said,

"Geri, I am so sorry that I came to your house for the first time and fell asleep within fifteen minutes and don't think that this shows how I feel about you."

Yep, that's what he should have said. But trying to listen differently to this new person in her life she accepted his "thank you."

"I do feel better." He searched her face as he responded. "How about you? How are you? How was your day?"

"Do you want an answer to all those questions?" She laughed lightly and leaned over to pick up the remote control. She couldn't decide whether to turn the music back on or turn off the TV. Just nerves, she knew. She turned off the TV.

"Which one do you want to answer?" Did she really mean her question or was she just not in the mood to talk after he'd fallen asleep? He was starting to feel worse about it.

"I'm fine. I just didn't realize that you were so tired. Maybe we should have waited for another time." She followed up with, "So, this is the real Ntheba?" She waved her hand over his sweater and jeans, the first clothing she'd seen him in other than his uniform. He laughed and gently pulled her to him.

"I love kissing you." He spoke while their lips were still touching.

"I love you kissing me." She pressed her lips to his after her words. Her sarcasm melted in the warmth of their kiss.

They kissed longingly, as if they were being reunited after an extended absence from each other.

"Hum. It seems like that rest did you justice." She smiled and continued with, "Would you like something to eat?"

Things were getting a little heated. "You came for dinner, right?" She smiled as she reminded him that he came for the dinner she'd cooked.

"Not yet. I just want to sit here with you. Unless you want to eat?"

"No, I'm okay. Just let me know when you're ready."

They talked about their day and how happy they were to finally be together this way. Geri got them a glass of the wine she bought just for the occasion. It was her favorite. They toasted each other before continuing their conversation.

"Do you want to hear my story tonight?" His tone was serious.

"Yes, I've been waiting to hear. it." Recognizing the serious tone in his voice she almost felt the need to brace herself. What he said next convinced her that bracing might be needed.

"It's not good." Nathan put his wine glass on the table as he spoke. He turned from her and leaned forward with his hands clasped.

"No problem. Go ahead." She could feel her heart begin to pound, wondering what he was going to tell her.

"You know I used to work for my government, right?" Nathan began his story.

"There were so many things that we were made to do. Some of them were okay, but others were not." He was choosing his words carefully as he spoke.

Geri could sense his ambivalence about how much he should tell her. "It's okay. Whatever you want to share is fine." She assured him understandingly.

"I saw so much corruption that it was hard for me to do my job with a good conscience. It got worse when I witnessed violence against people who were arrested just for speaking out against things the government was doing." Nathan was getting choked up.

"Nathan, you don't have to say anything else. I understand, really." Geri tried to comfort him with her words, but they both knew she had no way of understanding what he was talking about.

"No, it's fine. I just get so angry still when I think about it. I saw so much violence. And then one night it came to me."

He sat up straight and continued.

"One night I said 'No, I can't do what you are asking me to do'. That's when I was beaten and threatened. They even threatened my family saying if I could not be trusted, neither could they." He leaned back in the chair and took Geri's hand.

"I think that is all I can say right now." His words were again taut with anger and what Geri now understood as deep sorrow.

Geri put her hand over his. She did not speak because her thoughts were flashing back to what she saw in him the first time. There was that midnight sea she could not understand then. There was that pain she could identify with not even knowing how it emerged. Her heart spoke to her softly saying "You are familiar with pain. You are familiar with hurt and fear."

Releasing their hands, they held each other letting their feelings flow between them. Still holding her, Nathan said softly, "War is bad. War that's against your own people is even worst. You have nowhere to turn."

It all sounded surreal to Geri, but the pain that he felt as he shared was evident to her. He had done his job until he could no longer comply with the things they asked of him. The violence he witnessed and encountered, the fear for his life, made him have to leave his home.

As she listened, his words echoed with sorrow and heartbreak piercing what had been a place of serenity. No amount of candle light or music could erase the words from the room. In that moment, no words could make the reliving of the pain he felt go away. She could only listen.

"I can never go back. I never want to go back. I want to bring my family here." He pulled away from her as he spoke.

"I didn't even have time to say good bye to my mother, sister and brother. I didn't have a chance to say good bye to my daughter." Nathan's voice was now low and raspy.

"I have a daughter. Her name is Asha. She's now five years old. I had to leave her behind with her mother." As he said the last part he could see her body tensing. Before he could go any further, Geri interrupted.

"So, you're married." The question came out as a statement. It was as if she rose out of his pain to a reality she had not anticipated. She sat up straight and without speaking a word her body language insinuated itself into his story.

She'd searched his ring finger the first day they spoke in the parking lot. She was happy not to see a ring, but could not believe that such a handsome man could be unattached. How could she have let that suspicion fly out the window? 'Wishful thinking' was the response that flashed in her head. 'But didn't he say, "I'm free!" What the hell!' All of this ran so quickly through her mind that she had a sense of whiplash.

"No, I'm not married." He could see her expression changing.

"We were not married, but we were a family." He tried to take her hand, but she pulled it away.

"What do you mean?" Before he could answer, "You still love her." Another question-statement.

"I do love her. She is my daughter's mother and we were a family before I left. I just don't know what it means now." Answering her questions honestly he knew he was risking her saying that she did not want to see him again.

"Are you still in contact with her? Does she think you're faithful to her?"

Geri heard the barrage of questions come from her mouth, now on autopilot as the old tapes of her past relationships rewound and played fast forward.

"Yes. Geri, I…" Feeling his heart breaking, he tried to continue. She cut him off.

"Okay." She took a deep breath. "Why did you tell me you were free? Don't you remember telling me that you were free? 'I'm free' were your words."

"I know. I know. I don't know why I said it like that. Maybe because it's been so long since I saw her. We had planned to get married, but we did not have time before I was forced to leave. I don't know. Maybe I didn't want you to say no, you're taken."

The moment was slipping away from him. How could he have been so stupid, to wait until now to tell her this? Did he think it would make a difference being woven into the full story? The truth is although he meant to think about how he would tell her beforehand, he didn't.

Geri stared at him searching his face for something that might change the disappointment she was feeling. She asked herself, "How could I have been so naïve to think he wasn't attached to someone?" She watched him panic and thought how he deserved it.

"Geri, I didn't know how to tell you about her. I felt free because I wanted to be, because I've been here alone for years. I wanted to be able to be with you." He was thinking that he should just shut up. The more he said, the less she said. That couldn't be good.

She shook her head and thought about how transparent she'd thought their relationship was. More than that, she thought about how transparent she wanted it to be. What the hell was she thinking about going for the okeydoke? Her cynicism hit hard in those places that had become so tender by the touch of all his other words. She breathed deeply and turned away from him. She could not look at him and listen to him at the same time.

"Okay. Tell me everything." As she blew out the breath she'd been holding in, she was ready to continue the conversation. There had to be a way to make this right. She was not willing to give up what she felt as easily as she had in the past.

"I've been trying to bring my daughter and her mother here so they would be safe." As he spoke he looked at her hoping she would understand.

"I love and miss my daughter, Geri. She was only six months old when I left." He said nothing more about his child's mother.

"What about the rest of your family?" Geri was fully aware of the omission, but did not want to stop the flow of conversation.

"My sister is trying to get to the United States on her own, but my brother will stay behind to make sure our mom is okay." Nathan paused to read her face. He saw nothing.

"Usually the girl, the daughter stays behind. But Chandra, we call her Channi, was the one who always wanted to come here. To me, it didn't matter. It wasn't until everything started going wrong that I had to leave. Where else would I go? To France, to England?"

Nathan was trying his best to get through his story even though he knew she was still thinking about his daughter's mom.

"Why not those other countries?" Geri was curious.

"I guess I was supposed to come here to meet you." Nathan answered and smiled.

"Don't push it, Nathan." Geri was not amused.

"No. I'm serious. There's something with us Geri. I really believe that or I would not be here tonight." He tried to take her hand again, but she pulled it away.

"Okay. I understand. I just need you to know how hard it was to leave all of what I knew and loved. I didn't want to do it. They were going to kill me and my family if I did not cooperate."

Nathan stood as if to walk away from where they were sitting. He turned to Geri in the silence that had now captivated the room. Still standing he continued,

"All the politics. The brutality! I had to leave my own country to save my life. If I'm not there, my family will be safe. That's how it goes. It was not planned. It was necessary and quick."

He sat back down, this time closer to her. Looking squarely in her face he explained,

"My friend's people helped me escape. Geri, this was the friend I saw killed right in front of me! They said he was some kind of spy or something! It was hell, just pure hell!" Torment strangled Nathan's words.

Feeling his anguish, Geri began to cry silently. She had moved with him in his story and no longer concentrated on the woman he left behind.

"Geri, since I got here there's been no one. I just work. I have been so lonely. You may not believe this, but some nights I just cried myself to sleep. Trying to get my family here was all I could see."

"I'm so sorry Nathan." It was all Geri could say.

"I know. I'm sorry I didn't tell you this before. I just feel so much shame. Until you, I felt like I was being punished for leaving my family. I thought I was doing the right thing, but did I make it worst for them? I asked myself that every day and planned to live with the guilt. Then I saw you."

Nathan reached out for her hand again. This time she did not draw it back, but it remained stiff in his hand.

"I was not looking for anybody." He offered the words almost apologetically. "Sometimes I wanted somebody to just be with and sometimes I was not looking for love."

Nathan wanted so desperately for her to believe him. He was not sure if it would make a difference. He could not imagine losing her now.

"So what about her?" Geri asked about his child's mother by emphasizing the word "her". Nathan had not given her name. Not giving him the opportunity to answer, she continued,

"And just how do you see us – me and you – fitting into all of this?

What do you want from me Nathan?"

She needed concrete answers, but knew that there weren't any.

"Geri, I love you. I never knew that it was possible to love two people at the same time. My love for you is now. It is different than anything I've ever felt. So I don't really know how to explain it. I am not trying to just get with you." Nathan spoke so freely that even he was surprised. There was nothing hidden in his words. At that moment, he was allowing himself to be totally vulnerable. It was something he rarely did for any reason or anyone.

"I don't know what this all means, but I do know that I love you." He felt his heart pounding in his chest as he continued to speak.

Geri searched Nathan's face to see if there was something -anything that could make her want to walk away. She could see or feel nothing except her love for him and the belief that he loved her.

"Is it selfish of me to want you? Wait, don't answer that. Let me. It is. I know what my life is. I don't know how it will end up." Nathan was trying to answer the questions she now asked in her mind.

"Yes, it is selfish, but crazy enough, I believe you love me." She responded.

Hearing herself acknowledge his selfishness, she made the decision to be selfish as well. This time she would take the chance at loving and being loved the way it was. Life could be cruel whether it was in the politics of Angola or here in the U.S. People were dying, children were crying out, families were pulled apart by life's raw deals and underneath it all was some sort of selfishness that lacked love. Why not embrace the selfishness of love? Even if it lasted for just a short time, wasn't it worth it?

Nathan continued to share his story. He looked away when the details were wretchedly painful. Geri could feel those moments of agony without looking into his eyes. He ended by telling her how much it hurt him to be alone in her country and that his love for his daughter's mother was something he had for a long time. There had never been anything to challenge that love. Now here he was not certain what to do except hold on to her, Geri, for dear life.

"Geri, can you see any of this?" Now clinching what honor he had left and feeling the need to hold back some of his need for her, his question was a mask. He really wanted to say, "Please don't turn away from me. I need you."

"I'm so sorry you had to experience all of that." That was all she could say.

They sat in silence for what seemed an eternity. Both of them were replaying in their minds some of what had been discussed. Nathan had shared his story to the extent that nothing else needed to be said. Geri was doing what she did well, which was putting things into perspective. She was not quite sure what to do with the part about him loving another woman, regardless of the circumstances. She asked herself if she really cared about his other life. She believed he loved her and she knew she loved him. Loving anyone meant being vulnerable. As crazy as it seemed, at that moment she felt that he was a place where she could live and breathe, a place where she would be warm in the coldest realities of both of their lives. Maybe it was his passion for life. Maybe it was the compassion that she saw in him. Maybe it just was what it was, love.

They had moved through an emotional battle, but it seemed they had come through safely at least for the time being. They embraced and the rush that she felt during their initial encounter in the parking lot rose up in her again. It made her hold him tighter and he responded. They did not kiss and it seemed almost as if it was a conscious decision. Thinking that it was a good time to ask, she pulled away from him and broke the silence.

"Okay." She spoke with composed determination as she turned to look at him. "Are you hungry?"

"Actually I am. You cooked for us?" he asked with a look of delight on his face. Although he could smell the food when he entered her home, a lot had occurred since then. He was not sure if he was welcomed to stay for a meal.

"Yes, I did." What seemed to be his genuine response made her wonder whether her invitation to him had been to come to dinner or just come by. But she was glad that she had cooked. They would have a meal to settle them into the rest of the evening.

"I hope you like chicken and rice. Can I fix you a plate?"

"No. I'll do it. Let me fix yours too?"

She watched him go into the kitchen and then through the open area between the two rooms. He moved with ease. He caught her smiling when he looked over to ask where she kept the plates.

He smiled back and said, "Thank you", but the "thank you" did not seem to have much to do with directing him to the plates.

While he was in the kitchen she went into the bathroom, closed the door, and leaned against it. She closed her eyes, took a deep breath and blew it out slowly. As much as she had planned for a romantic evening with the soft music and scented candles, listening to his story had overshadowed the idea. She ran cool water on her hand and looked at herself in the mirror. This was not an 'it is what it is' moment. There was nothing cavalier about how she felt or her decision to stay with it. She turned off the water, dried her hands and stood up straight.

"This is what I asked for. Isn't it?" She smiled sadly at herself, recalling how she'd once stated that the person brought into her life did not have to be completely available. Mama always said, "Be careful what you ask for." Geri turned off the light and went back to the living room. Nathan was just coming out of the kitchen. He had already placed her food on the coffee table before she came out of the bathroom.

"Thank you. It's nice to have someone serve you dinner." She spoke wittingly and seriously at the same time.

"You are welcome." He handed her a napkin and fork.

After the intensity of their conversation, it was astonishing how they were able to laugh and share the way they had before his revelations. She turned on the music and the sultry sounds filled the air. She was still hopeful about their relationship. She wanted to be with him to give herself to him. Not something she would have even considered a year ago. In fact, a year ago she would have asked him to leave as soon as he told his story. She would have found a way to politely say, "I am so sorry about all of that, but I don't have room for more drama in my life."

She was not sure if it was Nathan that was different, or if she was changing.

It had been a long time since she let anyone get close to her. This one looked her in the face with a reflection that just might help heal the deep dark places that had been left by so-called love in the past. Yes, she would be selfish in love this time.

Resting now in his arms made it seem that everything would be alright. It also made her feel warmth she had not felt in a long time.

Knowing where that could lead, she raised her head to kiss him before saying, "Okay, you have got to go."

Geri sat up straight and patted gently on his knee.

"Are you sure?" He considered that the mood change had come from her concern about his life and questions he still could not answer.

"Yes, I'm sure."

He wanted to be with her all night, even if they did no more than lie together in each other's arms until they fell asleep. Somehow that might reassure her.

"I understand." He kissed her hand and sat on the edge of the sofa. "Thank you for listening to me tonight. It was good to finally talk with you about everything and to tell you how I feel about you."

Nathan stood and pulled Geri up to him. He hugged her tightly and gently kissed her eyes. When they stood apart she could see the exhaustion on his face. She understood how tired he must have been, but she was not ready for what she anticipated would come. If she thought that she could just lay with him and hold him through the night, she would have asked him to stay.

She walked him to the door and kissed him sweetly.

"Drive safely." Her words followed him out the door.

He smiled in response and said, "Talk to you tomorrow?" It was a question. He was not sure if she would ever talk to him again.

As she closed the door behind him she said, "Okay, Ms. Geri. Where do you go from here?" She knew she still wanted him, even with all the baggage that he carried. She believed that he had come into her life at this time to love her. The way he looked at her was how she wanted to be looked at, lifting the lid off of the things she had missed feeling, believing and oddly enough the things she'd missed knowing.

Chapter 11

That night she laid in bed thinking about the years of just giving her love away. She thought about how one day she made the decision not to let anybody have her love again. Eventually she realized that she just needed to be more deliberate about why she would give it and who she would give it to. She remembered something she wrote months before called "An Ode to My Sisters." The verses were now clamoring loudly in her mind.

"I am so tired of feeling that in the scheme of things I don't count enough for my love. My life gets turned upside down inside me just because I let him count too much. I am so tired of hurting, of crying, of needing that touch and of needing him to understand and appreciate who I am all by myself not because of him or because I'm with him, but all by myself because I do have the right stuff."

Would Nathan fall into this category? She moved from the question and shifted in the bed as if to allow him to get closer. She turned on her side and felt herself drifting off, but the thoughts kept coming, contemplations of her past. Her mind sunk deeply into areas she thought had been put to rest. Saddling the urge to remember, she got the journal from her nightstand and began to write,

"Love is an awesome thing. It can weigh you down or lift you up whenever it wants. It's like a force of nature, something that you have no control over. Perhaps love is its own thing with atoms, particles and shapes that fit into the size of its captives or creates obesity without the pleasure of consuming good flavors. At its best, love is a formidable companion. At its worst, it's hell on wheels. You have options about what to do with love. You can embrace it, leave it be, or just toy with it awhile until it decides what it's going to do with you. Yeah, love is its own thing. And if you don't do something with it, it will do something with you." She put the journal and pen on the floor.

Memories flooded her mind, even the one she very seldom thought about, her marriage. Whenever the subject of marriage came up in conversation with her friends Geri would say that she was married a long time ago not because she was now old, but because she was really young when she did it. "The girl-woman" as she put it had claimed her "boy-man" when neither of them were ready. Admittedly, it was not the smartest thing she ever did. Mark was one of those guys who could not keep his pants on. As she had shared with Kyra, Geri believed that if she opened the dictionary she may have found his face next to the word 'hoe' and she did not mean a garden instrument. He would have been there next to the word just smiling. Proud too! Mark was the epitome of a man who constantly and carelessly fooled around because he thought he should and could get away with it.

The craziest thing was she knew this about him before they got married. "What was that about?" is a question that she had since answered with much clarity. Sometimes childhood experiences can mess you up inside and out. The experience with Griffy for one lingered in her mind as something she did wrong and needed to atone for. Her father leaving them putting them out to be exact was something else that she wrestled with for years. How the latter became her plight was beyond her real comprehension, but she held on to it until she was able to let it go. There was no wisdom attached to any of it including the decision to marry Mark. She was twenty two years young making choices that reflected her lack of wisdom.

The sound of a big truck passing by her window interrupted her thoughts for a moment, but they were instantly recovered. She had written a poem about her and Mark before they got married, "*I walk around the corner and I see you, no younger or older than we be.*" Such elements of wisdom at the time she did not understand. If she had she would have known that the poem was saying, "Stop! Keep walking around the corner until you are older." The marriage had been a long, in and out journey that ended badly. But the end was a new beginning. She pushed her way into becoming more of who her grandmother once told her to be loving and strong with wisdom that balances them both.

Surprisingly she had peace in the midst of her remembering it all. She had forgiven Griffy, her Daddy and Mark. More than that, she had forgiven herself for ever believing that any of what they did was her fault. Embracing Ella's mantra had helped tremendously. And tonight it was evident. So what about Nathan? The question was one to rest on and pick up the next day.

Chapter 12

Geri could hear her phone ringing. She reached over to the nightstand, but it was not there. Fumbling around the bed she found it under the comforter. She raised up to look at the caller ID number. It was Nathan. She smiled and pressed the answer key.

"Good morning. Are you up?" His tone was warm and welcoming.

"I am up. Are you at work already?" She replied not realizing the time.

"I am. I get here between 6 and 6:30 every morning." He spoke cheerfully. "How did you sleep?"

"I slept well. I thought about you before I fell off to sleep." Did she really just admit that?

"Are you coming in?" He teased. She never missed work. "I can't wait to see your face."

She ended the call saying, "See you shortly" and thought how it would have been to wake up with him that morning.

On her way to work one of her staff called on her cell phone to say that there was a fire in a domestic violence shelter and one of the children was being brought to the center. Her mother was rushed to the hospital in critical condition and they had not been able to locate any family. The counselor on duty at the center was told that it was a temporary drop and that a social worker would be in to get her that afternoon. The child that they were bringing to them had not suffered any physical injuries in the fine, but had just gone to the shelter that week with her mother who had been badly beaten by her husband. They had to sneak out of the house in the middle of the night leaving everything except what they had on their backs. The little girl was nine years old, afraid and confused.

No matter how early she arrived, it never seemed early enough to head off emergencies. On this morning, the street that she usually took to get to the office was closed because of a bad car accident. Traffic was backed up three blocks and it was only 7:30 AM. By the time she got to the building after detouring three more blocks, it was almost 8 o'clock. She looked for Nathan, but he was nowhere in sight. This meant that she probably would not see him all day.

Rushing, Geri forgot to greet Gina who was covering the front desk that morning. "Where is the little girl?"

"I'm sorry Gina, good morning? Now where is she?" She apologized and went back to the concern at hand.

"No problem, Ms. Michaels. Tanya took her to get some breakfast. Also, someone is waiting for you outside your office door. It's the security guard from next door who helped you that day…"

Gina smiled as she saw her about to reprimand her for letting someone just go to her office.

"He said you were expecting him."

"Ok. But next time…" Geri smiled back with her warning.

As she moved toward her office she knew that she would only have a few minutes to talk with him.

"Good morning again." he said smiling and gesturing for her to walk into her office. "I have something for you." He stated while following her.

"Well, this is a surprise. Do you do this kind of thing often?" Geri was not sure what to make of the surprise visit and wondered what Gina thought when he asked to wait at her office.

"No, not too often. I hope it's okay." Nathan was now trying to read her response.

"So what do you have for me?" For the sake of time Geri moved on to the question.

"Can I shut the door?"

"Yes, you can." She wondered what he was up to.

He shut the door and took her into his arms and kissed her, then he moved from her saying, "Have a beautiful day."

"You too." Geri responded feeling a little flushed by the kiss and the idea that it happened in her office. It was a first. When he left she sat down at her desk with a big grin on her face. The phone rang.

"Geri, what do you want us to do with the little girl they brought in this morning?" It was Tanya.

"If she's finished eating, bring her down to me."

When she walked into the office, she held her head down and held herself tightly with her own arms. Geri gestured to her to come over to her, which she did. Without touching her, she asked "What's your name, sweetheart?"

"Meredith." The child's voice was low and trembling.

She lifted Meredith's head with the tip of her pointer finger, released it and smiled at her. Meredith did not smile back.

"Did you get something to eat, Meredith?"

The little girl shook her head affirmatively and asked, "Where's my mom?"

"Your mom was taken to the hospital so they can take care of her. They brought you here so we can take care of you. You'll see your mom soon." She shook her head to acknowledge her understanding of what Geri said, then lowered her eyes.

Meredith stayed in Geri's office for a good part of the morning. They talked as much as she would allow and drew pictures together. When it was time for her meeting, Geri took her to the playroom where staff would attend to her and asked them to keep her abreast of how she was doing. As the day progressed, it appeared that Meredith would most likely be with them overnight.

Throughout the day, she thought about how her dream to help children around the world had plopped itself on a street in Baltimore.

What happened to that dream? What happened to all the other dreams that poured through her fingers like grains of sand? Watching Meredith reminded Geri of her childhood and the promise she made to herself that she would do great things. Today Haven seemed just the beginning of what she had yet to think further about or plan. She needed to talk. It was time to talk with the person she knew would not judge or advise her unless she asked for either. She needed a sounding board. Although she had several girlfriends, the best one to answer that call was Renee.

"Hey, can you meet me for dinner tomorrow?"

"Sure. Where do you want to meet?"

"How about the Best of Soul? About 7:30?"

The Best of Soul was one of Geri's favorite restaurants. It reminded her of her favorite spots in Chicago where she lived years ago. She loved the food and knew that she and her friend could stay there for hours and not be pushed to leave.

"Sounds good. What's up? I can hear something in your voice." Renee paused and then said almost screaming into the phone, "You finally gave up the booty, huh girlfriend?"

"See where you go? You know you're not right." Geri laughed to herself. Only Renee would ask that question.

"I'll tell you when I see you?"

Renee Marshall was different from Kyra and Candace in many ways. Renee was sometimes almost irreverent about everything Geri stood for, but stood firmly with her when the need arose. She had often posed the question, "Are you happy with your life?" to Geri. Geri sometimes referred to her as her alter ego. They'd known each other since their college days at Howard and over the years Geri admired her ability to take risk. Renee had no problem letting go of what even resembled craziness about to happen, that is unless she thought she could calm it down.

I guess you could say that Renee took calculated risk that may have looked impetuous to some who did not know her. Geri knew her well and would often tease "When I grow up I want to be just like you!" They would laugh and Renee would respond "Fat chance!"

Geri and Renee could physically pass for sisters. Like Geri, Renee was tall and athletically built. The difference was that Renee worked out all the time and Geri hardly did. Geri once teased her saying, "I was just born with good genes."

Renee threw back the response, "So my genes aren't good?"

Both also had long thick hair that they knew came from their grandmothers' Native American heritage. Geri had let her hair grow back after years of wearing it shorter and from the back you could easily mistake one friend for the other. That is until they started talking. Renee had a tendency to talk louder than everybody else in the room. She claims it is because she grew up with six older brothers and had to talk loud enough so she could be heard over them.

Renee was hardly ever on time for anything. Tonight was no

exception. At least every other birthday her friends and family would give her a new watch. She wore them proudly, but not purposefully.

When the light on her phone lit up, Geri thought it might be Nathan. Interestingly enough she had not thought about him all day and gave herself silent kudos for not allowing him to occupy her mind. She smiled when she saw that it was Renee.

"Hey, I'm on my way." Renee spoke in her typical matter of fact tone. She also let her know that another friend of theirs would be joining them.

"No problem. I'll be here when you get here. I'm nursing this apple martini you and everybody keeps telling me is so good."

"Who?" Geri asked.

"Who what?" Renee quipped back evasively.

"You know what I mean. Who's joining us?" Geri knew that Renee was trying to avoid saying who, but wanted to be able to say that she told her there would be someone joining them when she showed up.

"Listen. I can't wait to catch up. See you in a couple." Changing the subject, Renee ended the conversation and hung up.

Immediately after Geri figured out that it was Leslie who would be joining them.

"No she didn't." Geri spoke aloud. She held back from calling Renee to say "Forget about tonight. I think I just need to go home and get some rest."

She felt badly about not wanting Leslie to join them. They had all been friends since college, but Leslie left before graduation to get married. She'd fallen head over heels about Mike and when he was offered a job in Arizona, no one in their circle was suprised. She was concerned about how she would react to the news about Nathan and she had not called Leslie since her stepfather died. She wasn't sure how to apologize and then turn around to talk about the new man in her life.

Renee knew that she hadn't spoken with Leslie in months. She also knew her well enough to know that the longer she waited, the less likely it would be that she would call. Inviting her was sort of a break the silence for everybody's sake.

Even though Nathan was the reason she really needed to talk with Renee, Geri felt herself second-guessing whether or not she was ready to talk about him. She wondered if she should keep it a secret at least until she really knew where they were headed. She thought about what Renee was going to say about him being African. She could imagine her saying, "I know you have lost your mind. You know how our African brothers are. I hear they want too much control too."

She also thought about what Leslie was going to say about her when she heard his story. Not being as vocal about things as Renee, she would probably say something like,

"Geri, are you sure you want to get caught up in something like this? Even if he's not married…"

With all of that going on in her head she almost missed Renee coming in the restaurant. She took her drink from the bar counter and met her just as she was walking away from the door.

"Girl, I am so sorry I'm late." Renee's expression was genuine. Looking at her with a 'you are always late' smirk Geri responded, "I am just glad to see you." Mindful of the drink, she gave her a one arm hug.

Melanie Driscol, the restaurant owner came over right away and walked them to their seats. Mel knew Geri through one of her board members. She was also quite familiar with the routine of Geri waiting for Renee to arrive. Both women spoke warmly to her. Geri asked for a table in the back where they could 'holler and act a fool if they wanted'.

Mel laughed and said, "Like that's new. I'm gonna sit you where I always sit you."

Renee rolled her eyes then smiled.

"Please. Renee you know that's right" was Mel's response.

Geri could feel herself getting a little nervous about the conversation they were about to have. She had a silly grin on her face when they slid into their seats.

"So what's up?" Renee said looking at her trying to see what had her grinning like a Cheshire cat.

Ignoring Renee's exploring eyes she asked, "Is Leslie still coming?"

"Yes." She drew out the word 'yes' putting several s'es at the end.

"Okay." Geri smiled and took a long sip of her watered down drink.

Leslie arrived in the midst of their small talk. When she got to the table, Geri leaned over and hugged her with an apologetic "Hey girl. How are you? I'm so sorry I haven't kept in touch."

Leslie returned the hug and said, "Listen, I understand. But when are you going to take time out for yourself instead of giving it all to that center?"

"Funny you should ask. We'll get to that." Geri stored Leslie's question in her mind as a segue sharing her information.

In the meantime, the three of them laughed and talked about foolishness for a while. Renee hit a serious note when she told them that she was about to leave Baltimore to move to Washington, D.C.

"Okay ladies." Renee spoke in a lower tone than usual, so they knew she was about to say something serious.

Leslie and Geri looked at each other and asked simultaneously, "What?"

"I am moving to D.C. I've been offered a job that I cannot refuse. It's at a corporate law firm." Renee waited for their responses.

Renee currently worked for the State of Maryland in the Department of Commerce, but grew tired of the politics.

"Hey, listen, I am happy for you!" Leslie spoke up.

"Congratulations girlfriend! I'm gonna miss you, but I'm happy for you also."

Geri got up and hugged her. She thought 'So this is why she invited Leslie."

"Group hug! Group hug!" Leslie yelled out and leaned over to hug Renee who was sitting next to her.

"How you gonna have a group hug when you only reached over to hug one in the group? Get up!" Geri laughed and reached out her arm to Leslie.

The two women hugged their friend then sat down.

"You two are so silly." Renee laughed as the words came out of her mouth, but she could feel the tears welling up in her eyes. She was going to miss her friends. She knew that neither of them left the state of Maryland unless it was for business or for an extended vacation that they rarely took.

"Renee you are only going to be up the street." Geri said as if reading her mind.

"Besides Diva, I don't see you that much anyway. So don't perpetrate." Leaning slightly over the table to make her point, Leslie chimed in to lighten the moment.

"So, are you going to tell us the name of the firm or what?" Geri asked.

"I guess that would be a good idea, huh? It's Marcoff, Dandridge and Dandridge. They're based in Boston but are expanding to the southeast region. I had three interviews and they made the offer on Monday." As she was sharing, Renee knew they were going to harass her for not saying anything sooner.

Almost on cue Leslie asked, "And why are we just finding out?"

"Really!" Geri added.

"I wasn't sure if I even wanted to make the move. Me, in corporate America?" Renee's response showed a side of her that was rarely exposed. Being uncertain about what to do was not her normal modes operandi.

"Please. Although they're not going to know what hit them, it will be a good hit for them." Leslie stated confidently.

"Okay, I can't believe I understood just what you said." Geri whispered as if she didn't want anyone to hear.

"I know. It was silly not telling you. But once I made up my mind you two were the first to hear it." As she spoke Renee threw them kisses like she was a movie star.

Geri responded with, "You're so stupid!" It was a term she heard the children use when they were kidding with each other. Oddly enough it was their way of sharing an endearment instead of an insult. And it seemed to fit Renee perfectly.

Leslie looked at both of them and in her spirit could see what neither saw was about to happen to them, especially Geri. Both women were about to leave to start a life they could never have imagined and all of them were about to enter new seasons in their lives. How Leslie knew this she was not sure and so she kept it to herself.

"I love you guys." Renee said assuredly to both her friends.

"So what else is going on?" When Leslie asked the question a chill ran through her and her body quivered.

Geri noticed and asked, "What was that?"

"I don't know. Maybe somebody ran over my grave." Leslie shrugged her shoulders and answered.

Seeing how they were looking at her she laughed and said quickly,

"You know that's an old saying. What?"

Geri and Renee looked at each other and rolled their eyes.

"Anyhow…" Renee spoke to change the subject.

"So what about your man? What's his name?" Geri asked still on Renee's page.

"You know that's not going so well." Renee answered. "It's no big deal anyway."

"I know you don't have the nerve to act like you don't care. I thought you liked him." Leslie pressed the issue but got no response from Renee.

Turning towards Geri, "So, why are we so glowy?" Renee asked, leaning back with her arms crossed and a smile on her face.

Geri looked at Renee without responding and then answered with a twisted smile on her face. "No you didn't go there."

"Yea, I did." Renee leaned forward.

"And you are not going to act like you're not gonna tell us." Leslie's voice had a hint of an incredulous tone.

"Okay, okay. I'm seeing someone." Geri replied. Shrugging her shoulders she added, "He's younger." She elongated the word younger.

Renee mockingly asked "How much younger?" Before Geri could respond she quipped, "And I know there's more to it. Look at you. Where did you meet him? What's his name? Where does he work? Does he work?"

At the question, "Does he work?" Leslie grunted "Unh".

Geri interrupted her friend's interrogation with a tone that brought a hushed silence to the moment.

"Can I say something?"

"Yes. By all means. Speak!" Renee responded with a similar tone while leaning forward and cupping her chin with her hands.

"Thank you!" Shaking her head at the whole exchange, Leslie responded for Geri.

"He's about seven or so years younger. And in fact, he is everything I asked for including that he fit into my schedule." Geri stated.

"What the hay does that mean?" Leslie asked in her none cursing way.

"It means that he is not completely available because of circumstances. And it means that it's exactly what I wanted. You know I was trying to fit a man in my already cramped up life. So I wasn't asking for anything serious…" Listening to herself Geri could not go any further.

"Okay, now I'm asking. What the hell does that mean?" Renee chimed n.

Before Geri could answer, Leslie continued with, "So what's the circumstances' Are you doing the do?"

"Stop grinning and tell us the damned information." Renee was getting impatient.

"Ladies, give me a chance to answer at least one question." Geri sat up as if to give a report at a board meeting. These women were tough and she knew she had to make everything she said sound right, at least as right as it could sound.

"Okay. First of all he's African. He's beautiful. He's humble and strong, and he makes my heart happy when we're together."

"Uh, uh!" Sucking their teeth, Leslie and Renee spoke at the same time.

"So, he's fine and charming and all that good stuff, but what's the situation? Why are you trying to be selective about what you're telling us?"

Leslie asked with a look of suspicion about what Geri had gotten herself into. She was the one who usually took the high road and was serious about everything being in order.

"He had to leave his home because of a political situation. He was by profession an engineer, but now works as a security guard in the building next to Haven."

Renee frowned then waved her hand down over her face to demonstrate wiping the expression off and up to turn it into a fixed smile. Geri sucked her teeth and kept talking.

"He has a family in his country, but had to leave them…"

Renee interjected with "Seriously, a security guard and already hooked up. Geri."

"It's been years since he's seen them. I don't know. Neither of us was looking for this. It just happened. And as I just told you, my prayer was to ask that someone special be sent even if he wasn't free to commit. I did not mean like this, but I prayed that prayer because I just felt like it had been so long for me that I would be happy just to have a little fling. Then he shows up, all that I want in a man…" Geri's tone was almost confessional.

"Geri, do you really need to hear a run-down of what you just said?" Renee asked rhetorically and then continued with, "Okay, here it goes. Number one, nothing just happens. Well, maybe a run in your pantyhose when you're getting out of the car. But even that don't just happen, something had to cause it. Two, you might have prayed about it. But who'd you pray to? God don't send no crazy stuff just to shut us up. You better look beyond Mr. Fine like chocolate man. Yes, I know you like the chocolate."

Renee smiled for a second with the last statement, but went right back to the seriousness in her voice. "I don't know Ger."

"What kind of family? I know it may sound like a stupid question, but what damn kind of family?" Leslie butted in. Her eyes were on Renee even as she posed the question to Geri.

"He's got a daughter and a woman back home. They're not married, but if he hadn't come here they would have probably gotten married." Geri went on to share more of the "situation" as Leslie put it. Afterwards, there was a very pregnant pause that seemed to bounce around the table like a bubble. Both waited for Leslie to go off, but their friend surprised them.

"You know what?" Leslie paused for another second and then said, "Go for it! Yes. My lovely friend. Go for it!"

Renee looked at Leslie in shock and said, "Now see, if that was me, you'd be calling me all kind of names and giving me all kinds of lectures. I can't believe this." Renee looked at Leslie with an indignant stare, then turned to Geri. She continued with, "You know I feel you, Geri. But if it was me, Leslie would call me…"

Leslie shot back with a loving laugh "That's because you always doing something crazy."

Renee continued with what was now a rant. "See, you two are not right. That's wrong. Why does she get to do it with Nathan and it be okay?"

"First of all, who said I did it with Nathan?" Geri broke in on their bantering.

"You did!" Renee spoke.

"No I didn't. You just think I did because I described him so well." Geri started laughing so hard she could hardly get the next statement out.

"Renee, don't be projecting yourself all up into my business!" Their seriousness was momentarily lifted as they burst into laughter.

Leslie blew a kiss to Renee, then turned to Geri and said, "Geri, life is so short. You know I just buried someone who I loved and still love dearly. Love is special." She placed her hand on her heart and finished with, "Don't turn your back on it. I know who you are. No matter how it may appear to others, you know who you are. Live in love as long as you can. Be good to yourself and love, and it will be good to you. Don't you remember what you told us your grandmother use to say? Well now's the time to use it."

At that point, Geri was in tears. They were bittersweet tears because she knew that Leslie was right. She was also touched by her empathy. Leslie seemed to always have something to say that they didn't want to hear. Even when she was kidding around, her words made you stop and take stock. Today her words rang crystal clear.

The lingering question was how long would their love last? Could it be sustained in the midst of what was so complicated? But feeling better about having the conversation and drying her tears, Geri lifted her tired and watered down apple martini to her friends with a smile. She had shared the new circumstances in her life with part of her sister circle. They raised their glasses back to her and then to each other.

Looking at all of their half empty and watered down drinks, Renee beckoned to the waiter.

"Can we get a fresh round?"

The rest of the evening they laughed and talked themselves to a place of sheer peace about their lives and new found decisions.

Geri drove home with her friends' words about her relationship with Nathan resting in her mind and her heart. The most promising words were "And, when or if it has to end and you fall apart even a little bit, we will be right here for you."

She smiled and began humming Luther Vandross' song, *Never Too Much*" to herself.

Chapter 13

Geri leaned back in her office chair and watched a leaf falling from the tree outside her window. As it floated to the ground she knew that for a while it would be no different to the touch. Thinking how at some point it would wither and die, she tried to recall ever caring about the transition until that day. It was a subtle sign of life that she would have missed a few months ago. The symbolism made her wince as she involuntarily connected it to the precariousness in her relationship with Nathan. Although taking things slowly, they had been seeing each other for months. After their conversation about his situation, they had become much closer than she could have imagined. Dismissing what might become of them, she turned her thoughts to what they already were. She cared deeply for him and believed he felt the same. They had conversations that skirted around the edges of what might become of them and periodically Nathan would kiss her in a way that made her want more. Besides the obvious about what more meant, she also understood that she wanted more in the sense of having all of him. She was not sure why she was so conscious about it all today.

Nathan called earlier that morning to see if he could stop by to see her on his afternoon break. He gave her no clue about why he wanted to see her mid-day, saying only that he missed her. They spoke over the phone every night, but their schedules had prevented them from seeing each other for several days. Still doing what she could to limit their engagement during the workday, particularly in her office, Geri suggested that they meet for lunch at the diner some blocks away.

Mabel's Diner was starting to fill up with the usual lunch crowd. Nathan was already there when Geri arrived and walked over to greet her at the door. He'd asked for a booth in the rear of the restaurant where they were seated almost immediately. Geri could see the seriousness in his demeanor through the brightness of his smile. He waited for her to slide into the booth and sat across from her. Geri looked around the room to see if anyone she knew was there. It was less her being concerned about being with Nathan than being seen having a leisurely lunch during the peak of the workday. She caught herself through his smile. He knew exactly what was going on in her mind.

"What?" She smiled and responded knowingly to his thoughts.

"You look as beautiful as ever." Nathan's compliment was warm and genuine.

"Well thank you. So do you." She gave the compliment back.

Beautiful he was.

Geri decided to only have coffee. Following her lead, Nathan initially ordered the same but added the breakfast special.

He watched as she sipped her coffee refusing to look up at him in the way it had become natural for her even when they were silent. Geri rubbed the roundness of her cup as her mind went back to the view from her window earlier that morning. She remembered the leaf drifting to the ground and how she thought at the time that it was symbolic of what they shared. Staring into the cup, she waited somewhat anxiously for him to speak.

"So how is your day going so far?" Finally Nathan spoke while salt and peppering his eggs.

"Fine. But I know you didn't want to meet me to talk about my day." She sat her cup down and leaned slightly towards him.

He offered her a piece of toast which she refused.

"You're right. I needed to see you. I've been trying to make sure that I'm doing the right thing. I know that I want to be with you. We are good together." His words ran together like a slow moving train.

She did not know where he was going with this and she wanted to be able to respond without being concerned about her surroundings.

"I have been so confused about everything. I love you so much. I can't imagine not being with you." Pushing his plate to the side, his tone was soft but resolute.

Still holding the cup of coffee in her hands, Geri looked at him as if to search his face for her own words. Saying what she thought at that moment would have been raw with emotion. They talked about many things. Sometimes it seemed they consciously avoided speaking about what he was now sharing so openly with her. Silence lingered between them.

"Geri, say something."

"I don't know what to say." As soon as the words came out of her mouth she wanted to slap herself. Of course she knew what to say. "I love you. I want to be with you. I can't share you. I won't share you. Just be mine. I can't do it any other way." Her thoughts were now running beside his train not willing to be spoken.

The silence reappeared momentarily.

"I can't let you go. It will be okay. I believe it will be okay." Nathan pressed gently at the cup in her hands. When she sat it down, he closed her hands together and held them.

"Can I get you something else?" Their waitress suddenly appeared at the table.

"I'm fine. Thank you." Geri answered feeling relieved that she had another moment to consider her response to Nathan.

"Yes, we're fine." Nathan smiled and nodded, then turned his attention back to Geri.

"Okay." Sensing that she had no intention of having the conversation with him, he wasn't sure what else to say. He drew her hands to his mouth and kissed them.

"Are you sure you don't want something to eat?" He picked up the menu and laid it in front of her as if they had just sat down and nothing had occurred beforehand.

"No. I'm okay, really. I'll get something from the cafeteria at work later. But, I do need to get back. Can we talk later?" The moment was awkward. She could not believe she was at such a loss for words.

Nathan stood as she walked away from the table without looking back. For a moment he was dumbfounded, but then thought about how he had put her on the spot. Did he expect her to confess her undying love for him? Did he even expect her to believe that he wanted to talk about their being together as a couple beyond what they had developed? He answered himself with "Yes" and beckoned for the waitress.

When she got back to work, Geri thought about what might happen to them? Lord knows the answers were marked on the pavement like a hopscotch pattern. Could they play this game and remain standing on one foot until the other dropped? Even if they could hop on one foot forever, when the rain came, the hopscotch blocks would be washed away. What were they doing? She did not have an explanation, but everything they discussed kept leading them back to the home in their hearts.

Their conversation haunted her all afternoon. She considered that the closer they became, the more intense the fear of losing him would become. If she told him how she really felt, it would make her more vulnerable than she cared to be.

"But what if?" She picked up the phone to call him.

"Pierce Bradley Building." His accent clipped through the phone.

"Hello, Pierce Bradley Building. What are you doing?" Hearing his voice made her smile. She asked the question while thinking she was ready to go all in.

"I'm working." He laughed lightly, but was still a bit stung by their conversation or lack thereof earlier in the day.

"Why?" He asked curiously.

"I was just thinking about you. I am so sorry about today. You just caught me off guard." Her apology came before the request she had not planned to make.

"I would like to see you."

"What about tonight?" He replied.

"Okay. Do you get off at 7:00?"

"Yes, but I want to stop home. So, I'll see you about 8:30 or so. Is that okay? Do you want me to bring anything?"

"No. Just yourself." "

"Sounds good."

"I'll see you later."

She hung up the phone and swung her chair around to face the window. It was not yet dusk, and she could see that there were no more leaves falling. The ones on the tree were gently waving to the wind that moved through the branches. She turned back to finish reading one of the documents on her desk.

When she got home she looked at herself in the mirror thinking that she would see someone different, someone who would reflect feeling so differently about a lot of things. But nope, it was her. She stuck out her tongue the way she did as a child looking for evidence of something different like the red color left behind after eating the cherry popsicles she loved so much. But like her face, her tongue was still the same. She looked directly into her eyes and said, "Ah, there it is." Her eyes spoke to her with a glowing certainty. She had been patient with herself and with him. This night would open them to another chapter in their story, moreover, in her story.

Nathan rang the bell at 8:25p.m. She walked towards the door feeling more relaxed than she had been when she got home. Her heart was racing with the excitement of sharing the evening with him. The contradiction of calm and excitement was an indication of how she felt concerning everything about them. She opened the door and received his kiss. They walked to the living room hand in hand with an unspoken expectancy about the evening. Without a word beyond their greetings, they sat on the sofa and embraced each other with the familiarity that still eluded her. Having already decided that she would move forward with him, she stood up and took his hand as they moved from the sofa. It had been years since anyone shared the sanctum of her bedroom, but tonight Nathan would. She had rehearsed the moment in her mind over and over again. She questioned whether she should. Tonight she said, "Yes".

As they moved into the evening it seemed almost surreal to her. It had been so long since such intimacy was part of her life. She was in the arms of someone whom she believed loved her in all the ways that he knew her. They joined together slowly and then breathed into each other. She cried silently as he showered her with love. Overwhelmed by what was happening, she buried her head in his chest and held him tightly so that her tears would not distract him. Her attempts to hide what she was feeling were unsuccessful. He lifted her face to his. He suddenly remembered her telling him in one of their conversations that she could never be with him in fear that they would combust. He thought it only humorous until that night. Was she afraid of bursting into flames or how it would all turn out? He kissed her forehead and held her without movement of any kind until he heard her whisper, "I'm Okay."

Everything stopped except the synchronized beating of their hearts and the silhouette in the moon lit room.

When he felt it was timely to speak, he whispered gently into her ear, "Are you alright?"

"Yes."

He kissed her forehead again and continued to hold her until they fell asleep.

The next morning Geri was awakened by the birds outside her window. The sun was on the horizon of the trees outside her house.

Nathan was still asleep, but she knew she had to wake him shortly. She turned quietly to her side and watched him. He now laid flat on his stomach revealing the strength of his back. His head rested gently in the bend of his right arm. She sensed that his peace was comparable to hers. As she watched him sleep, she remembered the night before and words of poetry began to sail through her mind. She closed her eyes and silently spoke her morning prayer. Although the night had taken them into complete surrender, she asked if their love was enough to override everything else. Or was she tempting her faith to prove that all things were not necessarily perfect.

Noticing that it was time for him to get up, she made swirling motions on his back with her fingers. He shifted a bit, opened his eyes, and smiled.

"Good morning." His voice was low and husky.

"Good morning back to you. Did you sleep well?" She answered feeling strangely shy about the moment and wildly happy in general.

"What do you think?" He responded with sleep still in his voice. "I wish I could just stay here all morning."

"Well, neither of us can. So, how about some coffee?" She kissed him and sat up reaching for her robe from the chair next to her bed. She left it there the morning before not considering then that she would wake up with someone in her bed. She was glad she had not taken the time to hang it up. She was not quite ready to parade in front of him.

Reluctantly Nathan headed for the shower. Watching him move so gracefully she wondered how he was able to be so free, a stark contrast to her now tying the belt tightly around her robe. Smiling at the beauty of his back, she said, "The towels and clothes are in the basket next to the shower."

While he showered, Geri went to the kitchen to make coffee. She didn't know what his morning routine was, but decided that she would fix a light breakfast of toast and scrambled eggs while the coffee was brewing. She placed the toast and eggs in the oven to keep warm and went back to her bedroom to see if he needed anything. He was sitting on the foot of the bed putting on his shoes. He looked up and motioned for her to sit next to him. He kissed her neck softly and asked how she was.

"I'm okay. How are you?" She waited for his response. "Just okay?" He turned to look at her.

"Yes. But okay in a great way." She kissed his shoulder and stood up. "Are you hungry? I made some eggs and toast. And coffee."

"Maybe a little." He glanced at the clock when he answered. His response had more to do with the time than his hunger.

They had coffee while he wrapped his breakfast to go. When he left she laid on her bed thinking about the night before. Taking a deep breath, she rolled over to her side and went back to sleep. The phone rang a little over an hour after she drifted off. It was a good thing, too. She had forgotten to set the alarm clock the night before and it was already later than she normally got up.

"Hello." She answered the phone a bit groggy.

"Are you up?" Nathan asked.

"I am. I am." She answered twice trying to convince herself. "Thank you for calling. I would've still been sleep. It was a good sleep too. Are you at work?"

"Yes. I'm eating my breakfast." His voice was relaxed.

"Aren't you at the desk?" She asked, now also feeling a little nervous about what he might be thinking about what did and did not happen the night before.

"Nobody's in the lobby yet. Anyway, it's under the counter and I'm savoring little pieces at a time." He whispered the last sentence as if to tell her a secret.

"You know what, I better get moving. We'll talk later?" Her tone was warm and hopeful.

"I look forward to it. Love you." Nathan responded and hung up before hearing her last words.

"Me too." She still couldn't bring herself to say the words "I love you" but she knew that what she felt was real.

As she got dressed to go to work, she found herself humming tunes that were unfamiliar. Maybe they were just songs of happiness. Moreover, maybe they were songs of the odd sense of freedom that she was beginning to feel about herself and her life. Nathan was only part of it.

Geri arrived at work feeling good about what the day would bring. Not that she expected anything special to happen, but just that it would be a good day. Maybe it was nothing more than the change in her perspective, and certainly some of it was due to her night with Nathan.

They did not talk until late in the afternoon, but every now and then she would have a flash back of the evening.

The day moved by smoothly allowing her to get most of her paperwork done, meet with a couple of her staff supervisors and spend time observing staff interactions with the children on the second floor. At 7:00 that evening she decided to call it a day and head for home. On her way home she thought about the poem she wanted to write about him. She marveled at how he made her feel and how that feeling made such a difference in her that day. After settling in for the evening, she sat at her computer and began to compose the poem. It seemed to just flow from her heart onto the paper.

"You inspire me to be whom I am in this moment... You inspire me."

Geri did not know if she would merely add the poem to her collection of writings or give it to him. The words expressed her love as well as what she believed he felt for her. The oddity was that she did not feel that it was a declaration of anything everlasting and that was strangely acceptable to her. It had only to do with that moment and what they shared the night before. She couldn't understand why she felt so much peace with it, but she did. She knew it was part of a beginning, her new beginning. How better to begin again than with love.

The following evening she decided to give what she had written to Nathan. She nervously watched him as he read and waited for his response. She knew that the words were powerful and was not sure how he would take them. Nathan's words broke into her thoughts.

"Geri, this is beautiful. Thank you so much. I've never read anything so beautiful. I've certainly never received anything like this before."

His gentle strength poured out of the expression on his face as if it had been stored up from the day they met. The deep dark sea within him that she sensed the very first time she saw him seemed to lighten and glisten under the strength of a warming sun giving rise to a light breezy wave. Moving with it and him, she remained silent letting the wave just roll.

"Thank you so much." As he spoke, she looked deeply into his eyes and felt his appreciation. A chill moved through her, she shivered.

"Are you okay?" He touched her shoulder.

"I'm fine. I don't know what that was." It bothered her that it happened when they were in such an intimate and loving moment. She leaned over to kiss him and he pulled her closer reciprocating with a deep and passionate kiss.

Feeling his arms around her pushed the concern out of her mind. That evening they talked about what they hoped for in their relationship as well as what each of them wanted out of life. They once again verbalized their agreement to take a chance on whatever they were to be. Their "being" was enveloping them sort of like a giant flower that had begun to fold around them. The petals were pretty and smelled mighty good, and the flower itself seemed strong enough to hold them. They did not question how long it would last.

"Each time I see you I just want to tumble in joy" she said to him without hesitancy.

Nathan was inspiring her to say things that she hadn't thought of saying to anyone, ever. But now all of her emotions seemed to be living their own lives and having their own say. They were free and in charge of their own expressions. She felt like a new vessel filled with new life to pour out in words and in ideas for her future. That book she always wanted to write was beginning to unfold.

Chapter 14

"To celebrate life is to embrace every experience with purpose and consideration about what might succeed in our experiences." Geri jotted this down in her journal one morning before leaving for work. The thought was ever present in the acceptance of her involvement with Nathan. It had been almost a year and she had fallen deeply in love with him. Still she needed to stay as grounded as possible by talking about the reality of their situation. She was beginning to sense that the end was drawing near. She had shared some of Nathan's story with Diana and decided that she would talk with her.

Diana could tell that something serious was on Geri's mind and could no longer wait for her to cough it up. While sharing a break one morning she posed the question.

"So what's going on, my friend? Looks like you could use an ear."

"Am I that transparent?" Geri asked. She was grateful that Diana inquired.

"Do you want to stop off after work?" Diana asked sensing what the answer would be.

"Yes. I could use a change in atmosphere and a glass of something." Geri smiled as she responded.

They decided to stop at a place that was central to both their homes. On the drive over she was trying to construct just what it was she wanted to tell Diana. There was a lot to say that led to the bottom line. Should she just skip to that point?

"There is always a catch. Why is there always a catch?" She opened her conversation with a voice of exasperation.

"This is about Nathan, right?" Diana had that "I have been waiting for the other shoe to drop" expression on her face. It was not judgmental or sympathetic, but an "I'm here for you" look that had been sitting on the shelf.

"LoDe, it's so good with him. Sometimes it feels too good." She felt a lump welling up in her throat.

"Geri, you know that if something seems too good to be true, it usually is. But is that really the case with you and Nathan. You've known the situation. And if there is or was a catch, so what? Catches get caught every day! Some even get broken. Hell, I just lost my favorite bracelet because the catch broke!" She smiled hoping that Geri would be amused.

"Come on, you know that was funny." Diana laughed at her own joke.

"Diana. See. There's nothing funny about this. And, what you said was stupid, not funny." Geri gave in and laughed at her friend's feigned attempt at being funny.

"It will be alright. Geri, it's already alright. Nothing happens without a reason. You tell me that all the time. You need to practice what you teach, Ms. Michaels."

Diana let her talk away some of her frustration. They laughed at the ironies of life and love while sipping on their wine. Eventually both ordered coffee. She raised the metaphor that every now and then you get a perfect cup of coffee. But even that was a rarity when all it took was coffee grinds and water that went through a filter. People and life were most often unfiltered.

They ended the conversation with her still having difficulty understanding how she could be so much in love with someone who she didn't believe she could have. Not only that, she had waited for years to share herself with someone. Although she did not regret it, the idea that they would probably not be together for long. Yes, she finally said the words. It seemed to be on her mind more and more, especially when they were together. It was also beginning to get on her nerves when he spoke about his family. Although she had encouraged him to talk about how he was feeling, she now regretted it. She was sick of his truth telling! She found herself falling into the same predicament of caring for someone while placing herself second. This time, however, she was so aware of it that there were moments when she had to tussle with resenting him and his family. One evening as they sat listening to music, she couldn't help but bring it up.

"Nathan, why do you keep talking about them? Are you trying to get me to walk away from you?"

"Why are you asking me that? You know that's not what I want." He seemed startled by her question.

"I know you have a family. It haunts me all the time. I don't want to have it between us when we're together too."

As she made the statement, she realized how ridiculous it sounded. Of course they were between them. The fact that his family was thousands of miles away did not change the fact that they were right there in his heart. She painfully acknowledged in that instant that although his heart seemed big enough to carry them all including her, the space was still too small for her. It was beginning to squeeze her in places that were no longer subject to being squeezed.

"Geri, I don't know what's going to happen. I just want my family to be safe. And I want you. Can I have both? I don't know." Nathan's ready response let her know that he had been thinking about it also.

He got up from the sofa and walked over to the window. It was late and for some reason the stillness shown outside the window reminded him of his homeland. He knew that no matter how much he loved Geri, a piece of him was still missing. He could not deny that to himself and sometimes he felt guilty about how happy he was with her. Maybe it was the guilt that made him bring up his family so often. He had also become more conscious of the fact that each time he did, it hurt her a little more. It had begun to put a wedge between them. Turning back to her, he spoke almost in a whisper.

"I love you, Geri. I love you."

Sometimes the very thing that you want so badly, no matter how good it seems, just isn't meant for you. No matter how much love they had for each other, the truth was that he had another life. Though it seemed that he had been a gift to her, it was clear that he was not God's good and perfect gift. He had come into her life at a time when she needed what they shared and was open to receiving it. Maybe Nathan was unknowingly preparing the way for that "good and perfect gift". Realizing this more every day she questioned him further about his relationship with the woman he left behind. It was really on her mind that night.

"One of the things we haven't talked about in a while is your daughter's mother. How do you feel now? We've been together for months. Has anything changed?"

"A lot has changed. Eleven months ago you couldn't have told me that I'd feel this way about another woman. Yes, I still care about her. But it's different. Just what it is, I don't know. But it's different."

"Are you still going to bring her here?" She spoke slowly as if she was trying to help someone understand a language that was not theirs. After all, she knew that he had not abandoned his efforts.

"I want my daughter here. Her mother comes with her, Geri. You know that."

"Nathan if I knew that, I wouldn't have asked you." Liar, she thought. "How can you say you love me as much as you do and still question whether you want to be with…?" She stopped short. As crazy as it sounded, he had never told her his daughter's mother's name.

"I do want to be with just you. But I don't know how to do both?"

"Both. You have acted like only one exists. Me. You've never even given your daughter or her mother a name." She hesitated as she saw the expression on his face, then continued. "I'm sorry. You did tell me your daughter's name. Asha. But what about Asha's mother?" Geri's exasperation was now laced with a bit of sarcasm.

"Tamara. Her name is Tamara." Seeing her frustration he was not sure how to respond. He hadn't even realized that he had not told her the name.

"At this point it doesn't matter, Nathan. It would only have mattered if you'd told me right up front that you already had someone. I would not have fallen in love with you. I would not have tried to convince myself that it didn't matter. I can't live this lie any longer, no matter how much I love you."

There was a long silence. She was waiting for him to say something crazy like "You still had a choice after I told you". That's what she would have said. Thankfully he did not. Although she'd been saying it to herself more often than not, she could not imagine what her reaction to his saying it would have been.

"I want you, Geri. I don't know what I feel about Tamara." He gave her name emphasis.

"You can't have both. You can't."

"I can't just forget about her. We went through so much together. She's been waiting for me for all these years."

"And, she has your child."

"Yes. She has our child."

"You cannot have both." Geri repeated the words. It was settled in her mind and now she needed to settle it in her heart.

She felt her eyes begin to well with tears she did not want to release. After all, she did know the situation early on. It was her choice to continue to see him. The cruel things that she thought he might say, she had already said to herself. She did have the choice. It had been a choice of loving and being loved. It was unfortunately caught up in his life, the one he brought to their relationship and her life, the one that was changing. It was indeed the manifestation of her prayer about not needing him to be available. The prayer had come back to haunt her and not bless her. Her mind flashed back to the day that he said "I'm free." She wanted to yell out her thought, 'Liar! Such a liar. Why did you lie?' She knew those words would have come from the frustration that was tied up in her sensing that the end was coming. She stifled the screaming in her heart.

"Geri, if you want to walk away, I understand. I don't want you to walk away, but I know that's just my selfishness." He touched her face and one of her eyes let go of the hot tear. As he watched her, he began to cry as well. He could tell that it was all about to end. He thought how his needing her hurt both of them. His loving her burned through his chest.

He put his arms around her. They spent the night together filled with the emotions of love and pain. His touch was tender. Her sighs were heavy from the burden of truth, but softened by the love she still felt. They slept in disquieted peacefulness that represented the paradox in their relationship. It was a contradiction for sure, but it was how they felt.

She did believe that he had come into her life for a reason. Though she was not quite sure what that reason was, she embraced it even now knowing that she could not stay with him. She knew that leaving him also meant putting an end to this chapter in her life. Ironically it was tied to the chapter that she had already been in the middle of when he showed up. It was almost as if she had to experience him before she could move forward into everything else. Was Nathan a necessary lesson? She wondered. It also seemed that her consciousness about an end drawing closer for them was simultaneously connected to her work at becoming increasingly more tiring. She considered that it might have been different if she could have planned a life with him. Accepting that it could not happen the way she wanted and thought she needed, she began planning the rest of her life.

While fighting back the desire to cover her ears Geri had listened to Nathan the night before. As childish as that seemed, it was the only way she thought she could block out the noise of completion.

That leaf that gently fell to the ground without a sound some months ago, the one she watched from her office window it seemed just the other day, now fell with a loud and thunderous sound. Night had turned into morning and she was still in love, but in a different place. Fortunately she concluded that she was not the leaf. He was not her life source. No. She was the tree rooted deeply in all the love she'd received from her mother and grandmother Ella. She remembered how excited she was when she shared with Renee and Leslie that she'd met this special man. He was still special, but could not be hers. She remembered too what her friends had said, "We will be here for you if it doesn't work out."

Chapter 15

"It's time for me to leave" was echoing tirelessly through Geri's mind. She understood that it meant leaving Nathan and her job. The idea was daunting.

After wrestling with the thoughts for two days, Geri awakened Sunday morning and decided to visit her family's church. She could not remember the last time she attended anybody's church, but that morning she knew it was where she needed to be. Wondering how she would be received by members who'd been there for years, she searched her closet for the most conservative suit she could find. "No." Speaking out loud she stopped her search and pulled out her favorite.

Though she loved hearing a good sermon and listening to sweet music, Geri had not been to church for a while. It was mostly because Sunday's were the only days she could rest. To compensate for her absence, every now and then she would send a substantial check to what she knew was their ever ending building campaign. But today as she prepared to go she recalled the wanton glances she'd received from her pastor of twenty years the last time she was there. The looks were disturbing. She now remembered how not once did he look at her face as they talked after service. She left feeling too uncomfortable to return and let her schedule be her excuse. Today, however, she did not care. Her initial idea to dress down was chastened by her burgeoning desire to just be herself, red suit and all.

The service was wonderful. It reminded her of what she had been missing the last two years. To her surprise she found out that the pastor who covered her body with his eyeballs had attempted something even more disturbing with a young girl and had been asked to leave the church. There was a new pastor, The Reverend Patricia Monarch. As Reverend Monarch entered the pulpit it was another sign that things do change.

Geri had not spoken with Nathan since their conversation on Thursday evening. To her surprise he had not called. Although she was not concerned about what he must have been thinking the last couple of days, she did feel somewhat worried that he was not sick or something. She decided to call him the next morning.

"Hey. How's your day going?" There was deliberateness in her voice.

"It's alright. How are you?" Nathan responded recognizing the tone in her voice and trying to hide his. He had left her knowing that the end was coming.

"I need to talk with you. Can you come over tonight after work?" She asked.

"I'll see. I'm real tired and wanted to go straight home. What do you want to talk about?" He knew.

"Me. Us. Everything. I really need to make some decisions. I need you to come by."

"Okay. I'll be there around 8?"

"See you then." Geri gently hung up the phone letting her hand rest momentarily on the handle. She realized that her heart was racing and took a deep breath.

That night Nathan rang the doorbell then stepped back. He leaned against the wooden rail that faced her door. This was different. He was usually standing almost eagerly at the door waiting for her to open it and receive the anticipated hello kiss. She could see that he was dead tired.

"Hi" was all that came out of his mouth.

"Hi, back" she said putting her arms around him. She knew that his coming that night was a sacrifice. He had put in his fourteen hour day. There was always a part of her that felt guilty about loving him and even more so about his loving her. She could not imagine how difficult it was for him to split his life in two not knowing if either half would ever be reconciled. She had a dream one night about his working himself to death and her taking his body back home. When she arrived, his family was there waiting. As dreams go, when they took him off the plane he was cut in half hanging on a meat hook. She woke up in a panic. The crazy thing about it was that it demonstrated how much he loved both her and them, and had divided himself in two.

They were barely seated when she spoke.

"This is not working for me." Geri allowed the words to move out of her mouth without hesitation.

"What do you mean?" Caught off guard by her abruptness, his question was more for the sake of gaining his composure than getting an answer.

"You are never available." As bold as she was trying to be, this was also her stalling tactic. She knew that at that moment he would think she was talking about his work schedule and their not being able to see each other as often as she would like.

"It's not just you're not having a lot of time. It's that this is crazy. I'm thinking that I'm being a little crazy and stupid too. Crazy I can get, but I'm not a stupid woman." Geri turned slightly away from him and stared into space.

"Geri, you're the smartest woman I know. Why are you saying this? What do you want me to do?" He knew it was a rhetorical question, but it was all he could think of to say.

"I want you all to myself. I'm tired of pretending that it's okay the way it is. It's not. But I'm not going to ask you to change your life. You have to do that, Nathan." Her words were penetrating.

"But you know my situation. I have always told you the truth." As he spoke, he realized that it was not entirely true.

"Well, not really. Remember the 'I'm free' declaration?" Now she was irritated.

"I know. I know. I've told you how sorry I am about that. I just didn't know what else to say to you at that time. But I've tried to be clear…" His voice was apologetic, but without hope.

She put her fingers to his lips. She didn't want to hear anything else. She did not want to get angry. Anger was what may have made her walk away months ago, but now what would be the point? Yes, he had been very clear about some things. She admittedly had been unable to wrap her heart around that clarity right away. The irony was that now it was not what he told her that made things clear, but what she told herself. If she could not have him completely, she wanted him to be with his family.

She knew how much he missed his daughter. He talked about her often. But she also knew that it was a complete package. About Tamara, he said to her once, "I cannot forget about her. We have been through too much." She wasn't sure what that meant, and decided that it was none of her business.

On this evening, though, she wished that she had asked what he meant when he said it. Was what he felt for Tamara love or responsibility? Her answer to herself was, "It doesn't matter".

"Nathan, I know. But we have been together for almost a year. We're in some kind of fantasy that has us together in a way that I don't think either of us expected."

"I've got to walk away from this, from you, now." Geri's voice was resolute, but her heart breaking.

He pulled her close. "Geri, no. I love you. It will be okay."

As he spoke of his love, she remembered him telling her that they were like a rare wine that spilled from a broken wine glass. He told her that the glass did not shatter, but was broken into two pieces.

"The first time I looked at you it was as if I was picking up a part of the glass as you picked up the other and walked towards me. Then we put the glass back together."

Now it seemed that the vision was pure nonsense. What did it mean in the scheme of both of their lives? As they held on to each other, she saw the glass falling to the ground again and held him tighter as if to prevent its shattering. The intensity of their physical expression of love moved them close to the combustion they had laughed about. Only it was not the two of them who would eventually combust. It was their relationship.

Resting deep into the sofa, they held each other knowing that would most likely be the last time they were together. They could not escape the moment, but felt solace in each other's arms. The truth had finally broken into both of their spirits. Geri could feel the wind that blew across their faces the first time they spoke. She wondered if he could feel it too. They fell asleep in silence, resting through the night on the sofa. Her dreams were peaceful, even as she watched the wine glass fall to the ground and shatter into tiny little pieces, there was not sound.

When he left the next morning she closed the door behind him knowing that they had really said good bye. As usual, she'd gotten up while he was in the shower, fixed a light breakfast, and packed something for him to eat during the day. That morning they were both silent. They walked to the front door and kissed in their usual way.

"I'll talk to you later" were the familiar words that he spoke, but her "good bye" held the truest meaning.

By the time she got to work, her focus had changed to her whole life. Her first conversation would be with her Director.

"Diana, can you come to my office?" Geri called her on the intercom.

"Give me about twenty minutes?" Diana was in a meeting and replied with the question.

"Okay." Geri responded almost relishing the delay.

Her decision about departing from Haven had been made. She would give three months' notice. She wanted Diana to take her place as the center's executive and hoped she would agree. Geri would have to sell her board on the idea, but did not think it would be a hard sell. Diana had been with her from the beginning. She was highly capable and demonstrated the same passion about Haven's purpose.

When Diana came in the office, Geri was working on a letter that needed to get out that day.

"Hey. Have a seat. I'll be right with you."

"Family Services wants us to expand. I'm writing to tell them that we will consider, but I need to evaluate whether an expansion will diminish or enhance what we're doing now. I'll talk more about that with you later. How are you?"

"Good." Diana said studying her. She could see something else going on.

Geri looked up from what she was doing and hesitated for a moment before saying, "Okay. Here it is. I'm leaving."

Diana's expression signified her lack of surprise. "I was wondering when you were going to tell me. What are you going to do? Are you moving away? What about Nathan?"

"Can I answer one question at a time?" She laughed because Diana knew her so well and all of the questions were appropriate.

"I want to leave in December. And, I want to propose to the board that you take my place."

"Geri, I don't know. This is a huge responsibility. You know how I feel about this place, but my husband is already complaining about my hours." Diana sank slightly back in her chair.

"Who are you telling? Listen, think about it and talk with your hubby. I know it's a lot, but I know you can do it." Geri answered a little disappointed that Diana did not just say "Yes".

"Okay, so what about my other questions? What about Nathan? Is he going back home?" Diana could see Geri's concern about her answer, but wanted to move past it.

"Why would you think he was going back? You know his situation or at least enough to know that he shouldn't go back." Geri responded.

"I don't know. It just came to me. You know life is strange. Anything can happen." Diana was now sitting upright in her chair.

What she said had caught her a little by surprise as well.

"Well, I don't know what he's going to do. I just know that I'm feeling like our story has ended. Not because he's done anything different, but because I'm feeling differently about who I am in it." Geri smiled as she uttered the last few words. She could not articulate it, but she knew that something was happening. She felt the need to get out of the way - her way and Nathan's way.

The dream about the bus and it's not having a driver crossed her mind that morning. The dream had not repeated itself since the night before she met Nathan. She was glad that it had not, but wondered if she would still be alone on the bus if the dream reoccurred.

The thought moved through her mind again as she and Diana continued to talk about her plans. They left for the evening with Diana agreeing to seriously consider accepting the recommendation to the board.

On the ride home from work she decided she would leave Haven on December 23rd and spend the month of January recovering from the exhaustion she was feeling. For some reason her thoughts were being pulled in the direction of moving back to Chicago.

"Humph. Maybe I'll write my book in Chicago."

Chapter 16

After a little questionable resolve about being ready for the reactions, Geri decided to share her decision to move with everyone who might be affected. She started by calling her mother before leaving for work that morning.

"Hi mom. How are you?"

"I'm okay. You're calling early. What's wrong?"

"Nothing's wrong." She drew a breath and continued. "I just wanted to call to let you know that I've decided to leave the center and to leave Baltimore."

"What are you going to do instead?" Victoria asked with a concerned tone.

"Well, a couple things. One is I'm going to finally write the book I've been putting off for years."

Her mother was clueless about this, which made her explanation even less palatable.

"How are you going to live?" Victoria asked still trying to wrap her mind around her daughter's news.

"It's going to be fine mom. I'm excited about finally starting to live my life for me." Geri responded knowing she had to tell her mother in a way that left no room for discussion. It was now time to get out of the box she had so neatly crafted for reasons other than "herself".

Still Victoria received the news as if she was telling her that she was flying to the moon. Geri understood her concern, but could not let it influence her decision.

She finished the call with her mother, but didn't hang up. Although she felt they had already said their goodbyes, she felt the need to let Nathan know about her decision. It was true that the right and wrong of their relationship had moved with them like the soft curves of a question mark, but now everything was definite.

Just as she was about to call his number her phone rang. She saw his home number on her caller ID and couldn't help but think that it was some kind of premonition.

"Wow. I was just about to call you."

"Hi. I need to talk with you." He did not respond to her statement. The usual weightlessness in his voice was heavy with something that made her switch gears from wanting to share her information to being concerned about what he was about to say.

"What's wrong?" she asked.

"Can you meet me now?"

"Yes. Where?"

"I'll pick you up in front of your building in about 20 minutes."

"Okay. Are you okay?"

"I'm alright. I'll be there in a few minutes."

There had to be something wrong. Although they did not try to keep their involvement a complete secret, he'd never asked to pick her up in front of the building. When she got in the car, he took her hand and kissed it before saying "Fasten your belt." The silence was deafening as they road along a familiar street. He drove to the nearby park where they went periodically to sit and talk. It was the middle of the day and there were not a lot of people around. It would have been perfect for one of their "I'll meet you in the park" rendezvous.

"You know I love you, right?" Nathan had barely turned off the ignition when he looked at her in a way he had never before.

What's he getting ready to say? Geri's heart was pounding.

"Yes, I know you love me. Why? What's going on? Nathan, what's wrong?" The words were almost choking her as she spoke them.

"I have to go home. I have to go back to my country." Nathan spoke slowly trying not to sound too alarming.

"What do you mean? Why?" Geri asked. "Is it safe?" The alarm had registered.

"My family is in trouble. They arrested my brothers. Tamara took Asha to stay with her parents a few towns away. My mom called to say she was afraid that the police would search for them. I have to go. I have to get my brothers, my family."

"But how are you going to do that? Why are they holding them? If they are being held because of you, don't you think those bastards know that you will come back so they can get you?" A flood of questions compounded by the images of what could happen came out of her mouth.

"I know. But you know I can't let them hurt my family, Geri. I can't." He hit the dashboard with his hand and said something in his language that sounded like hard, angry cursing.

"I called my friend who's getting me a way to come back. His cousin will help me get in safely." He paused to look into her eyes as if to search her soul when he said, "I have to leave tonight."

She tried really hard not to cry, but she burst out uncontrollably thinking that he would be killed. It's one thing to say 'Goodbye. We can't see each other anymore', but it's a whole other thing to say, 'Good bye' because of death. There was nothing for her to say except, "I understand."

He kissed her so hard that her lips felt bruised. His hold was tighter than ever which was in contrast to her feeling limp and almost numb. He told her how much he loved her and how sorry he was for causing her to love him. In the midst of it she kissed his eyes and forehead the way she touched them that night he fell asleep in her lap and said, "I would not have missed this for the world. You came when I needed you. I love you, Ntheba. Please be safe."

They dried their eyes. He shifted his position and started the car.

"Do you want me to take you to your car?" He paused and looked at her as she touched up her makeup. Her beauty was still astounding to him.

"No. I need to go back to work. I'll leave a little early, but I have to meet with Diana first." Geri hesitated then continued with, "I guess I should also tell you that I'm leaving and will probably move out of the area. So, I don't know if we will see each other again."

What had fallen apart between them was now rendering a new perspective. This was how it was to be. The mere cycle of things was creating a new season for both of them.

Once more, Nathan took her hand to his mouth. As they drove off Geri laid her head on his shoulder and silently prayed for him and his family.

He left that night.

Chapter 17

Talk about new beginnings. It was as if Geri had been waiting to step into herself, into her liberation, and into the world that had been prepared for her. Victoria ultimately gave her blessings, her townhouse sold sooner than she had expected giving her a nest egg to take with her and Diana got the position. Geri's move was in full motion. Everything was working together.

In all of her planning she had not stopped to think about how she had vowed never to return to Chicago because of the cold weather. She shook her head when she remembered the promise as she headed out in the cold of windy March. She had arranged to stay with a distant cousin and his wife until she could get her own place. She found out a couple days before she was scheduled to leave that her cousin's mother-in-law was about to have emergency surgery and would have to move in with them while she recuperated. Geri was further convinced that it was the right move when she was able to secure a sublet rental within hours of receiving the call from her cousin. It was a furnished studio downtown with a year's lease. That was even better than staying with her cousin because it would give her more time to get settled. She knew she would miss the treasures she had collected over the years, but having already resigned herself to putting everything in storage except the absolute necessities, staying in a furnished space was now just part of the transition.

Excited and a little scared, Geri started out on her new venture. Driving from Baltimore to Chicago was no small feat, but her excitement kept her moving through the bouts of snow and sleet she encountered on the way once she crossed into Midwestern territory. She stopped a couple of times for coffee and to go to the bathroom, but other than that it was nonstop Chicago bound.

Geri was pleasantly surprised that her new accommodations were tasteful and above all super clean. The space was also larger than she imagined a studio apartment would be. She guessed she was thinking about the ones she had heard about in New York. She had always been intrigued about living spaces and was determined to one day have the space of her dreams.

As soon as she settled in, she began writing her book. It made sense to draw from her relationship with Nathan. Thinking more about it she was not quite convinced that she would be able to put what she now understood about love into words. It was more of a feeling than a declaration. Ultimately, the words for the book emanated from Nathan's life story as much as how she felt about him. It was a love story and unbeknown to her at the time, it was one that would swing the door open to her new life. The heroine was named after her friend Diana. She changed the spelling to "Dianah." Dr. Dianah Cartwright was a pediatric neurosurgeon who met the man of her dreams at a conference in Kenya. He lived in London at the time of their meeting, but was in the process of transferring to the United States when their chance encounter occurred. Their cross Atlantic love grew after the conference. It was spellbinding. Dr. Celestin Conrad was part of a group of doctors throughout the world who traveled to third world countries to consult on establishing community clinics. The plot had unfolded with Dr. Celestin's death. Just prior to moving to the United States he and three others in his convoy were ambushed and fatally wounded during a visit to the Sudan. Geri was struggling with how to end the story in a way that paid tribute to the doctor's plight.

She was leaning toward having Dianah travel to Kenya several months subsequent to his death to touch the ground where they met and discussed the possibility of a future together. Since their meeting had felt like fate, Geri thought Kenya would be the place to tie the story together. Although there were parts she still had to develop, the epilogue would involve Dianah raising money to open a clinic in a small village. The clinic would be named the C. D. Community Clinic. The story would end with Dianah sitting on the front porch of the clinic looking out into the sunset smiling and thinking about her lost love.

Writing was forcing Geri to explore her deepest feelings about life and the luxury of just breathing. She uncovered an inner source of healing that had laid dormant for years. After many revisions and more than the six months she had given herself to write at least half the book, she was ready to share the first few chapters. She decided to send them to her friend Sonia who was a published author and playwright. They too were friends since college, but Sonia lived in California so they did not see each other or talk that often. When they did, Sonia had great words of wisdom and encouragement to give her about following her dreams. Geri thought she was the perfect person to read and comment on her work.

Sonia called as soon as she finished reading the chapters.

"Geri, this is awesome. How did you come up with the idea?"

"Really? Are you sure?" was all she could say right away.

"Please. You know that you have always had the gift. It was just about doing it. I am not only impressed, I'm almost jealous. How long did it take you to write these chapters? Two minutes!?" Sonia joked with her, but was genuinely impressed by the timing.

"So answer my question. How did you come up with this plot?"

"To tell you the truth it was a little embellishment of my own experience. Plus you know I like intrigue. So you really think it's worth continuing?" Geri responded.

"Absolutely!" Sonia's voice was like an applause.

"Okay, so what do I do next?" Geri asked.

"Look, let me give you my agent's number. I hope you don't mind, but I already spoke to her and she's waiting to hear from you." Sonia was prepared to respond if Geri scoffed at her moving on her behalf without talking with her.

"Are you kidding? I'll call her tomorrow morning." Geri's answer was filled with appreciation and a little disbelief.

"Good. I think you will like her." Sonia was relieved that she was not upset.

"Enough about me. How are you doing? What's new?" Geri asked. "You know, husband, children, sometimes me" was the short answer.

She continued with, "Did you hear that Sabrina got married?"

"I haven't talked to anybody in months. I can't believe she didn't invite me or at least tell me."

"Please! She didn't tell any of us until it was done. You know she married some no account that we would have been all over her about. I just hope she'll be okay." Sonia paused and then said, "Have you heard from Nate?"

"Nate? Where'd you get that from?" Geri laughed, but knew it came from their mutual friend, Renee.

"Isn't that his name?" Renee had told her the whole story or at least her side of it. Sonia was not as accepting about the idea of "Nate" as Leslie or Renee and certainly not Geri.

"No and no. His name is not Nate and I have not heard from or about him. I try not to think about what might have happened."

Geri inhaled and exhaled. "I believe that if he was hurt or killed I would feel it. We were brought together for a minute for both our sakes I guess. I see Renee told you the story."

"I know, my friend. You know I'm not trying to be insensitive." Sonia could almost hear Geri saying "Really?"

"But look at you now! You probably wouldn't know what to do with him if he showed up at your front door today."

"I know you know better than that. I'd know just what to do with him!"

"And what's that?"

"Well, aft that" she said half serious and half joking, "I would invite him in for a cup of coffee listen to his story then send him on his way."

"Really?" Sonia was surprised.

"Yes. Believe it or not, really. I probably wouldn't even be tempted to do the first part." Listening to herself, Geri was actually surprised.

They talked a little longer, sharing news about their cirle of friends. They hung up after agreeing to keep in touch more frequently. Geri promised she would contact Patti.

After the conversation, Geri remembered that she met Patti Cohen a couple years ago at one of Sonia's dinner parties. She recalled her as being a very fashionable and somewhat aggressive woman who could knock doors down with her voice, let alone her presence. She reminded her of a person you would definitely want on your side. No way could she have forgotten her.

The next morning she called Patti and found out that Sonia had already sent her the chapters.

"No she didn't! I did not ask her to do that, Patti." It was one thing to discuss the work, but she was not sure she had been ready for Patti to see it. That was the part Sonia had left out of their conversation.

"Geri, you know Sonia. Once she sets her mind to something, she moves on it. I'm glad she did. It gave me a chance to read it before I spoke with you. It's really good for a novice. Better than most. This is what I would like to do." It sounded like Patti did not take a breath in her response. She went on to the next steps.

After talking with Patti, she knew it could take a while before her book was published. In the meantime, she would continue working on the manuscript. For now, she also needed to decide what her next life step would be. Should she look for a job and start scoping out a place to live? She had convinced the real estate agent to give her a six month lease. She had three and a half months to find another place. Now that she had a better idea about how she needed to schedule her writing time, there was nothing to stop her from adding to her "to do" list.

Later that day Geri walked to the corner store to get a couple of newspapers. Before looking at the help wanted ads, she went to the real estate section and was elated by what she saw. Ten years ago she had cut out a picture of her dream house from a magazine article about an up and coming architect. The same architect was being featured in the paper.

His new work was in condos and townhouses. The article was about the small developments he had designed for major urban areas. Believing that it was not a coincidence, she tore out the article and hung it on the refrigerator with a magnetic butterfly.

Turning to the employment section she tried to remember the last time she went through the exercise of finding a job. She realized that it was when she last lived in Chicago. Just as she was getting discouraged by what was available, she saw an ad for the same organization she worked for then. She mused about how her search in the paper was beginning to feel a little like kismet. She circled the employment ad and decided to go to the office the next day. It was not the conventional way to respond to a professional want ad, but she was not feeling very conventional nowadays.

She walked into the lobby of her old place of employment not knowing what to expect. Her interest in the job took a slight turn as she approached the receptionist desk. Wasn't there some saying about never being able to go back home? Before she could give it more thought, the voice from behind the desk startled her.

"Geri?" The receptionist leaned back in her chair and gave her a big smile.

"How are you? It's been a long time."

"Hi..." She could not remember the woman's name and her name plate was turned at an angle she could not view.

"It's good to see you. I can't believe you're still here looking like you looked ten years ago." As soon as that came out of her mouth, she hoped she had not offered her. She was just surprised to see her still in the receptionist position. What kept her there? Geri was genuinely happy to see her. Now remembering that she was very good to her when she worked there before, she also remembered her name, Sandra. It is amazing how many thoughts can go through your mind all in the course of saying 'Hello'.

"Shoot girl. I have two kids in college and one at home that wears a size thirteen shoe. Can you imagine how much it costs to fill him up with just with milk and cereal?"

"I know that's right. You look good, Sandra. Who else is here?"

After catching up, Geri let her know that she wanted to apply for the job in the paper and thought she'd just stop in to see what was going on.

"It's different but the same." Sandra raised her eyebrow and whispered, "Are you sure about coming back?"

Geri leaned across the receptionist desk. With a little chuckle she replied, "No, I'm not sure. But I need a j-o-b."

"We have a new Executive and guess who his second in commnad is? The position reports to her."

"Humph." She knew exactly who Sandra meant, but didn't want to get caught up in any drama before interviewing for the job.

Reading her signal, the receptionist picked up the phone. "You know what? Let me call the HR Director to see if she can see you. Since you're an old employee, maybe she'll make an exception and see you."

"Thank you, Sandra." Geri smiled and sat down. A few minutes later, the HR person walked through the door.

"Ms. Michaels? Hi, how are you today? Why don't you come back to my office where we can talk?" The woman smiled politely and gestured for her to walk through the glass doors. As she moved past her, she realized that she had forgotten to ask Sandra the woman's name. She followed Ms. X into her office and saw her nameplate on the desk – Mrs. Dottie Connors.

She gestured for Geri to have a seat and said, "I'm sorry. I didn't even introduce myself. My name is Dottie, Dottie Connors."

"Good to meet you. I'm Geri Michaels – as I'm sure Sandra already told you." Geri laughed at herself and said, "It's one of those days."

"I know what you mean." Dottie responded.

They discussed the position, the work Geri had done for the organization before and of course, her work at Haven. It turned out that the job involved managing a short term community project. It was right up her alley, particularly because it was part time. As the conversation continued, Geri shared that she was writing a book and intended to get it published, so flexibility was important. Dottie indicated that they were in the initial stages of interviewing for the position, but she seemed like the perfect fit. Geri thanked her and let her know that she was deeply interested.

Sandra was on the telephone when she walked back into the lobby. She waved good bye as she walked out the door. She smiled, buttoned her coat, and headed for the elevator.

Chapter 18

Living in unfamiliar surroundings helped Geri move forward. There were no reminders of lost loves of any kind or the occasional guilt she felt about leaving *A Haven for My Children*. Her days were filled with writing, work and a lot of solitude– in that order. Getting the project management job helped to re-root her in the city she loved. She even started thinking that her memories about Nathan were a bit exaggerated. Still, from time to time she was tempted to call his sister to ask about him. Today was one of those days. Concerned about how she might respond, she decided against it. She wondered if Channi felt she was somehow partially responsible for Nathan's family trouble. Did she think she was a distraction causing him to drag his feet in bringing his family to the States? Geri remembered how awkward it was the day they met. She spotted them in the mall one Saturday afternoon. They were laughing and pointing to something in a jewelry store window. His arm was around her. Geri stood motionless trying to decide whether she should turn and walk the other way. Questions about who the woman was, why they were there looking in a jewelry store window and what was so damned funny ran through her mind like bumper cars crashing into each other. As if he sensed her presence, Nathan turned to see her looking at them. He said something to the woman and they walked towards her smiling. When he hugged her he could feel the tension in her body. Teasingly, he asked if she was at the mall to buy him a gift. The woman beside him was looking at her as quizzically as she looked at them just moments before.

"Hi, I didn't know you would be here." Still smiling and trying to read her, Nathan peered intently into her eyes. He reached for her hand.

"Well, you never know." Geri smiled, but her voice held a hint of sarcasm. She pretended to adjust the shoulder strap on her bag so she would not have to take his hand. She turned to the beautiful young woman at his side and nodded politely.

"Oh." He touched his sister's shoulder. "Channi, this is Geri the friend I told you about." Apparently he hadn't said any of that to his sister when they were walking towards her. She seemed as surprised as Geri.

"How are you Geri? I'm pleased to meet you." Her voice was lyrical and very pleasant.

"Hi. I am happy to meet you as well." Geri smiled almost feeling foolish about thinking his sister was "another woman" and then looked at him. Why hadn't he told her that she was here? Did his sister really know what their relationship was? 'This is the friend I told you about.' Right!

"Where are you off to?" Still trying to lighten the moment Nathan continued. "We were just going to get something to eat. Can you join us?"

Geri could hear that Nathan's accent was even more pronounced. Maybe it was because he had been talking with his sister just moments before. Sometimes when you are in your own environment, your accent comes out fully. Even her Baltimore accent had a tendency to be more prominent when she was at home with her family. Being with his sister was being in his own environment.

"Actually, I was just on my way to a meeting. Can I have a rain check?" Geri politely declined with a false excuse– a lie. She was not about to be placed in an even more awkward situation. He should have known that. What would she have to talk about with the two of them? Her wish that his other life never existed?

"I should be home later this evening if you want to give me a call." She spoke to Nathan and then turned to extend her hand to his sister.

"It was so nice to meet you. I hope to see you again soon."

Without verbally responding, Nathan hugged her. Geri smiled and headed towards the mall exit. She walked away challenging herself not to look back. She could feel that one or both of them were looking at her. She wondered what he had told his sister about her and them.

"What the hell?" was all she could think to say to herself as she drove home.

He called late that evening. They talked about why he had not told her his sister was there.

"I don't get it? Why would you not have told me? I thought we agreed to be honest with each other."

"Geri, this is all so complicated. I wanted to let my sister know first how I felt about you. If she didn't accept it, I didn't want to bring her into the picture at all. She has nothing to do with us. My sister…"

"Run that by me again." She cut him off, "How can you say it has nothing to do with us and then turn around and say you wanted to make sure that she accepted us? If 'us' is the case, then it has everything to do with us." She was getting irritated, but tried to calm down so they could continue the discussion.

"Okay, help me understand."

"Yes" he said. "I should have told you. I'm sorry." He knew she was annoyed and even though she never did before, he was afraid she might hang up on him. He explained that his sister had come to the United States a few weeks ago, but had only come to visit him for the weekend the night before. He went on to tell her about the conversation he had with her about the two of them. He went so far as to tell her that Channi had warned him that the relationship could not work because his love was spread too thin. It was the last thing Geri remembered him saying about his sister.

Anyway, fast forwarding to today and thinking about it all, Geri decided not to call her. Instead she got the article about the condo development she saw in the newspaper and called to set up an appointment. The recording on the other end of the line began with "Welcome home. Your keys are just a conversation away."

Chapter 19

Patti was having difficulty making a publisher connection for Geri's manuscript. Her writing had a different twist and the two publishers she contacted first were afraid to take a chance particularly because she was new. Finally, she encountered some leeway with a publisher looking for a fresh new writer. They struck a tentative agreement with the understanding that it was ultimately up to the author. Pleased about the prospect, Patti called Geri immediately.

"Darling, are you sitting or standing?"

"Sitting. Why?" Geri had been relaxing with one of her favorite books, but sprung to attention at the tone of Patti's voice.

"How does a $2500 advance on this book of yours sound?"

"Patti, are you serious?"

"As a heart attack! How's next December sound for a kick off of your first book tour?" She had already mapped out the timing.

"Yes or no, lady?" was Patti's response to Geri's silence. She had gotten to know Geri a little better and understood her analytical side could create a lot of discussion.

"Yes! Are you kidding? Yes!" Geri also knew Patti well enough to know that she did not want to chit-chat about how surprised she was.

They agreed on a time to talk later that evening. Geri did a happy dance and then fell to her knees to thank God for all that was being done in her life. She called Sonia afterwards and they both screamed on the phone.

"That's awesome! And they're pushing so it will be ready for Christmas? Girl, you know that's just God! Unh!" Sonia was beyond happy for her friend.

"Okay, details!"

"I don't have all the details, but I know that I have a check coming. I'll talk with Patti later tonight."

"So when do you start working with an editor? Do you know who it will be?"

"Didn't I just tell you I didn't have details?"

They laughed again and Sonia assured her that Patti would be good looking out for her. Everybody's best interest was on Patti's plate every time. This was why Sonia liked her so much.

Patti was a fighter and would not settle for "mulch" as she would say. And just knowing what she knew about Patti so far, Geri's response was, "I know that's right."

Geri waited anxiously to talk with Patti that evening. She took sometime between writing a report for her job to write in her journal. She had not been consistent with writing in her journal, but on that day she knew she had to record something. First, she had to locate where she saw it last. It was under the bed. She sat on the floor and recorded, "I am sitting quietly after wearing myself out with thanksgiving, reflecting over the last two years of my life. I'm thinking about how it all could have gone so differently if I had not been willing and able to respond to the urging to step out on faith.

Recently I thought about Ntheba in a way I hadn't for months. Still trying to figure it all out, I wondered how I could still be blessed after sharing my life with someone whose life was not free for me to share. But then I remembered what made me go ahead with the peculiar pull towards him. Many may never understand, but it was just the experience of real love. It had no mystery or tainting, it just was. How I wish I could share the news about the book with him. I pray that he is well and experiencing his own joy."

After she finished her journal entry, she called her mother to tell her the good news. Victoria was thrilled and like Sonia had a lot of questions. Her response was "I'll let you know when I know."

Patti called late in the evening. Geri had fallen asleep, but was fully alert during their conversation. The details were still unfolding, but a meeting had been set with the publisher. She could not sleep after talking with Patti on the phone and wished she still had Nathan to talk to until she could. She turned on the television with the sound really low. When she began to feel sleepy, she said her prayers.

The next day Geri met with the person she worked with on the consultant project to discuss its completion. Being able to step right in and get to work so quickly after accepting the job had allowed her to get quite a bit done already. Her work was impeccable and they off her the possibility of periodically taking on small consultant projects in the future. She accepted their offer. After all, she had yet to become the best-selling author she hoped to be and she could use a flexible income.

Two weeks after the conversation with Patti, Geri bean working with the publishing company. They were headquartered in New York, but had a satellite office in Chicago. Geri was assigned to Eileen Golden, the new Acquisition Editor who had just started with the company. Grandville's Chicago office was small in comparison to its New York headquarters, but large enough to have an impressive caliber of editors and staff.

Eileen was hired to head up the "New Author" division and as Patti explained to Geri, she was looking for diverse "fresh, new authors."

The meeting included Eileen, Pam Grayson who was a junior staff editor, and an intern named Peter Mumford who looked like he was ten years old. It was a relaxed and comfortable setting. Something she had not anticipated. Patti was at the meeting, but would not attend the following ones unless otherwise requested. Eileen shared that she enjoyed reading what had already been submitted and wanted to know the inspiration behind the story.

"My last relationship inspired me to write about love – not just romance – but the challenges that can come with it. I like espionage and intrigue. I want to use them at the heart of the story as unexpected twists." Geri heard herself using the language Patti had indicated Eileen used in their initial conversation. It was not purposeful. It affirmed for Geri that she had been matched with the right editor.

Geri continued to describe the plot as she now knew it. Some of it mirrored her relationship with Nathan at least the love part. Although the characters' lives were different from the two of theirs, in her heart their story was the impetus for writing the book. Looking around the room it was evident that everyone had become caught up in the story. Patti acted as if it was the first time she had heard it. Grant you she left out the very personal details, but embellishing the piece about Nathan's political struggles made the story even more compelling.

"That's some story, Ms. Michaels." Still in strictly professional mode, Eileen responded.

"I just hope it sells." She smiled as she looked around the room and then back to Eileen. "Would you call me Geri?" Everyone had been introduced using first and last names. Since Geri hadn't referred to Eileen yet by name, she had not even considered needing to call her Ms. Golden.

"Sure thing. I'm not one for formalities unless they're called for. Call me Eileen."

Eileen had taken a few notes while Geri told the story. She rested her pen on the tablet and leaned forward just enough to signal more engagement. First names notwithstanding, she kept things very businesslike. She made some suggestions about certain portions of the manuscript of which Geri jotted on her tablet. She was given an eight week turn-around to edit what she had submitted and add three additional chapters. Parts of the conversation made Geri think about her college English Literature professor who thought she knew more about her story than she did. Although Eileen's comments were not so coarse, Geri felt herself stiffen a little and almost waiting for the same thing to happen.

Eileen discerned a shift in Geri's body language and said, "I am used to writers not always trusting my judgment, but this is a cooperative relationship. So let's agree that nothing said is personal. We both have the same objective to release a best seller! Yes?"

Eileen picked up her pen and leaned forward again. Relaxing a bit, she drew a smiley face in the middle of an empty page and pointed back and forth to Geri and herself.

Geri thought "The woman is either crazy or crazy intuitive." The "she's good people" attribute came from how she sometimes drew smiley faces in the center of her blank pages when she knew enough had been said during a meeting. In other words, "Done." Finally responding to Eileen's question, Geri leaned slightly forward, smiled and said "Done!"

The next topic of discussion was a title for the book. The group agreed that *In Our Time* the title Geri had suggested, was not an attention grabber. In addition, it didn't really give a clue about the story.

A couple of titles were suggested, proving that everyone was tuned in to her story content presentation.

"What about *Remembering Kenya?*" Eileen spoke up.

"Or what about *The Crescent Moon?* That has a mysterious ring to it." Someone else in the room asked.

In total agreement that *In Our Time* was a little dull, Geri said she liked *Remembering Kenya*.

Everybody agreed that *The Crescent Moon* and *Remembering Kenya* were both good suggestions. It was decided they would try out the latter and the design department would begin working on a suitable cover.

Eileen's final remark to Geri was, "Again, don't get hung up on my critiques to the degree that we get hung up in the editing process. We are writers and editors. The key is to communicate our work through communication with each other."

Geri responded with "Deal."

"Deal." Eileen smiled, stood and said her goodbyes.

The meeting was over and everybody shook hands. Something that Geri had dreamed of for so long was coming to fruition. She wanted to dance and lose control, but decided to keep her wits and dignity about her until she got in the elevator with Patti.

"A-W-E-S-O-M-E!" She sang the word in full bravado. Patti tried to chime in, but had to clear her throat. By the time she finished the song was over. They hugged and both simultaneously said, "Thank you." A relationship was being forged that would in due course measure up to every girlfriend connection Geri ever had. As for Patti, she sensed it might be a rare experience.

That night Geri went to bed wondering what people would think when they saw her face on the back cover.

She wondered how many women would identify with her story and how many who couldn't identify would still be able to understand? She also wondered if Nathan would ever see or read the book. How would he feel about her telling portions of what could be their story? To her astonishment she wondered if she really cared.

Chapter 20

"*Silhouettes*, here I come!" Geri applied the finishing touches to her makeup, took a deep breath and smiled the way she planned to smile at her readers as they handed her their books to be signed. "Signed. Do you believe it? Signed by Geri Renee Michaels." She'd already sent copies to her family and some of her friends. But this would be different. The people would actually be there she hoped waiting for her signature. They would mostly be people she did not know who would know her from that day forward.

The tour began at *Silhouettes,* a local bookstore in Baltimore. It had expanded and relocated from the downtown area to the mall. Geri purchased her first book as a teenager at the store when it was just a block away from her grandmother's house. She remembered searching the shelves and thinking intently about the kind of book she wanted to read before making her purchase. She knew she would know just which one by the title, cover and reading a couple paragraphs. To her delight, she saw that there were little synopses of the story and about the author on the back or inside covers. She was disappointed by what the store had to offer for girls her age. She swore to one day be on a *Silhouettes* shelf as an author of a book about a girl's life. Her book would be inspiring and full of the knowledge packed in her head just waiting to come out.

Today Geri mused when she remembered that promise to herself. Clearly *Remembering Kenya* was not necessarily for teenaged girls, but she believed that it pulled from some of that early knowledge even the wisdom from her grandmother Ella. She had contacted *Silhouettes* herself to request that the store be her first book signing engagement. When asked by her mother "Who would have thought your next visit home would be as an author?" Geri remembered the promise to herself. She smiled and said with confidence and humility, "I would have." Baltimore was a success. She was happy about the turnout. People she had not seen in years showed up. From Baltimore she headed for D.C., San Francisco, Detroit, and then back to Chicago for a December 23 and 24 signing at *Borders*.

On some level all of it seemed like a dream. For one thing, she knew how difficult it was to get a book published, especially your first book. The icing on the cake was ending up at Borders on Christmas Eve. That meant the publishing company thought they had a good and maybe even best seller. The thought of doing a book signing on that day was more than exciting. She was giving what she considered a gift of words to the world. To think about it that way might sound vain to some, but in her heart that's what she truly believed. Remembering Kenya could open doors for women to love in a different way, especially those who were still struggling with the idea that the kind of love they wanted and deserved was a chimera or an illusion. Would they be able to see the realism embedded in the story? It was truly about two people who gave of themselves to themselves, to each other and to the world at the same time. She had written the story hoping to illuminate possibilities as purposeful. It was not just about romance.

As excited and grateful as she was, Geri thought that four stops in less than a month was a lot, but she trusted her publisher. Patti would join her during her two East Coast stops. Although it was unusual for an editor, Eileen planned to stop in San Francisco while visiting her family for the holidays. They had spoken just before she went on tour and both thought it would be a good idea. Nothing official, just support. It would also provide Eileen the opportunity to gage the public's response to the book. Geri wasn't as excited about that as Eileen was. What if it tanked?

Chapter 21

The book tour was going well. Today she would be at her friend Renee's in D.C. Renee had moved from Baltimore to Washington for her job and as was her personality had already positioned herself on the social scene. She was more than happy and proud to hold a book signing at her home. She would introduce her to some "important folks" as she put it. She also wanted to show her just how much she was in her corner.

Renee greeted Geri when she arrived at the gathering. "Girl I am so happy for you and to see you! Who would have thought that all this would happen? And I might add that you look fabulous!"

"I know. I feel so blessed by how my life has turned out. And, looking around this room, you don't seem to be doing so badly yourself. Where'd you get that chair? Who is that brother in the black shirt? Since when do you like white furniture? Where did all these people come from?" Geri whispered with a barrage of questions. This was her first visit since Renee moved to Washington a few months before she herself had left Baltimore. And like her own life, everything about Renee's life was new to her.

They squeezed each other tightly. When they let go, Renee looked slyly at the man in the black shirt.

She leaned closer and said, "Well, the chair I got from Tanya Brace's shop. You would love her stuff. Now, the brother on the other hand, I met at an art show. I think he likes guys like we do."

Geri sucked her teeth and said, "Why is it like that? He's so cute!"

Just as Renee got ready to answer, she saw Christian Nounkwa, the Ambassador from Cameroon, West Africa moving towards them. She whispered in Geri's ear, "Don't look now, but this one's fine and from what I've heard, available."

Geri smirked, glancing at him then looking right back at her, Renee answered.

"No, I have not slept with him, Ms.Thing! I can just tell that he's a special man. Sweet and sensitive when it counts, but also strong when necessary and sometimes unnecessary. One side is for him personally, the other for him professionally. Huh, what I just said was profound don't you think?" Renee laughed.

"Yes, you are so profound. And how do you know all that?" She smiled wittingly at Renee. She was also thinking about the ambassador's physique.

"I'll tell you later." Renee cleared her throat to warn Geri that Christian was now walking towards them.

He was looking directly at Geri. As he got closer she tossed her head back in laughter partially over Renee's last remark, while the other part was for affect. The result was a flirt that surprised both her and Renee. Renee looked at her friend and smiled.

"Good evening, my name is Christian Nounkwa." Speaking directly to Geri and taking her hand, he did not acknowledge Renee.

Renee spoke up with "Well, Mr. Nounkwa, am I chopped liver?" She asked teasingly and put her hand on her hip while she waited for his response.

"I'm so sorry. I was just taken by Ms. Michaels…" He looked down at Geri's hand to see if there was a wedding ring.

"It is Ms. Michaels, right?"

"Yes it is. I'm happy to meet you Ambassador." Geri responded before realizing that she was giving away that they were talking about him. He did not introduce himself as "Ambassador".

With that said she glanced over at the signing table and then back to Renee. "You know, I think it's time to start the signing." Turning back to him, she said "It was nice meeting you."

"Before you walk away, I have to tell you that I enjoyed your novel. Was there any truth to it?" Christian asked.

She wanted to ask why, but decided not to play the cat and mouse game that she believed was coming. "Some."

"You seem to be a woman of few words this evening. Is that because you poured all your words into your book?" Christian laughed at his own wit, but Geri was not amused.

"I'm sorry. That was rude. Can I make it up to you over dinner tomorrow night?"

"Your apology is accepted and I'm leaving early in the morning which cancels out the prospect of dinner, not that it's necessary anyway." Geri responded thoughtfully. She was happy that she was leaving the next day so that she could not be tempted by his offer. She liked him from the beginning, but another African man? She didn't think so. And where did he get those dimples? I bet they work well for him every time he smiles and opens his mouth. Bam! Dimples and an accent.

"Well, take my card just in case you're back in the area." Geri took the card. Like a magician's trick it seemed to appear out of nowhere. He smiled as she took it from his hand and said, "Or, if you are so inspired you can call me at any time. You never know, dinner can be arranged in other ways."

Like a final act, Christian kissed her on each cheek. Nathan once told her it was the polite kiss of an acquaintance used in some African cultures, more personal than a handshake while not as personal as a greeting shared between family and friends. But come on. Really?

In the meantime, Renee was still there like a fly on the wall. She was impressed by his approach and startled by Geri's response. She had taken the card while looking into Christian's eyes without expression, then smiled and turned towards the book table. As she walked away, Renee shrugged her shoulders and said, "Don't mind her. She's just really focused. Maybe you two can talk later. I can see that you would like that." Renee let the thought linger for a second then said, "Excuse me, Christian, I need to announce that the signing is getting ready to begin."

He smiled nodding at Renee and turned immediately to look at Geri getting settled at the table. He thought she was beautiful. She smelled like a rare flower that could only compare to the smell of jasmine combined with some authentic scent that he did not recognize. He loved the scent of jasmine, but sensed that what he captured from Geri was something that came out of her spirit and not from a glass bottle or a stem. From that moment he decided that she would be his and he would rename her 'Jaz' - short for the scent of jasmine that came from her, and the attitude that she blew at him like the sound of cool, sweet, and mellow jazz from a tenor saxophone.

Because of her initial response to him, he thought he would just move to the side and watch her a little longer. He would move to the table to get a book signed later.

After watching her for a while, Christian was even more convinced that he had stepped into something special, into a possibility. It was ironic though, because he did not realize until that moment that he'd been looking. Initially he just thought he recognized her from some other place. As he stood watching and sensing who she was, he knew that the other place was some place he had never actually been. As that thought went through his mind, she looked up and caught him giving her the once over. She smiled, and at that very moment John Coltrane's horn spoke from the stereo. They smiled at each other, he lifted his glass to her, and turned away. Thinking nothing of it, Geri went back to what she was doing.

"I hope you enjoy the book." She spoke cheerfully to the person she handed the signed book to, and beckoned to the next person in line.

Looking up again, she saw Christian saying good bye to Renee. As he walked out the door, she refocused her attention. The young woman standing over her was beaming.

"Geri, I have already read your book. This one is for my mother. Is this your story, sister? It's powerful."

"Thank you so much. But no, it's just the story that I believe so many of us dream about."

Saying those words made her think about Ambassador Nounkwa. Perhaps she should have given him a little more attention. Shaking her head she said quietly to herself, 'I refuse to go anyplace near there again'.

"What did you say?" Renee had moved behind her while she was in deep thought. "Are you over here talking to yourself, girl?"

"You know, I am getting a little tired. I think I've signed all the books that we brought with us. Could you just ask if there are any more to be signed? If not, I'm going to call it a night."

Call it a night. That's what she had been doing for over a year. Working and then falling asleep just before she could begin to think about Nathan. But tonight might be more challenging because of Christian. He reminded her of him. What was it? "Okay, stop it. Stop it." It was time to say good bye to her guest and her host.

"My friend, thank you so much for tonight. If you don't mind, I think I'm just going to go back to the hotel. My flight leaves tomorrow morning at 7:00." Geri spoke apologetically.

Renee asked her to hold on a second. Announcing the closing of the book signing event, she gave everyone a chance to say good night. After closing the door behind her last guest, she went over to her friend. She had recognized the look in Geri's eyes. She could tell that Nathan had entered her space. Renee gave her an assuring touch on the arm and said, "No baby, I don't mind at all. But I know why you really want to go. Christian spooked you, didn't he?"

"Yeah, he sure did. I keep thinking that I'm okay until I realize that I'm not. I'm so tired of missing him, Renee. You'd think that with all that's going on in my life I'd get over it." She had placed him far enough in her past so that she did not think of him constantly, but it still remained hard to remove him from her heart. She considered that he might always have a corner there and that she would have to figure out a way to deal with it. Tonight she didn't feel like dealing with anything else but rest. Christian Nounkwa was part of the 'anything else'.

Renee suggested that she spend the night there, but Geri declined saying that she still had to pack. Tuned in to her friend's emotions, she didn't push.

"At least let me drive you to the hotel instead of calling a car service."

"Okay, that'll work. Let me have that Coltrane CD you were playing earlier so I can play it on the plane?" Geri winked at Renee and said, "You know I love ya, right?"

"Hell, you better if you got the nerve to ask me for my music." They laughed and hugged on that lighter note.

"Love ya too!" Renee quipped as she went off to get her bag.

When they arrived at the hotel she got out of the car and leaned over to gesture for Renee to open the window.

"Listen, if Christian says anything about me to you, you can tell him a little about my situation. I think I was a little rude to him. You never know. Just in case we run into each other again, I don't want him to think I am some diva witch."

"But you are!" Renee burst out laughing as she saw the incredulous look on Geri's face. "Girl, you know I'm kidding. There can only be one of those in this friendship. Don't worry, I got you covered."

After blowing a kiss to Renee, Geri went into the hotel. She had the odd feeling that the night clerk was waiting for her when she approached the desk and understood why when she saw a copy of her book in his hand. He had seen her in the hotel the day before and was waiting for the opportunity to meet her. A native of Baltimore himself, he thought it would be great to have her autograph a book. He had purchased his book from the gift shop for his wife.

"Hi, do I have any messages?"

"Good evening Ms. Michaels. Let me check. Would you mind signing a copy of your book for me?"

"Not at all. Jack, right?" She saw his name on his uniform bar. He smiled and nodded.

While she was signing his book, he took the messages from her box. She had asked that they take written messages when possible. She absolutely hated listening to long voice mails and thought a person would be less apt to leave a long message if someone had to write it down. That was just one of her idiosyncrasies and hotels generally accommodated her.

"Yes, you have a couple of messages." He handed them to her as he thanked her for signing the book.

As she walked away from the desk, she read the first message. It was from Patti reminding her that she should confirm with the car service that was to pick her up from the airport when she got back to Chicago in the morning. The second message was from…"Huh. That's interesting."

Chapter 22

It was as cold as she believed hell was hot when she got back to Chicago. True it was December, but sometimes December was a lot gentler. Walking to the car with her driver she laughed when she saw the breath coming out of her nose turning to what looked like frozen air. The lenses in her sunglasses fogged up as well. "I think Chicago is a test and a testimony. If you can get through the winter, you've passed the test so that in the spring you can give the testimony." The driver laughed and opened the car door for her to get in.

As they drove from the airport, she stared out the window and fell deep into thought. She remembered the lean days when she lived in Chicago before. Between the consultant work she continued to do and the modest royalties from the book, she was well situated. Life was pretty good. In a couple of days she would have her Chicago book signing. This year she would also open her holiday with a big party. She couldn't remember the last time that she even attended a party, let alone gave one. She looked up to the sky and said, "It's alright." She believed that if God could and would do what was being done in her life now, that all things really were possible. All she had to focus on now was getting gifts for the people she loved. She would be able to give some of them at her party, but most would be mailed to family and friends back home. At the top of each person's list would be a signed copy of her novel.

"That's an easy one" she said thinking out loud.

"What did you say, Ma'am?" The driver turned slightly to look at her.

"I'm sorry. I was talking to myself." Geri laughed as the words came out of her mouth. She realized how excited she really was.

"No problem. We all do it sometimes." The driver answered back out of the comfort that he felt with her the moment.

They were already on Lakeshore Drive. Reaching into her bag to get her phone, she realized that she hadn't turned it on when the plane landed. Several messages had been left including a couple by Renee asking if she had heard from Christian.

"Geri, where are you girl? Call me back. Oh, did Christian call you? Turn on your phone. Are you back in Chicago? Did Christian call you? Call me back. Love ya!"

Geri's response to herself was "No. And I don't expect him to." She thought this even though part of her wished he would call, while another part did not. She kept imagining falling for him and then finding out that he had a family at home like Nathan. Or that he would leave to go back to his country for a cause and she would never hear from him again. The questions 'what if he did and what if he didn't' danced in her mind every time she thought about the evening of the book signing. Right now she was busy and happy with her life. She didn't need or want any drama. But, what about that dinner remark he made at Renee's party? It had been three weeks since she left D.C. She had half expected that he would call, particularly after leaving the message at the hotel. "It was a pleasure meeting you, Ms. Michaels. Have a safe trip back Christian Nounkwa." She still could not find out how he knew where she was staying.

Sitting on her sofa and pulling off her boots, she could feel the exhaustion from her schedule fall over her. She laid back and closed her eyes just long enough to almost fall asleep when the phone rang. It was Patti.

"Hey, Patti. Yes, I just got in."

"You sound exhausted."

"Funny you should say that. That's just what I was telling myself. Listen, can we shorten the time for the book signing tomorrow?"

Patti agreed to cutting down on the time for the signing and let her know that she would settle the last of the arrangements with the store about how they would move the book.

When she arrived on Christmas Eve the bookstore was bustling with last minute shoppers. It was thrilling to see her picture in the store window and the set-up for the signing because both were decorated with holiday props and shimmering icicles. Her book sat in the center of the likes of some of her most favored writers. Decked out in a red cashmere sweater with her hair caught up in a high ponytail, she settled in her assigned space. She looked festive and sophisticated at the same time. The ponytail was pulled together with a rhinestone covered band and her own excitement seemed to make the stones bounce off her head as she greeted each person that approached the table. Eileen had given her a set of red Mont Blanc pens for a Christmas present and told her she had to use them to celebrate the day's signing. It was Christmas Eve, one of her favorite days, and everything was good, real good.

The night before she had slept well and woke up feeling energized and excited about the days ahead. She couldn't wait to get to Borders for the book signing. Everything seemed to be in order. Even the party for Christmas night was set to perfection. She'd chosen a caterer that she would use for years to come. His specialty was a mix of Creole, African and Caribbean cuisine. Geri knew him when they both had lean days and big dreams. Now he was doing quite well for himself. His business was in great demand. Not only could Chris cook, but he would bring the help needed for serving and setting up. For the first time she considered that she would be dressed when her first guest rang the bell.

By the end of the book signing, almost all of the books had been sold. All that was left for her to do was go home and get some rest. Once in she would call Patti who had left to go back to her hotel room. She also needed to call her mother and others she would not see during the holidays. This meant she would not have to do it on Christmas and could just relax before getting ready for her evening soiree.

Leaving the signing she decided to stop at the toy store in the same block to pick up a few gifts to drop off at a homeless shelter for families. She had managed to work a couple of hours a week at the shelter when she was in town. No matter how successful she became, she would always be concerned about children. Her belief that every child in need was a child who belonged to everyone and with that came a responsibility was unwavering. Before leaving town, she had taken over clothes and toiletries for the families, but having had such a magical day herself, she wanted to share some of the joy with the children. Along with what she knew was an extravagant bundle of toys, she wrote out a check that would be put to a more practical use.

Her driver agreed to wait for her outside the store and then take her to the shelter. Patti's company contracted all the drivers for her clients, but Geri asked him as an off the company clock favor. Getting out of the car in front of her building she gave him a hundred dollar bill.

"Merry Christmas. Thank you for helping me take the toys over."

He smiled and said, "Merry Christmas to you, Ms. Michaels. Thank you also for the book."

Leaning against her door was a long white box wrapped with a red velvet ribbon. She automatically assumed that it was from her mother or one of her friends that could not come to Chicago for the party. She smiled, again feeling blessed and happy. She unlocked her door and picked up the box, juggling it with her purse and the shopping bags. She put everything except the flower box on the dining room table and headed for the kitchen. As she opened the box, she smiled broadly. Beautiful long stem roses lay perfectly inside. They reminded her of a beautiful silk bouquet painted to perfection. They were a deep shade of pink crowned at their tips with a hint of crimson. The scent was heavenly. Geri lifted the ribbon tied bouquet from the box and unconsciously began counting each one admiring its beauty.

"Hum. There are only eleven. I wonder what that means." She asked the question before searching for the enclosed card.

"These are not from my mother." Geri laughed at the thought and said, "Nope. This is not from my mother." Instead of a card she found the cover of her book with writing on the inside.

"Congratulations on your success! I re-read your wonderful book from cover to cover in one night. Here's the evidence (smile). And by the way, you will get the other rose when I see you. Merry Christmas. Let's see each other in the New Year. My best to you, lovely lady. Christian Nounkwa."

"Oh my God." She sat down at her kitchen table holding one of the silky roses in her hand, brushing its fragrant flower against her cheek she whispered,

"Here's one for you, Ambassador Nounkwa."

Just as she began to get lost in the moment, the phone rang. It was Renee. "Hey Diva. Can a sister catch a cab in Chicago? Who are all these people coming to this cold ass city on Christmas Eve? I've been out here for a half hour waiting for the next fleet of taxies to drive up. I was trying to surprise you, but hell, I might need you to come get me."

"You know you're insane, don't you? Girl, this is a wonderful surprise. What airport?"

"I'm on the Southside. You know I hate that other crazy place."

"OK. I'm leaving right now. And have I got some conversation for you! Wait a minute, you probably already know."

"Already know what? I don't know what ya talkin 'bout, Sissy." Renee laughed after using her pitiful African accent. "I'm at the Continental baggage area. Love ya!"

"Right. Love you too. I'll be there shortly."

She should have known that Renee had something to do with this. But she was happy for it and even happier that Renee was there.

The drive to the airport was challenging. It had started to snow again and the road was slippery. Traffic was bad too, probably last minute shoppers trying to get home.

"What time was it anyway? Oh shoot, it's 9:15p.m. I hope there are not a lot of drunken folks bringing home last minute trees."

She remembered the Christmas that her father and uncle fell into their house drunk and singing with a scraggly old tree that they probably took off some lot that had already closed for the night. She was four years old and still believed in Santa Claus and reindeers. Her mom was pissed, but she recalled it with fondness and humor. It was also the last Christmas that she remembered being so happy. Her mother let her stay up while she finished baking the butter cookies and gave her a couple to sample.

"Oh my God!" Her scream rang hollow in her ears.

As she tried to get control of her car, she skid off to the opposite side of the road. Several cars had piled on top of each other's bumpers in the middle lane. Her car smashed into the right side guardrail as the airbag unleashed itself against her face and chest. The impact knocked the wind out of her. The next fearful thought was that the cars behind her would careen into her. She did not know they already slowed down and began to stop minimizing the threat of them ramming into her car. On the radio she could still hear "I'll be home for Christmas" playing as if nothing had happened. For a moment she thought the car was moving, but then realized it was not and neither could she.

Trying to pull herself together, she let her head relax against the airbag. She thanked God for sparing her life, and then began to pray for the others in the cars ahead. Just as she was praying, someone knocked on her door and yelled out, "Are you alright?"

She had not completely caught her breath and couldn't answer back. When she tried to shake her head in response, she felt dizzy.

She felt the tears rolling down her face. Suddenly a vision of Nathan came to her. She saw him standing at the door and like a dream, she recalled in an instant their final holiday spent together. She wondered if it was her life passing in front of her face as it all came back the meal, the conversation and the love. She heard the voice outside her car again and this let her know it was just an illusion.

"I want to open the door to get you out. Can you reach to unlock it?" She looked up and saw a young woman leaning her face close to the window.

She tried to manually unlock the door, but couldn't seem to get her fingers to work. Again, she saw Nathan's face. This time he smiled at her, shook his head affirmatively then turned and walked away. She was finally able to speak and said to the person standing outside the door "I can't. It's stuck." She began to cry harder.

"Try to open the door using the handle. Take your time. Just act like you're getting out of your car as normal."

"As normal." She was able to push down the handle and the door opened. The airbag was still pressed against her. There were now two people trying to pull her gently from the car.

"Do you feel any pain?"

"No. I think I'm okay. I feel a little dizzy."

An ambulance pulled beside her car and two paramedics rushed to her with a stretcher and some other equipment.

"Ms., we're going to slide you out. Just relax."

Within minutes, she was out of her car and onto the stretcher.

They began asking her questions about different symptoms. She said she felt dizzy. They placed a brace around her neck and band around her head.

She had calmed down and was thinking about Renee who was probably going crazy. She told the paramedic that she was on her way to the airport to pick up a friend.

The man responded, "You can call when we get to the hospital."

"Okay." Geri answered but was worried that it was all taking too much time.

As they drove to the hospital, the sound of the siren began to dilute her calmness. She did not believe that she was in any physical danger, but she could not help but think about what this all meant. She had such a wonderful day and evening for that matter. She asked the paramedics if they knew how the other people in the crash were doing. The response was that they didn't know. Would they have told her if they did?

Somehow, by the time she arrived at the hospital, Renee and Patti were there. At first she thought she was dreaming, but when they rushed to her side she knew it wasn't a dream.

"Geri, are you alright?" Patti asked in a tone that seemed to say that if she wasn't, the person who did this would pay. Patti sounded tough on the outside, but on the inside she knew she was afraid for her.

Although she knew she probably would not get an answer, Renee felt the need to inquire about her. She went over to one of the paramedics to ask if Geri was okay and to figure out what happened.

The commotion of several people being brought in on stretchers distracted Renee. The ER doctors and nurses moved swiftly to assist. Geri was wheeled behind one of the curtains. She looked out of it. Renee and Patti tried to go with her, but they were stopped by a nurse.

"She needs to be examined. Someone will come get you after that. Are either of you a relative."

"I am." Renee said wondering why they would include Patti in that question seeing that she was white and pretty pale given the circumstances. "I'm her sister."

"Good. We may need you to fill out her insurance papers."

A few minutes after she was wheeled behind the curtain, the nurse came out to let Renee and Patti know that they could go in.

"The doctor said I'm going to be okay. I didn't hit my head, but I may have whipped my neck in the impact of the crash."

"Honey, we are just glad you are talking. Thank you, God." Renee took Geri's hand and kissed her on the forehead.

"How did you get here? How did you know about the accident?" Geri asked, glad that she and Patti were there.

"Hey, I knew something was wrong. I could feel it. When I called your cell phone some guy answered and said you were taken to the hospital. He said you left your phone on the car seat and he heard it ring."

"Of course she then called me at the hotel." Patti was staying over for the party.

"How did you know Patti was at that hotel? What are you two up to?"

"Right now, all you need to do is rest. Don't worry about us?" Renee pulled out her cell phone to make sure it was turned off. "I don't want anybody in my face about nothing, so let me turn off this phone."

Geri laughed. The dizziness was still there.

A few minutes later the doctor came in. "Ms. Michaels, it looks like you're fine. To make sure though, we want to do some X-rays and a CT scan to see if you have a concussion. Do you feel any pain or dizziness?"

"No. pain. A little dizziness though."

"A technician will be in to take you for the tests. It shouldn't take long for the tests to come back. Your friends can wait for you here or in the waiting room."

"Take my bag. The nurse already took my insurance card. Make sure she gives it to you." Geri instructed Renee and Patti.

"Still bossing, even with the brace on your neck." Patti teased. She took the pocketbook and moved outside the curtain.

Renee leaned over to whisper in Geri's ear. "You know I told them I was your sister."

Geri whispered back, "Hey, you are."

Getting into the wheel chair was a little more difficult than she imagined. The difficulty was not a physical one. She felt a rush of sadness that brought tears to her eyes and weakened her legs just for a moment. Not wanting to focus on her emotions as her friends smiled lovingly and thankful that she was alright, she smiled back and gave a childlike 'see you later' wave.

As the attendant wheeled her into the elevator she thought of all the times she had gone to the hospital to visit other people.

What a difference it was for her at this hour. She had faced her own mortality in the car accident and the sadness she felt was really a strange sense of loneliness. What if she had died in that car? She was alone as usual. She closed her eyes. She could not help but wonder why she had been spared. Was there something that she was supposed to do that she hadn't? She made a promise to herself as she heard the elevator bell ring.

"Whatever it is, I will do it."

Chapter 23

It was about 4:00 a.m. The doctor gave her clearance to leave after the tests came back normal. He let her know that there was no sign of a concussion. It was probably just the stress of the accident that caused the dizziness. She should, however, try to stay awake for a couple more hours to be on the safe side. With the neck brace still on as a precaution and a prescription for Tylenol they left the hospital.

They took a taxi to her place. Renee helped her friend put on pajamas and reminded her that she needed to stay awake a little while longer. She and Patti borrowed Geri's sweats to change into. The three sat up talking until sunrise. Deciding it was okay for Geri to sleep, they blew kisses to each other and said "Good night."

Renee walked behind Geri as she moved slowly to the bedroom. She teasingly tucked her in and headed back to the living room. At her insistence, Patti would sleep in the spare room and she would sleep on the sofa.

Geri was the first to get up. She felt a little sore, but otherwise fine. She took a hot shower and put on fresh pajamas. Trying not to make noise, she walked quietly into the kitchen to make coffee. Careful with the way she moved her body, she leaned into the refrigerator and took out the dough she'd prepared the day before to make her Christmas Cinnamon Buns. Although it was in the refrigerator longer than it should have been, the dough had risen well. One of her spices fell from the shelf while she was taking the brown sugar from the cabinet.

Renee woke up and ran into the kitchen. Hearing Renee, Patti stumbled from the bedroom behind her.

"Are you okay? What are you doing in here?" Renee approached the kitchen concerned that Geri may have fallen.

Geri stopped what she was doing and looked at the two of them with an amused expression on her face. "Good morning, my lovely sisters. Merry Christmas!"

"What the hell's funny? What are you doing? What time is it?" A little agitated Renee repeated her questions.

"I'm doing my usual Christmas morning thing. Why?" She turned from them to place the spice back in the cabinet.

"Geri, I don't want to have to call Santa Claus and tell him to come take back your presents." Renee looked at her with a parentally raised eyebrow, now feeling the humor in it all.

"Are you kidding? Santa likes me. Look at my roses." The roses were on the counter where she left them the night before. She had not put them in a vase before she left to get Renee at the airport, but the little tubes of water they came in had not yet evaporated.

"You both need to stop that Santa stuff. What would Jesus say?"

Patti laughed and shook her head.

"So why are you in here making noise and making a mess when you should still be in bed?" Patti spoke to Geri, lifting her hands in a manner of questioning.

Geri ignored the question and said,

"Girl, you don't know nothin' about Jesus or Santa. You don't know what you been missing all these years with your wonderful Jewish self."

"Okay, I'll bite. Who did they come from, Geri?" Renee picked up one of the roses.

"Please! Don't even try it. You know who sent them." As soon as she said it she could see that Renee really didn't know. That was actually a good thing because it meant Christian didn't get any coaching from her. This may have been his idea.

"They came yesterday from Christian Nounkwa." She emphasized the pronunciation of his last name.

"He did call to get your mailing address. I didn't think you'd mind since you had been waiting to hear from the man." Renee tilted her head back and smiled. "Well, bless his heart! That was sweet."

"And who told you I was waiting to hear from him?"

"You did, every time I asked if you'd heard from him. I know your ways, girl."

"Anyway." Geri rolled her eyes and turned to look at Patti, "I say Merry Christmas to you, both of you. I am so glad that you were here last night. I can't imagine having to go through that alone. I could have been just coming home from shopping or something."

"I'm glad I was here too." Patti was taking baking ingredients off the shelf. "Sit down. I'm going to make you some Jewish sweet rolls in place of your Christmas buns. They're called Zemmels. They won't be Kosher, but neither is Christmas." She laughed at her own joke.

"They're sort of like your cinnamon rolls, but better!"

"Zemma who?" Renee asked, and then looked at Geri. They both laughed.

"You won't be laughing after you taste them. You'll be begging for more." Patti placed her hand on her hip and winked with confidence.

'Thank God for them and the laughter'. Geri thought as she sat down. Renee handed her a cup of coffee.

They sat at the kitchen table sharing stories, laughing, drinking the Christmas Blend coffee from the corner cafe and eating warm Zemmels late into the afternoon. And yes, the Zemmels were fabulous!

Determined to celebrate her Christmas the way she had planned, she was careful not to do too much that afternoon. She and her friends watched television, dozing off and on. She was heartbroken when the news reported that ten people had been involved in the collision, three were fatalities. She was also mentioned. Her phone rang continuously with inquires about her wellbeing and whether the party was still on. She talked with her family, but shared only a modest account of the accident.

The caterer arrived at 7:00 p.m. She was always delighted to see Dale. He was one of her favorite people and he made every occasion a wonderful affair. Her guests started arriving around 8:00. For once she was dressed on time and able to greet them instead of yelling out from her bedroom that she would be right out. In the past she prepared the food, set up the space, and then rushed to shower and change a few minutes before the first guest arrived. She would run out of the bathroom to open the door, then run back before they entered. Her greetings from the bedroom were to people that the first guest let in. Tonight was different.

The evening was amazing. It was topped off by a surprise visit by one of her favorite people in the world. Jack, a friend from her job in Chicago showed up with his new fiancé. Geri screamed when she opened the door and saw him. The woman on his arm was a little taken aback, but by the end of the evening she was fine.

"I can't even tell you how good it is to see you." She hugged him carefully and kissed him.

"How are you? I heard about the accident. What the hell were you thinking about out there in that weather anyway?" Jack admonished her knowing how she hated driving in the snow and rarely did.

"How did you hear?" She didn't have to ask. Ms. Busybody Renee had called him.

"Hey, don't fuss at her. I told you it was my fault." Renee overheard Jack's question.

"You know what, the only person at fault was the one who was drunk and caused the whole chain reaction. Unfortunately, he paid the ultimate price. His daughter was one of the persons who died in the crash. I'm just happy to be here with so many of the people I love."

She mouthed to Dale to come over. It was time for him to start serving the 'really good' champagne. They'd been drinking 'good' stuff all evening, but it was now time for the toast with her favorite bubbly.

"May I have everyone's attention?" The room became quiet. When her guests' eyes were on her, she thanked them for coming and said that there were gift bags with their names on them under the tree. She had invited eighteen people and fifteen came. Each had a personalized bag with things she remembered they liked. She remembered the bottle of the 25 year old Scotch given to her by a board member at Haven and put it in a bag for Jack. She knew it was one of his favorites. She would suggest that he share it with his fiancé.

Dale's helpers filled the glasses as she asked that everyone raise them for a toast.

"This is to all of you. . . " Before she could finish the toast the doorbell rang. "Who in the world?"

"Hold that thought." She laughed and went to the intercom to ask the front desk who it was.

"Yes?" She expected to hear the desk attendant's voice telling her the name of the person coming to visit.

"I hope you always say Yes."

Geri was surprised that she recognized the voice and was even more surprised that it was him. "Christian?"

"Yes. I will probably sometimes say 'No' though." Christian answered teasingly.

When Renee heard Geri call his name, she walked over to her with a suspicious look.

"Did you know he was coming?" The question came out of her mouth almost accusingly, but she held back the full accusation that Geri had kept it from her just in case she had to go someplace else in support of Geri. The someplace else was 'How dare he just show up uninvited!'

Geri hadn't told anyone that she'd called the Embassy to invite Christian to her party. First of all, she couldn't believe that she did it. Secondly, she did not expect him to respond because of the lateness of her invitation. She had only called last week. The possibility of his coming was such a farfetched notion that she had literally put it out of her mind. Even when she received his roses she just thought it was a result of Renee's maneuverings. But now, here he was.

"Well are you going to buzz him in or what?" Renee recognized the expression on Geri's face. Guilty as initially charged! She didn't budge. Renee pressed the buzzer and whispered in her ear, "heifer." Renee smirked and began walking away. "We'll talk later Ms. G."

"Oh shut up." She opened the door to wait for Christian to get off the elevator. Some of her guests' eyes were focused on the door as well. Renee went over to Patti and Jack who were standing together, to tell them what was going on.

"That's my sister." Jack said laughing with his arm around his fiancé. Geri stepped out into the hallway as he approached her door. This was her effort to avoid everyone seeing the greeting and to let Christian know that she wasn't that surprised that he showed up. 'Liar', she thought aft making the second mental statement.

"Well, look what the cat dragged in. Or should I say what Santa dragged in?" Ms. G., as Renee had just called her, trying to make light of what was utter surprise, took the chance that he would not be offended by her familiarity. After all, she didn't really know this man.

"I'm happy to see you too, Ms. Michaels." Christian went with the banter. Putting his arms around her, he felt her wince. He pulled back apologetically now thinking that he was being too familiar.

"Oh no. It's not the hug. I was in a car accident last night. I'm a little sore." Geri kissed him on the cheek and took his hand to bring him inside.

"Are you alright?" Christian asked as he held her hand the way you do to make somebody stop moving. "I mean I know you look alright, but is everything okay?"

His concern was genuine. He wasn't concerned about greeting her other guests.

"I'm fine, just a little sore. Come on in and meet my friends." Geri responded.

She smile and pulled at his hand to keep moving, then took his arm after giving his coat to one of the caterer's staff. She introduced him as Ambassador Christian Nounkwa. Why the formality, she wasn't sure. He said hello to everyone and that he was sorry for his late arrival. He followed it up with,

"I guess when you come late you get your whole name called."

Everyone laughed but Geri. She gave him the look like "I am not amused." He smiled and winked.

Christian's late arrival seemed to create a second wind for the party. It was almost 2:00 a.m. when the last guests left. That did not include Renee who was staying with her or Christian who just couldn't seem to tear himself away. He was at the Chicago Hilton and kept kidding with Renee about her taking his room and letting him stay with Geri. While he was laughing about it with her friend, Geri interrupted in a sing-song way saying, "Hello. This is my house and you are a leaving guest. My sister here is the sleep-over guest."

Geri gave both of them the eye and they started laughing.

"Anyway, good night lovely people." Renee decided to turn in. She kissed Geri and told Christian it was good seeing him again. As soon as Renee left the room, Geri felt a little nervous. She felt the need to have small talk. The idea was not far off because she remembered she had not thanked him for the roses.

"Have I thanked you for the beautiful roses?" Geri asked knowing that she had not.

"Well, no." Christian responded with a fake incredulous look.

"What if I say I wanted to wait until we were alone?" She smiled flirtatiously.

"That would be good. Is that what you did?" Christian answered.

"Yes." Geri responded sincerely.

"Good. Because I left something for you outside your door." Christian spoke then got up to get the box he left in the hallway.

"Where are you going?" Geri asked.

"Ah. It's still here." Christian did not answer her question. "What? Stop playing." Geri laughed curiously. She had not seen him lean the box against the wall near her neighbor's door.

A twinge of pain ran through her back as she leaned over to see what Christian was getting from the hallway.

"Here it is. It's for you my lovely lady." Christian smiled as he handed her the box.

Sitting down next to her, he waited anxiously for her to open the box. It was the twelfth rose. This one was almost completely crimson in color. It was as if it had been developing on its own in a special way just waiting for the moment it would be delivered.

"You are really something. This is as beautiful as the others." Geri smiled and gave him a kiss on the cheek.

"Am I?" Christian asked teasingly.

"Yes, you are." Geri answered.

"I will take that as a wonderful compliment, Ms. Michaels." Christian responded and continued with, "I could think of no better way than to knock at your door with something that still needed to be finished. The eleven were to let you know that I have not stopped thinking about you. This one," he gestured, "I wanted to give you this one personally and tell you how glad I am to see you again."

Geri held up the single rose as she spoke. "It's a little deeper in color than the others. It's more like the crimson tips of the others."

"Ah, you noticed." Christian responded and smiled broadly.

"Thank you, again Christian. They are all beautiful." Geri answered.

There was a brief silence after her answer. As if with intention, neither of them spoke any more about the roses. For a moment after commenting on the different shade of the single rose, Geri thought about how it had its own color, its own life. It made her think momentarily about how her life was unfolding. It was as if he knew more about her than she had shared.

"So, tell me something about yourself Christian." Geri broke the silence with her request.

He answered many of the questions she had about who he was. She made a mental note of it all, beginning with his growing up in Cameroon where his father was in the Diplomatic Services. She was fascinated by how as a young boy he knew he wanted to follow in his father's footsteps. It was not so much because of the work he thought his father did, but because he wanted to travel around the world. It would be his ticket to get out of his small village in Cameroon. His father stayed mostly in the Capital away from the family and traveled to places like the United States more often than anyone else he knew.

As their conversation continued Christian was quite forthcoming with information much more so than Geri. She listened to him with an ear of caution as he shared personal details. He had six sisters who were married with children. His oldest sister's daughter worked in New York at a foundation. He was engaged to his college sweetheart who was killed in a car accident two weeks before their wedding. It was fifteen years ago, but the devastating effect had kept him from dating anyone seriously ever since.

"I mostly work." Looking at her as if to confess, he continued. "My parents grew up together and had a happy marriage. I wanted to duplicate it, not completely, but at least the essence of it. My father died when I was fourteen and being the only son, I believed that it was my duty." He laughed as he heard himself use the term "my duty".

"Why are you laughing?" Geri laughed nervously as she asked the question.

"Wow. I can't believe I used that word! Duty!" He looked intently at his hands. "That's not what I think marriage or relationship is. Ms. Michaels, I believe you just pointed me to a revelation about myself."

"What?" Geri leaned back in the sofa.

"Ah. Not to share, Ms. Michaels. At least not yet." Smiling, he took her hand and changed the subject. "Am I keeping you up?" He offered to just call her in the morning.

"You know what, I am just happy to see you. And who knows when the next time will be." She was enjoying the conversation and his company. Both were easy.

"Do you want some coffee?" Even though she didn't want their time to end yet, she was getting tired. The coffee was mostly for her sake.

"I could use a cup." He stood up. "Let me make it, looks like you could use some down time."

"Are you sure?" It was like Deja vu. But she would not think about Nathan tonight.

"Not at all. Take advantage of it because I'm not a kitchen kind of guy. I can hardly boil water, but I make a mean cup of coffee."

And that he did. It was strong and hot the way she liked it. He put a couple pieces of the Zemmels on a plate and put it all on a tray he'd spotted on the kitchen counter. When he came back into the living room, she was slightly curled up on the sofa. She'd placed the throw cover over her legs and was feeling quite comfortable - quite happy actually.

"I hope you don't mind. I saw these in the refrigerator when I was getting the milk."

"Actually, this is perfect."

They continued to talk until daybreak. It was a perfect ending to a wonderful evening. He seemed to be a nice guy. They did not return to the subject of marriage or relationships – or his revelation. At first she was hesitant to share with him, but the more he shared the more comfortable Geri became.

She told him about how she had always wanted to be a writer. She even told him a little about Nathan. He asked if she had heard from him. She answered shaking her head 'no' and as he had done earlier, she changed the subject. If there had been a count of how much she shared versus how much he shared, she would surely have lost. As much as she liked him, she was super cautious and in many ways suspicious. After all, Nathan was a nice guy who she liked too.

"I'll be leaving for Cameroon this evening. I took the opportunity to layover in Chicago for a few hours so I could come to your party."

"You have family there?" Although she heard the story about his fiancé, Geri sensed that his revelation had something to do with the gap in time between then and now. Christian looked at her perplexed. Hadn't he just told her that his mother and sisters were still there?

Before he could answer she followed up with, "Do you have children?" She was determined to get off the train at the first stop this time. Positioning herself to pull the cord to get off she heard Christian say "No one but my mom and sisters. If I didn't mention it before, I'm in the middle. Can you imagine the hell I caught with them growing up?" He laughed even though he sensed a little tension in her question.

When Geri did not laugh with him, he got it. Although she had not gone into detail about Nathan, he made the connection and wanted to put her mind to rest right away.

"I haven't really had time to focus on a personal life. When I said earlier that 'I work', that's really about it. My life has been about my country and career. What about you Ms. Secretive? You've given me a little bit of this and that, but nothing for real. What about your family? What about this Ntheba Nathan person?"

"What do you mean? I'm not secretive." She found herself being coy as she explored the structure of his face, his eyes, nose, mouth and chin were strong and beautiful. Raising her eyes back to his she could tell he had been looking at her intently as she studied his face. Christian did not respond to her question. His silence was appreciated.

"It's alright." He kissed her on her forehead, but before he could hug her, she retreated.

"I'm sorry, I forgot about your shoulder."

"Humph, I think I am just about beat." She gave him her best smile. Christian took the hint and said, "No, don't get up. I'll get my coat.

I saw where your servant put it." He laughed at the indignant look on Geri's face.

"You know he was not my *servant*. And neither are you Ambassador Nounkwa." She got up to go to the closet. "Besides, I know you've got servants up the ying-yang!" They both laughed and went to the closet to get the coat.

"Is it alright if I call you tomorrow?"

"It is tomorrow!" No matter how comfortable it was with him, she just could not give in. "Have a safe trip. I'll keep you in my prayers."

He smiled, before kissing her gently on the cheek. And just as he walked away from the door, he turned around to Geri and said, "Take care of you, Jaz."

As she shut the door quietly behind him she could still feel his lips.

Sliding the chain across the door she hesitated, "Jaz?"

Chapter 24

"Look at you." Renee's voice woke her out of a deep sleep. After Christian left Geri fell asleep on the sofa with the throw wrapped around her body like a shawl. Renee stood over her laughing. Geri opened her eyes without lifting her head. Renee's knees were staring in her face.

"Geri?"

"What? Leave me alone." She managed to get one arm out of the wrap and pushed at Renee's leg.

"Okay, girlfriend. But I'm getting ready to leave and I have all your jewelry in my suitcase." Renee continued to tease her until she looked up.

"I know that's a lie. But where are you going, it's early." Geri started pulling herself up and realized that the throw was really tight because it had gotten tangled around her shoulders.

"Baby, it's almost 11:30. I been up, ate breakfast, showered, and now I'm ready to go."

"Oh my God. Renee, why didn't you wake me up?"

"Please, it looked too good. Whatever you were dreaming about, it just looked too good to disturb. Besides, you needed the rest. When did your boyfriend leave?" Renee laughed.

"He is not my boyfriend. But he didn't leave until daybreak. And yes, it was good." She stretched the arm from the shoulder that wasn't sore and smiled. "The dream. The dream, Renee." Geri responded to Renee's signifying look that she was talking about Christian.

"Hey, it's alright with me." Renee replied.

She got up from the sofa and walked to the kitchen still talking to Renee. "What time is your flight?"

"It's at 3:30 I just want to get a head start. And you know you got to get to the airport a zillion hours in advance nowadays."

"But you've got, what? One, two, three hours?" She counted on her fingers as she tried to pull herself out of the fog left from her deep sleep.

"Come on, let's have breakfast." Geri asked pouting.

"I had breakfast." Renee responded.

"Well, let's have another one. Besides, I know you want to know about Mr. Christian."

"Okay, I'll bite. No pun intended."

The two women sat at the kitchen table and talked about more than Christian. They shared the 'what next' dreams for their lives and promised to see each other more often. When Renee left for the air- port, they hugged knowing that their promise was going to be hard to keep. Before the elevator door closed Renee called out "Love ya!" and she called back, "Back at ya!"

Geri shut her door and turned to look at her living room. It seemed really empty after so much love had filled the space. She sighed and was headed for her bedroom when the phone rang. She rushed to get it and answered wistfully, "Hello."

"Hi, I'm at the airport getting ready to board. Did you get some rest?" Christian had ignored her put-off about calling.

"Yes, I did. I thought we agreed that you wouldn't call."

"We didn't agree to anything. I really like you, Geri. Don't push me away."

"Christian…"

"Listen, if you want I can try to track down Nathan's whereabouts. Would you like me to do that?"

Geri was quiet for a moment, but then spoke. "Yes, yes I would like you to do that."

"I will. And I'll let you know the minute I hear something. Geri, hear me. Don't push me away."

"Christian, have a good trip. Call me when you get settled. And thank you."

Just as she said thank you, she heard the boarding call at the airport. She heard and felt his hesitation to say anything else, but he finally said, "We'll talk soon."

When he hung up, she held the phone to her chest and began to cry. She didn't know if she was crying because she believed she would find out about Nathan after so much time had gone by or if she would miss Christian just knowing that he was so far away. Certainly the latter didn't make sense, but as she placed the phone on the receiver she realized that it was both. She sensed the end and the beginning trying to break through her unwillingness to embrace either.

Still a little exhausted from the events of the last several days, Geri felt the need to sleep. She laid on the bed and pulled the comforter over her shoulders. Falling snow met her in her dream. It was a quiet gently falling snow that stuck evenly on whatever it touched. As it covered the ground it seemed to harden just enough to allow her to walk across it without sinking too far. She walked across an open field leaving her footprints behind, but did not turn to see their pattern. She was headed somewhere. Where she didn't know, but she had to go.

The phone rang disturbing the serenity of the dream. Sill half asleep the ring sounded like wind chimes blowing in the distance. It was her cell phone that rang like chimes. Eyes closed not wanting the dream to end, she reached for the phone. "Hello."

"Hey, what are you doing?" It was Leslie, her friend from back East.

"Hey, what a surprise! How are you?" Voice groggy with sleep she greeted her friend.

"I'm okay. How about you? Did I wake you?"

"Girl, I'm fine. I had a little car accident a couple nights ago, but

God is good. You just caught me napping instead of working. I was having this dream about snow."

"Snow? Don't you have enough snow in Chicago not to have to dream some up?" They both laughed. "But what about this accident? Are you sure you're fine?"

"I really am. I missed you this Christmas. Sorry you guys couldn't come out."

"Geri, I'm sorry too. And unfortunately it would not have been 'you guys'. Mike is sick. That's why you haven't heard from me. I haven't told Renee yet. Don't say anything to her."

"What do you mean? Is it bad?"

Leslie began to cry. "I'm sorry. I thought I was ready to talk about it without crying. They found a tumor in his brain a few weeks ago. It's operable, but the chances of full recovery are slim. It's in a place that may cause him to lose his sight or if something goes wrong, his life. We talked it over and decided to go ahead with the operation."

"Oh, Leslie. I'm so sorry." Geri sat up. "When is the operation?"

"Tomorrow morning."

"How are Mike's spirits? How are you, really?" She knew how strong Leslie always felt she had to be.

"Geri, this one is rocking me a little bit. You know how much I love Mike. I'm trying to be positive and strong in front of him, but it's so hard."

"Leslie, you know I will do whatever you need. Who's going with you to the hospital?"

"His sister. My mother will stay with the kids while I'm at the hospital. Listen, I just wanted to reach out to you to let you know. I left a message for Renee to call me. I'm going to try again when I hang up from you. You know we miss you, right?"

"I know. I miss you too. Please give Mike my love. I'll keep you both in my prayers. Call as soon as you are able to let me know how the surgery went. Love you."

"Love you, too."

She hung up the phone and once again thought, 'Life is its own thing'. As soon as she thought it, she said aloud, "Then be in it, Geri, be in it."

It was early evening. She decided to get up and get dressed to walk to the corner for a cup of cappuccino and sit for a while. She took her notebook so she could do a little writing. The writing wouldn't necessarily be for her book, but whatever came to her.

When she walked out of her building snow began to fall lightly like the fine dust of powdered sugar.

She could smell the cold in the air and feel the soft crystals land gently on her nose and eyelashes. Remembering Leslie's remark about not needing to dream about snow when Chicago had enough in real life, she laughed quietly. The stillness on the empty street gave life to a setting that was almost dreamlike, like the dream she had earlier. Her heart now racing, she considered that her dream was a premonition of some sort. Was this walk in the snow part of a premonition? She was afraid to look back at her footsteps because the dream seemed to be specifically saying not to. She kept looking ahead until she reached the Café.

Once inside she settled down at her favorite table. It seemed to always be available. Maybe that's because she usually went in the evening when there were few people. Tonight she decided to believe that it was because she would have some kind of a revelation at her table. The coffee was hot and creamy the way she liked it. Claude, the owner, was behind the counter reading a book while at the same time keeping an attentive eye on his customers. A couple of them she recognized as frequenters. It seemed like they had their own tables too. Her table was at the window that faced her building. She could see that the snow had stopped falling.

The visible images of bare tree silhouettes and the glow of the street lamps were almost haunting. Just before opening her note book, she heard Christian's request that she not push him away. She heard the fear in Leslie's voice and then the promise she made to herself about fully embracing life. This time she made the promise to God. She would live as best she could in the life that she had. She sipped her cappuccino and dated the empty page. 'So much for aimless writing' she thought. Deciding to work on a chapter in her new book she shift her focus. Out of nowhere she heard the words spoken by her second grade teacher saying, "Be better tomorrow." Picturing Ms. Hayes' face, she laughed softly. She would use that statement in her book. But right now she asked the question, "Will it be better tomorrow?"

Her new novel was about a group of women friends who had remained closely knitted for many years. They went through the joys and pains of their lives as sisters. Their unspoken covenant was to always be there for each other, no matter what. She thought about her own friends when she was developing the characters in the story. Tonight she especially thought about Leslie and what she was going through. 'How do I write about someone's pain in a way that lifted them and not the pain?' When Leslie read the book, she wanted her to feel good about what was being said. She wanted her to be victorious and not sad. Just as she wrote her first book based on love in her life, creating a new story out of it, she wanted to do the same with this one. Would snow have a place in the story? She didn't know.

Ms. Michaels." She heard Claude's voice calling her out of her thoughts.

"Oh, I'm sorry Claude. I was so engrossed. You're closing?"

"Yes. I hate to disturb you." Claude said.

She laughed, "Please, I know it's that time. You know what? This is a wonderful place. I'm glad you're on this corner."

"Thank you, Ms. Michaels. I'm glad you like us. See you soon?"

"You sure will. Good night."

As she walked to her building, she sent up a prayer for Mike's recovery and Leslie's heart. She whispered a prayer for their children and blew into the air as if to confirm all of their blessings in the universe.

She stopped and looked up at the sky. Her heart was filled with prayers. Certainly one of them was for Christian's safe journey. He should be in the air at that point, but it would be several hours before he landed in Cameroon. Kicking up the snow in front of her, she smiled and said softly "Why not? Why not take another chance?" That was part of the prayer concerning the Ambassador.

Geri went right to bed when she got home. Unlike many nights, she felt fully satisfied with what she had completed that day.

She fell asleep as soon as her head hit the pillow and did not wake up until her alarm went off.

Patti called just minutes after Geri set up her writing space for the morning. *Remembering Kenya* was climbing on the Best Seller lists in the US and UK. Geri was astounded. It was her first book. Although she wished it would, she hadn't seriously considered the possibility that the book would make a best sellers list anywhere.

Patti told her that the attraction abroad was probably due to the cross continental and humanitarian aspects of the story. The publisher had marketed the book in London on a small scale, but it took on a life of its own.

A story that began with a profound love affair between a man and a woman ended up being a story about a village of starving and sick people. Unaware to her or Patti when they spoke that morning, *Remembering Kenya* was being recognized by a private international foundation that supported socially conscious literary works. Every four years the foundation awarded grants to new writers from all over the world. The reviewers were impressed by the content of the book and how it addressed the realities and the possibilities for change. Geri was being considered as one of the recipients for a two year fellowship to write her next novel. The opportunity would allow her to market *Remembering Kenya* and speak abroad.

Chapter 25

The conversation with Patti that morning made Geri reflect on how well her life was going. In the midst of it she thought about calling Leslie. Instead, she decided to wait until she heard from her or Renee. Leslie had promised to call to let her know how the surgery had gone.

The phone rang and she assumed that it was Leslie or Renee. "Good morning." She spoke with a familiar greeting.

"Hello, can I speak with Ms. Michaels?" A pleasant, but unfamiliar voice was speaking causing her to look at the time. It was only a little after eight.

"This is Geri Michaels. How can I help you?" Geri was sorry that she hadn't looked at the caller ID.

"Ms. Michaels, I'm so glad I caught you. I hope it's not too early. My name is Lynette Goddard and I'm calling from the Wright-Goddard Foundation. Do you have a few moments?"

"I do. What's this in reference to?" Geri was trying to be polite, but wasn't sure she wanted to talk to anyone except her girlfriends.

Lynette Goddard continued with news that made it difficult for Geri to contain herself. She hung up the phone and started doing a little dance. She could not believe that this was happening. Of course, she would go to New York to meet with the head of the Literary Department at the Foundation. Of course, she would not mind if they made the reservations and arrangements for her stay on their end. And of course she would be able to come in the next day or so.

The news from the Wright-Goddard Foundation helped her to think more positively about Mike.

She got dressed and went back to the kitchen, her favorite writing spot. She placed the phone next to her on the table, again contemplating whether to call Leslie instead of waiting. Deciding again to wait, she turned on the computer.

A couple hours went by. The phone rang. It was Renee. She was crying and her words were not audible.

"Renee, what's wrong? Take a deep breath. Tell me what's wrong." It was a rhetorical question. Her heart sank knowingly.

"Geri, Mike didn't make it. There were complications during the operation. Oh my God. It's too much! She was just beginning to heal from her step dad passing."

"Renee, Renee, calm down sweetie. Did Leslie call you or someone else?" It really didn't make a difference but she was trying to get Renee to calm down.

"Her mother called. She said Leslie was still at the hospital with Mike's sister. Mike's father was on his way to the hospital when it happened. So they should be leaving soon." Renee took a deep breath. Her words were becoming clearer.

"Listen, I'm coming to New York tomorrow afternoon for a meeting. I'll take the train to Baltimore as soon as the meeting is over. In fact, I'm going to try to move it up earlier so I can arrive to Baltimore sooner. What are you going to do?"

"I'm taking a train in this afternoon. I think I'm going to just get there instead of calling. I'm not sure what Leslie has to do." Renee was clearly thinking it all out as she spoke. "Maybe I'll call the house. Her mother might be there."

"That makes sense. I'll call you on your cell when I get to New York. If you talk to Leslie, let her know I will be there as soon as I can. Love you."

"Love you, too." Renee said, softly.

The phone still in her hand, Geri went to the living room and sat on the sofa. Thinking about how such joy and such pain could occur in that short span of time was giving her a headache. One minute she was feeling on top of the world, the next she could barely move from the weight of the news about Mike.

"Oh, Leslie. God please be with her right now." She cried out as tears ran down her face. She had not cried tears of pain in a long time.

As soon as she was able to pull herself together, she phoned the Wright-Goddard Foundation to see if she could reschedule her meeting to an earlier time. She spoke with the same woman she'd spoken with that morning, Lynette. They were now on a first name basis. Lynette understood and agreed to an earlier meeting. Afterwards she called and left the message for Renee that she would arrive in Baltimore later that evening.

Packing for her trip, she wondered if her being patient by waiting to hear from Leslie had been the right thing to do. She did not come up with a real answer and decided that it didn't matter. Perhaps that was the answer. It didn't matter. Life is what it is in its own way and in its own time. Geri stopped what she was doing as that thought entered her head. The tears came again, this time softly.

The foundation made reservations for First Class. She was happy to have the kind of privacy that it offered. She brought her journal and Renee's Coltrane CD to listen to during the flight. She would have the free glass of champagne to silently toast to Mike.

It takes only a couple hours to fly from Chicago to New York. So why did she feel like she'd been flying for days. Her idea about writing and listening to music went out the window as soon as the plane took off. She stared out the window during most of the flight, dozing off a couple times into the snow dream.

Wright-Goddard had a car waiting for her. Approaching the baggage claim area, she spotted a well-dressed man holding a sign with her name and a bunch of roses. She was impressed.

She walked over to him. "Hi, I'm Geri Michaels."

"Yes, mum. I recognized you from your picture."

'Mum? What's up with that?' was her thought, but she answered,

"Yes, I'm she. I wasn't sure if you were waiting for me because of the roses." She gave him a big smile.

"Oh, yes mum. These are compliments of Mrs. Goddard. There is a card inside. Do you have more luggage?"

"No, this is it. Thank you." She had learned to travel light, everything she needed was in the small rolling suitcase.

"For you." The driver handed her the flowers as he took her suitcase handle and gestured toward the exit.

As they walked out of the airport terminal, she felt a sense of excitement. For the first time after the initial call from Lynette, she was excited again about the writing fellowship. Her energy level changed from feeling drained to being ready for what she sensed was a new and incredible journey. Leaning back in the seat, she closed her eyes hoping to relish the moment, but instead she thought about the anguish Leslie must be feeling and the pain in Renee's voice when they spoke on the telephone. With her eyes still closed, fighting off more tears she whispered softly, "God keep her."

Chapter 26

The lobby of the Wright-Goddard Foundation was breathtaking. The upholstery on the oversized arm chairs was rich in hews of purple and red. The texture resembled velvet, but did not look like the kind she was used to. She could tell it was smooth to the touch. She had the urge to walk over and run her hand over it. A bronze sculpture of a woman with striking characteristics stood in the corner to her left. Her features were not quite full, but very pronounced. What looked like wings, were resting at her sides. 'Why weren't the wings spread' she thought. 'Why have wings if you don't use them?' The sign on the wall behind the receptionist greeted her with, "Believing is the beginning." It was fitting for this occasion.

She took all of this in before she approached the receptionist desk, a deep mahogany half circle around the women behind it. After giving her what seemed to be the privacy to observe the room, the woman looked up with a smile to acknowledge her approaching.

"Hi. I'm Geri Michaels. I have an 11:00 o'clock appointment with Lynette Goddard."

"Oh yes. Ms. Michaels. Let me ring her for you."

The young woman was strikingly beautiful. Her skin was a beautiful dark brown that seemed to glow. Dimples sunk deeply into her smile. She had an accent. Where was she from? Those dimples reminded her of someone, but she could not remember who.

"Please, have a seat Ms. Michaels. Can I get you something to drink? Coffee or water perhaps?"

"No thank you." Geri responded, then added, "You have a beautiful accent. Where are you from?"

"I'm from Cameroon. My family lives in Douala. Are you familiar with my country?"

"Yes I am. I have an acquaintance from Cameroon. I think he was born and raised in Yaoundé." She smiled generously as she thought about Christian, but did not pursue further conversation with the young woman.

As Geri sat down, another woman came out and sat behind the ark-like desk. It was not clear if she was relieving the woman from Cameroon or if it had been the other way around. As the first woman left she smiled at Geri and went through the mahogany double doors. The second woman let her know that Mrs. Goddard was taking a phone call, but would be with her shortly. This woman had no accent, but was as pleasant as the other young woman.

Waiting for her new patron, Geri decided to read the literature on the sleek glass table in front of her. It was interesting how each chair had its own table with different magazines and reading material. There was just enough to spark interest, but not cover the glass. To Geri nothing was a coincidence and this room was arranged with beauty and purpose. She had done a little internet research about the foundation before leaving for the airport, but wished she had time to have done more. The latest annual report was on the table along with a sundry of picturesque brochures in different languages. She started to reach for the report, but decided to look at the French written brochure instead. Although her French was minimal, the brochure drew her interest more than the financial state of the foundation.

"Geri? Hi. I'm Lynette. I'm so happy to meet you." Lynette extended her hand and gestured for her to go through one of the heavy mahogany doors. For some reason, Geri recalled the doors to the Wizard's hidden room in Oz.

The meeting took place in Lynette's office. The Literary Department Director and the foundation's Public Relations Manager were called in after they had taken a few moments to get acquainted. When everyone was assembled, Lynette opened the meeting with introductions. The Director explained that her novel had been nominated as one of the prolific readings of the year by a new writer. Remembering Kenya was selected with two other novels.

The other authors were from France and Bangladesh. The nominations were confidential. Her appreciation would be afforded that person by her continuing to do outstanding work.

A $75,000 fellowship was to be used to write the novel and for research purposes, travel to the country she selected for the story venue. The fellowship would be awarded to Geri and the other recipients at a formal dinner that would take place in six weeks. In the interim, they requested that she choose the country and give them a briefing on the focus of the book so that it could be announced at the dinner. They shared that their concern was to make the connection between countries by showing that people are just people and have much in common. Though fictional it should raise the level of consciousness about how love fosters determination to do justice in an unjust world. It could be similar, but not mimic her first book.

We live with challenges and triumphs no matter who we are or where we are from. As simplistically as it was presented, and although her fi book embodied much of what their expectations were, the idea that she received the grant was a bit daunting.

The expression on her face must have been a little obvious. Marc, the Literary Director, tried to put her at ease by saying how her expression was "normal." He also offered to give any help he could as she sorted it all out. They promised help, but would not interfere with her writing in any other way. The fellowship was hers because of what she had already done. Stipulations had less to do with the content of her new story, but more to do with the timeframe for completion. They trusted that her new work would have as much imbued integrity as her first novel. She had to sign an agreement to that effect.

When she left the foundation, she walked across the street to pick up the rental car that had been reserved before she left Chicago. She had not driven a car since her accident and was a little concerned about how she would feel behind the wheel.

There was no snow in the forecast for the next several days and she wanted to make sure that she would have a way of getting around once she arrived in Baltimore.

She had decided to wait until after her meeting with the foundation to call her mother to share both bits of news. Before driving off she made the call to let her know that she was on her way, but would go directly to Leslie's when she got into the city. Her mother was at once elated to hear about her fellowship, but deeply saddened by the news of Mike's death.

Instead of driving straight through, she stopped a couple of times for coffee and just to rest. Her first stop was in Newark where she decided to drive into the Brazilian neighborhood to buy a couple of cakes to take with her to Leslie's house. She thought it would have been rude to show up empty handed no matter where she was coming from and she remembered how good their fruit filled cakes were. A colleague who worked at Haven the first year it opened sent them to the center every year on the anniversary date. That colleague's sister had been sexually abused by their father and now directed a place called Safe Harbor in Newark, New Jersey. Geri was reminded of how something good and sweet could come out of something so heinous. The cakes made her smile and her staff loved them.

Geri rewrapped the roses Lynette Goddard gave her to take as well. The description of the roses that Geri's heroine kept in her home reminding her of divine beauty inspired Lynette to give them to her as a welcoming gift. She was doubly inspired knowing of Geri's friend's death.

There were several cars parked in front of Leslie's house when Geri arrived. She recognized a couple of them and was relieved to see Renee answering the door to let someone in when she drove up.

"Dammit, I forgot to call Renee."

Suddenly the reason for her visit flooded Geri's mind. Leslie was the solid rock in many of her loved one's lives. Now, they would have to be solid for her. They would have to in some way let her know that she did not have to be the rock this time.

After taking the cakes and flowers out of the car, Geri turned to see Renee walking towards her.

"Hey girl. I'm sorry I didn't call."

"Look, I understand. I'm just glad you're here. How was the drive? I thought you were taking the train."

"I was. But, just in case there was any running around to do, I wanted to be mobile. How's our sister doing?"

"You know Leslie. Trying to be there for everyone else, still. Maybe you can get her to lie down for a minute. She's only gotten a couple hours sleep since yesterday morning."

"I'll do what I can."

Leslie was happy to see Geri and tried to assure her that she was all right. In the midst of that assurance, she broke down and cried as if her soul would change into a river of tears.

"Geri, I don't get it. I just don't get it," was all she could say as she dried her eyes with Mike's handkerchief she'd held all day.

There was nothing for her to say to Leslie that would make a real difference so she just held her and whispered "Leslie, I'm here for you for whatever you need from me. We will all be with you through this."

"I know. Thank you. Thank you for letting me fall apart for a minute." Wiping her face, Leslie laughed a little with the sadness still caught in her throat.

A few days after the services were held at the church Geri grew up in. The funeral was sad and beautiful as funerals tend to be. What an oxymoron! Many came to show their love for Mike, and love and support for Leslie and her family. It was a long and draining day for her. She could not even imagine how her friend was feeling. No. She could not write about this.

It was hard for Geri to leave Baltimore after the funeral and after spending time with her family. She realized how much she missed her mother and tried to convince her to come spend a week in Chicago sooner than later. They decided that she would come in the spring and maybe spend two weeks.

"Geri, I am so proud of you and all that you've been able to do. But mostly I'm happy that you are happy."

The words that her mother spoke to her the day of Mike's funeral helped Geri sleep through the night. She found comfort in lying across her mother's bed as they watched television and ate ice cream. When her mother fell asleep, Geri quietly turned off the TV and light, and went to her old bedroom. Her mother had changed the furniture and used the room for everything that didn't fit anywhere else in the house, but the spirit of the room still embraced her childhood. She felt comforted and comfortable as she remembered.

The next day Geri decided to drop the car off at Baltimore-Washington International and fly out of D.C. instead of driving back to New York. She was able to book a flight that would get her back to Chicago around the same time. Flying back she felt anxious, like something else awful was going to happen. She thought about the last few days and decided that her feelings were probably normal. Appreciating the First Class accommodation even more, she reclined her seat. She fell asleep almost as soon as she settled in.

"Geri, Geri."

"Yes. Who's there? I hear you, but where are you?"

She was in a deep sleep when the snow dream started again. This time the wind was blowing and she could hear the tinkling of wind chimes. The sound was melodic and grew louder as she moved toward *the voice she heard.*

"Geri. Don't be afraid. You don't need to see…"

"Ms. Michaels. Ms. Michaels." The Flight Attendant touched her shoulder gently. They would be landing in 20 minutes and she'd noticed that Geri had slept during the entire flight. She wanted to wake her to let her know she needed to start getting ready for their arrival in Chicago.

"Yes?" Trying to get her bearings, Geri's voice was a little woozy when she answered the Flight Attendant. "I'm so sorry. Had you been trying to wake me for a while? I was really out."

"No problem. I just didn't want to startle you. We will be landing shortly. You need to put your seat upright. Can I get you a glass of water?"

"Oh, no thank you." Geri answered as she sat up in her seat.

She sat up trying to remember what she had been dreaming about. All she could remember was snow and a voice calling her. She thought the voice might have just been the Flight Attendant's trying to wake her up.

PLEASE FASTEN YOUR SEAT BELTS AND TURN OFF ALL ELECTRONIC DEVICES.

As the sign flashed on the screen above her head, she turned her attention from the dream to preparing to land. She took a quick glance at her makeup. 'It is what it is.'

"Thank you for flying with us. Welcome to Chicago."

As she got off the plane, she turned on her cell phone. Almost immediately it beeped letting her know that she had a message. Juggling her bag and pulling her suitcase with one hand, she used the other to retrieve her messages. There was one message.

"Hi, Jaz. How are you? I tried calling you at home a couple times, but didn't get an answer. I hope you were out doing something special for yourself. Just wanted to let you know that I've gotten settled and whether things are all right with you or not, I miss you. I left the details about how you can reach me on your home voice mail. Hope to talk with you soon. Oh, it's Christian."

She was amused by his ending. "Oh, it's Christian." She shook her head and thought, "He has no idea."

To her surprise, Connie, one of her mother's younger cousins, was waiting for her when she got to the end of the arrival corridor. She waved and yelled with a big smile on her face. "Surprise. I called your mom's to talk to you. She told me you were headed back. I decided to come get you."

They hugged and laughed just at the pleasure of seeing each other.

"Connie, thank you. You have no idea, I was not looking forward to standing in that taxi line."

"Is this all your stuff?"

"Yep, this is it." Adjusting her bags so nothing would be between them Geri bumped Connie with her upper arm.

On the ride home, she shared what happened in New York and

about the funeral. Her Cousin didn't know Leslie or Mike, but felt Geri's pain. Geri had spoken briefly with her before leaving for New York. Connie thought that she could use a friendly face when she got back home. They decided to stop to get something to eat. Connie convinced her to try a new rib place that had opened a couple months ago.

"Hey Connie. Welcome back." The owner of the restaurant saw them come in and whispered a greeting to Connie as if they were old friends. She was on the phone and gestured that she would be with them in a minute.

Geri leaned over to whisper in Connie's ear. "I thought you said they just opened up. How many times have you been here? Didn't you say…" Before she could finish the question Connie cut her off.

"Hush. She is my cousin on Aunt Lee's side, so she's kinda yours too. And I've only been here once!"

"You know why I'm laughing? Who else you got stashed away as cousins? And do any of them have a vegetarian restaurant?"

A couple of months ago Connie said she was going to become a vegetarian.

"What?" Connie pretended not to know what Geri was talking about. She turned her attention back to Debra and mouthed, "Can we sit anywhere?"

Debra was now off the phone. "Sorry about that. Yes, sit where you want. Bobby will be over in a minute to get your order. I'll be right back."

She came back to the table with her coat in her hand and looked at Geri. "Hi, I'm Debra. I wasn't trying to be rude. I'm running a little late for an appointment." Debra touched Geri's shoulder.

"I'm glad to meet you. Congratulations! Connie said, you just opened."

"Thanks. Don't be a stranger with or without my cousin. See you." She waived at them both and headed for the door.

"So, how are you doing?" Connie turned to Geri.

"Connie, it's all good. Some way or another things work out. Right now, I'm just praying for my friend Leslie and her children. What about you? How's that husband of yours?"

"Girl, your friend is good. He's still refinishing furniture. Getting ready to open the store next month. Do you believe we were finally able to convince him to stop doing it for a hobby? I have to say, he's good."

"I know he's good. I've been waiting for my piece for how many years? Tell my brother that I'm coming to get what he promised me before he tries to charge for it!" Geri laughed.

It was great spending time with Connie, especially after all that had gone on the last few days. She shared about the foundation fellowship and ran some ideas about the new book focus by Connie. Although her enthusiasm had been a little side tracked, she knew she would regain it after some much needed rest. She needed to refocus and start on the Wright-Goddard Foundation project. This also meant that the "girlfriend" book had to be put on the back burner. She would ask Patti how to proceed with her publisher.

Connie tapped the table and said, "I am so proud of you. Hey, this can be your first celebration. The ribs are on me!" They both laughed.

Geri told Connie how grateful she was for the opportunity to celebrate with her while the hot sauce dripped off her hand. They stayed in the restaurant for a couple hours. Debra walked in the door. Geri told her again that it was nice meeting her and shared that she enjoyed her meal. When they left the restaurant the cold air brushed against her face and she felt a chill run through her body. She started to tell Connie what she just felt, but decided to end on a lighter note with a tight, happy hug.

"Don't be a stranger. I don't care how much work you have to do!" Connie dropped her off at her building and drove away thinking how glad she was that Geri had come back to Chicago.

The person at the desk greeted Geri when she came in. As she approached the elevator he remembered Carl's request that he tell Ms. Michaels about the packages. H called out to let her know. She pressed the elevator button before going to the desk.

"Do you need some help, Ms. Michaels?"

"No. I've got it Harry. Thanks though."

She entered the elevator with a sigh. One of the packages began to slip from under her arm. She noticed that it was from her aunt whom she did not see while she was home. "I have got to call her."

Chapter 27

Geri did not bother to unpack when she got in. She left her bag, packages and mail in the middle of the living room floor. The next morning she looked at the pile and kept walking to the kitchen. All she wanted was a hot cup of coffee and something to eat. She thought that eating so many ribs the night before must have stretched her stomach. But what could she eat? All that was in her refrigerator was the food left over from her Christmas party and she did not feel like getting dressed to go down to the corner café.

"Well, looks like Patti's Zemmels are getting more than their fair share of consumption," she said under her breath as she took the last piece from the refrigerator and put it in the microwave. When the coffee and roll were ready, she moved to the living room and began to sort through her mail. It dawned on her that she had not listened to her voicemail since she got in either. Remembering that Christian said he'd left messages, she reached for the telephone and sat back in the chair and relaxed.

"Hi Geri." It was Patti. She went on to ask her to call as soon as she had the chance. She remembered that Patti didn't even know about the writing fellowship. "I'll call her later." Erase.

"Hey sweet lady. How are you? I'm all settled. The flight was long as usual, but good. I hope all is well with you. I'll call you back later this evening, your time."

"Hi. This is Christian again. I forgot to give you my information. Just in case you need or want to call, my number is..." She pressed the button to hear the number again while she got a pen to write it down on one of her mail envelopes. After writing it, she pressed the button to save the message. There were a few more messsages that she skipped until she got to Christian's last message that said he sensed something was wrong and asked her to give him a call when she got the message. He gave her a rundown of his daily schedule telling her the best time to catch him at home.

"At home." The sounded strange to her. "I guess that really is his home. D.C. is just a place where he lives."

She laid the phone next to her and finished eating her roll and sipped her cold coffee. The phone rang just as she put the last bit in her mouth. She swallowed it quickly as she answered.

"Geri?" It was her aunt Viola.

"Oh, hi. Can you ever forgive me?"

"I suppose I can. Your mother told me about all that is going on. Are you alright?" Leave it to her aunt to turn her guilt into a moment of focus on how she was doing. She appreciated this about her.

"I am. How are you? How was Christmas?"

They chatted for a while and then her aunt asked what she had done for New Year's Eve.

"Oh shoot. I guess I missed it." She responded to her aunt with a bit of amused irony in her voice. In her travels from New York to Baltimore she kept hearing it talked about on the radio and television, but her focus had been on Leslie. By the time she got to her mother's house, New Year's Eve had come and gone. No one was in a particularly celebratory mood. It's funny how holidays are only important if you believe in them and stop to acknowledge them. Other than that, what significance did they have in the scheme of life's cycle? With that question she considered how New Year's Eve and New Year's Day would be for Leslie and her family from now on.

When she got off the phone with her aunt, she looked at the clock. It was evening in Cameroon and a time when Christian said he would be in. For some reason though, she could not bring herself to call him. She barely knew the man and felt uncomfortable calling him with so much news. "I'll call later."

Going back to her mail and packages, she opened the one from her sister. It was a small brown angel with spread wings. The enclosed card read, "Have a wonderful Christmas. Know that you are loved and missed. Debbie."

She was happy that she at least had the good sense to send Debbie's gift in advance. When they talked her sister expressed how much she loved the scarf and the book. She asked Geri to send her a couple of autographed books for her friends. "Of course, no problem" was her response. She just had to make sure that she took the time to send them.

The second package was larger with foreign postage. She shook the box a little and heard nothing. Her name was in a hand writing she did not recognize. But then she saw the return seal of the Embassy. "Oh, no he didn't!" She found herself giggling as she opened the package. Christian's note read "Let this keep you warm until I come back." It was the most beautiful throw that she had ever seen. She wrapped it around her shoulders and brushed the end against her face. It was so soft. It was also very clear that he had taken the time to know her taste. Standing up and tossing it across the arm of her sofa she marveled at how it was the perfect accent to the pillows. She couldn't wait to thank him.

After getting settled, she placed the call to Cameroon. She found herself holding her breathe as the phone rang. She exhaled at the sound of his voice.

"Bon Jour." It was her first time hearing him speak French, but she knew it was him. "Bon Jour back."

"Geri. How are you? I've been waiting to hear from you. Is everything all right?" Hearing him was special in a way that she had long forgotten.

"Everything's fine I was out of town. I'm so sorry to have caused you concern. Thank you so much for the gift! It's beautiful!"

"I'm so glad you like it. It reminded me of you the moment I saw it, and I knew I had to buy it and send it to you. Tell me, what's going on? How was your New Year's Eve?"

Christian's question opened up a conversation that would last for two hours. She shared all that had happened since he left. When she was sad he comforted her with his words. When she shared the news about the fellowship, he laughed heartedly and celebrated with her saying, "Congratulations! Have you chosen the country you want to visit? Will you spend time there writing?"

Their time was about sharing what each was up to. Her heart was open and cleared for him to step in.

Geri was once again ready to get back into her writing, but had difficulty concentrating on the story because of the foundation's criteria. She went into her office and spun the globe that was sitting on her oversized desk. Closing her eyes she stopped the spinning with her finger. She found herself in the Atlantic Ocean very close to the continent of Africa. She laughed hard and long. What a coincidence. Or was it?

She left the room and plopped down on the living room sofa. She pulled Christian's present around her shoulders. Caressing it as she hugged herself she asked, "I don't feel like working today. What should we do?" She hadn't taken a day for herself in a long time. Deciding to go to the movies, she removed the throw from her shoulders and laid it on the arm of the sofa. She looked at it with the longing desire that the one who sent it was there in its place. Speaking in the tone of a whisper, she ran her fingers over the fabric.

"I sure wish you were here."

Chapter 28

Her "Geri Day" ended up being a good one. The movie helped to take her mind off everything. Afterwards she stopped at a restaurant she'd passed by for months and wondered why she waited so long to try out what was touted as the best burgers in town. She got home just in time to watch her favorite TV show then went to bed knowing that she was going to have a good night sleep.

The next morning she woke up feeling fresh like the brisk air that was coming through her window. She sat up in the bed, took a deep breath and said, "So this is how it feels when you can see bigger parts of your life in fuller view." Christian was moving in where Nathan had moved out and for some reason that morning she remembered a stranger telling her a long time ago, "Books will flow from you." She finally understood what he meant. With the fellowship came a new and different kind of enthusiasm about completing the next one. She was almost dizzy with contentment.

"Humph, what country will I choose?" Geri thought about Christian's question as she headed for the kitchen.

She turned on the television and saw that BBC World News was reporting on an uprising in Angola. As she watched, she considered what it must be like to live in constant turmoil and instability. She thought about Nathan and what he'd described as even greater than what the news reports. Being told only pieces of the story was another violation against a people who could not report on it themselves. She shook her head in sadness.

"Maybe I'll use Angola. That's Nathan's home. Perchance I could get to see him…" Her feelings for him were lessening every day, but she could not separate the idea of him from where she was currently in her life. Her consideration to write about any African country had much to do with him. Though the soft blanket of denial she slept under during the brief period that they were together had fallen off, she still missed him sometimes. Still she knew that wherever he was and whatever he was doing was how it was to be.

She thought about how his family had never seemed real to her when they were together. With him gone and her being able to look at their relationship with new eyes, she saw them. She saw him and his family together and whispered, "God forgive me for not seeing and bless them as I now see."

The phone rang breaking through the moment. "Hello." She answered and muted the T.V.

"Hey babe. How you?" It was Candace sounding all cheerful.

"Hey back! I'm good girl! How are you? Where are you? You sound really close." The clarity in the phone connection sounded like Candace was in the next room.

"We just got a new phone carrier so maybe that's what it is." Candace replied. "I just heard about Leslie's husband. I am so sorry." She continued.

"It was so sudden we're all still reeling from his passing."

"So how are you doing?" Candace asked.

"I'm doing well, real well as a matter of fact." She remembered how grateful she had just been. As they caught up she glanced periodically at the silent television. Realizing her distraction, she clicked it off.

Candace suggested that she might be able to visit in the spring. "The spring" for some reason now sounded like a foreign concept. The winter had been so full and so long, that it seemed like spring was too far off to wait to see anyone or do anything. Still, they agreed that they would talk in a few days to establish an exact date. Both women were conscious of their calendars and planning was essential.

"I can't wait to see you."

"Me too. Love you." They talked for a good while and hung up with the promise to do better at keeping in touch.

There was a lot to do that day. Housekeeping concerns had gotten away from her. She thought she would spend the rest of the morning paying some bills, doing laundry and finally putting food in her house. Later she would do research on her new project.

Before doing anything, she went back into her bedroom and got on her knees. She thanked God for her life and her loved ones. She also prayed for the people of Angola and others around the world who were suffering. She thought about and prayed for Diana as well.

She ended her prayer asking that she be encouraged and strengthened to do what she needed to be fully in her life. Confident that she had been heard, she began her day - again.

It was a fruitful day. She was able to return several phone calls including the one to Patti who was overly thrilled about the fellowship. They talked about the ramifications for her publishing contract and agreed that Patti would get in touch with Eileen that afternoon.

After seriously considering Angola, Geri decided to go with Cameroon. Oddly enough, it was not because of her relationship with Christian. It was a place that she had wanted to visit for years after becoming acquainted with one of the nicest and most interesting people she had ever known. They had met at a conference in Boston over a decade ago and she understood from mutual colleagues that he now worked in Chicago. There was a story to be told about the people and the country that would provide a positive glimpse to her readers. She was excited to tell Christian about her decision.

Chapter 29

The days and weeks seemed to whiz by as she became immersed in her new project. Her initial decision to write about a young American woman involved in goodwill work traveling throughout Cameroon took a dramatic turn. She found herself moving toward the mystery of the life of an underground radical who falls deeply in love with the son of a prominent politician in Yaoundé. The story line challenged her imagination and willingness to delve into a life that was completely different from what she considered during the early stages of her research. Her new protagonist was a historian whose research had gained worldwide renown. She was fluent in several languages, politically radical, and trained in self-defense to flip a man two times her weight over on his back. She was also stunningly beautiful with a charming demeanor that contrasted the gutsy description that Geri assigned to her personality. Geri had yet to come up with an appropriate name for her femme fatal. For now she was Ms. M.

Ms. M. was a native of Cameroon who had studied at Harvard and perfected a New England accent that suggested her being born there. After living abroad for ten years, she returned to Cameroon at the urging of her family. The family had been stripped of all they owned in a governmental seizure of property that took place with the seating of the new government. Upon returning, she was introduced to a group with whom her brother had become involved. She decided to join them in the underground movement to recover their political and financial status.

Ms. M. met her love interest while masquerading as a wealthy heiress from America who was visiting Cameroon as a freelance photographer. She claimed that she was there to take pictures depicting the "upside of the country." Her brother was an attaché for the government though secretly involved with the underground group. He managed to get an invitation for her to a black tie political event. Ms. M.'s elegance allowed her to present herself as one of the not so common Black American's with wealth that would be highly regarded in that circle. Geri admitted that this was a little far-fetched, but considered that in this day and age almost anything was possible. She continued to work day and night to unfold the story as realistically as possible while giving it the intrigue and glamour of a highly rated fictional novel or maybe even a movie. In either case she would make sure there were numerous disclaimers about it being fictional and in no way factually based.

Underneath all of the mystery, however, there had to be an inspiring story with the integrity that she brought to everything she accomplished. The idea that it could be a movie made her laugh momentarily. The laugh changed to a "Huh, you never know."

Geri and Christian spoke a couple of times a week and were looking forward to seeing each other. He had prolonged his stay in Cameroon from one month to two months. He told her that he had an assignment he had to complete before returning to the States. Although vague, she accepted his explanation. Besides, she needed to focus as much as possible on completing the first draft of her book. He might be a distraction. She had hoped to complete a final draft within the next month. Perhaps she might even be able to time her second visit to Cameroon when Christian was there.

Feeling the need for a different writing space, she checked into the Chicago Hilton for a couple of days. She considered that if someone tried to reach her on her home phone and couldn't, they would call her cell. She worked, slept and ate without a schedule for three days. A couple friends and her mother called, but she hadn't heard from Christian in five days. She thought about calling him but didn't want to interrupt her writing rhythm. To her delight he called the morning she was going to check out. Groping on the bed for her cell phone she almost missed the call.

"Yes."

"Good morning sunshine. The sun is shining there, right?"

Regardless of the hour in Cameroon, his voice always sounded as if he was fresh and alert to all that was going on in the world.

"Is it?"

"I think so." He could hear the smile in her voice. His heart grabbed it.

"How are you? Help me to get up. I have too much to do today to stay in bed even though I'd like to."

"Maybe you should. Do you want me to call you later?"

"Are you kidding? Where have you been for the past five days anyway?" She pretended to be annoyed when all she really felt was happy to hear from him.

"I told you I had an assignment that I was working on. I'll be able to share more with you in a day or so. I think I'll be able to come in earlier than I'd expected. You know I miss you. I can't wait to hold you for the first time, I might add." His heart swelled with the thought of seeing her again.

"Didn't your mother tell you that the best is worth waiting for?" She teased him this time knowing exactly what he meant. She had been dreaming about him for a couple nights now. She couldn't wait to see him, but considered that his coming back early would mean that she would not be able to meet him in Cameroon.

"How's the book coming? Did you give Ms. M. a real name yet? I don't know why you don't just call her Geri. It sounds like you might be trying to live vicariously through Ms. M."

Christian laughed knowing that she was going to take his head off a little for the mere thought.

"You know what Christian?" She responded the way he'd expected.

"No, tell me Jaz. Hey! That's it, call her Jaz."

"Why would I call her Jaz? I don't even know why you call me Jaz."

"Well, I guess this is a good time to tell you."

"Thank you. It's about time." Her laughter skipped lightly over her curiosity. She had been trying to figure out why he called her that for weeks.

To call her 'Jaz' because she liked jazz was too obvious. Christian was not an obvious kind of guy.

"Do you remember the first evening that we met?"

"Yes."

"What scent were you wearing?"

"Christian, come on. Stop playing."

"No, I'm serious. I recognized it immediately because it is one of my favorite scents. What was it?"

"Oh, wow. It was one of my favorite scents - jasmine. I wear the oil when I am not trying to do a perfume thing. It speaks to who I am in an odd sort of way."

"I know. And it spoke that night. You are Jasmine. You are one of the loveliest creatures that I have ever met. Yet you are strong and distinctive. Like the jasmine flower there is a mystery about you, a mystery that's hidden in the beauty of your scent. Not just the flower, but also the scent. That's who you are and who I fell in love with immediately."

Tears rolled down her cheeks. Her guard was completely down. Was it because she was still tired or because she wanted to be vulnerable to him? Her silence caused Christian a small bit of alarm.

"Geri?"

"I'm here. Do you know that you just touched my heart? Will you please hurry back?"

"I'll be back as soon as I can. But for now, promise me you'll give yourself another couple hours of rest."

"I promise." She hesitated for a moment wanting to say "Christian, I do care about you." Instead she said, "That's what I'll call her. Jasmine."

"I miss you, Jaz."

"I miss you too."

With that, they hung up. She turned over to try and go back to sleep. As she welcomed the soft feel of the pillow against the side of her face she realized. 'We didn't say goodbye.'

A knock on the door woke her out of a sound sleep. "Maid service."

"Can you come back?" There was no way she'd be able to go to sleep after that. She checked out, pleased with the work she'd been able to finish and happy that she had spoken to Christian.

There was a Fed-Ex package in front of her apartment door. She opened it as soon as she got inside.

"No she didn't." Sonia had sent the manuscript for her new play.

She hadn't told her that she was working on anything the last time they talked.

"So that's why she was so concerned about making sure we set a date for her to come out. The little sneak. She knew she was going to send this right before she came."

She removed the remaining paper from the binder. She could see what it was after tearing the top portion. It was clearly labeled. The note taped to the cover read "Got ya! Hey sister, I know that you are so busy. But could you take a minute or two and read my new work? All wonderful comments will be greatly appreciated. All others will be accepted too. Talk soon. Love you! Sonia."

She decided to go all the way and use this day as a break from her own writing. She would go down the street to the café with Sonia's play and sit there until she completed it. Well, almost completed it anyway. How exciting!

It was a good day. She found out what 'Jaz' meant to Christian and liked it. Sonia's new play was fabulous. And, Ms. M. was given a name - Jasmine Moudime.

Chapter 30

Being able to name Ms. M seemed to open the path to her full adventure. After doing a little research about last names, Geri named her Jasmine Moudime. It was a strong name that would lend itself to the strength that this woman would need to confront the mountains in her life. Of course, there were several twists and turns that continued to unfold without Geri's knowledge about how the story would end. What would happen to this woman or with her love affair? She sensed that she would know sooner than later. Could it be because she now anticipated Christian coming back any day? He called to let her know that his assignment was coming to an end and he just needed to take a short trip to complete the information gathering portion. She still had no idea what the assignment was, but decided that it must be some state secret or important matter. Whatever it was, she was glad that it was ending.

Two days before Christian was to arrive in Chicago, she received eleven crimson roses. Her excitement grew as she prepared for his visit. She thought about all the things she had learned about him during their telephone conversations. The information she found on the internet filled in some of the professional pieces, especially what he had accomplished as the Cameroon Ambassador to the United States. She was impressed by all of his credentials. Christian was an inspiration to her on a personal and professional level. He pushed her gently to care more about herself and the world in a different way.

The announcement that Christian's plane had landed made her heart pound like crazy. She had managed to convince an airport customer service person to let her meet him at the gate. As passengers came off the plane, she could not understand why he was taking so long.

'I know he flies first class, so he should have been one of the first off the plane' she thought as she anxiously waited. Just as the thought entered her mind, she saw him. Not expecting her to be at the gate, he started walking in the opposite direction.

"Hey Mr. Ambassador," she called. When he turned around, she said, "Can you give a girl a hug?" Geri laughed as he looked at her with surprise and delight.

"Wow." Christian walked over and flung his arms around her. They kissed longingly unconcerned about anyone near them.

"Surprise." She whispered.

"Why didn't you tell me you were coming to meet me?"

"Did you just hear what I said? Surprise, as in you were not supposed to know." She laughed.

"Man, I have missed you! This surprise is the best I think I've ever gotten. Let's get out of here." Christian's voice was strong and filled with a longed for happiness.

"I parked my car in the lot. Let's go get your bags. I have some more surprises for you." Geri nodded affirmatively as she replied.

"Oh, you do, do you?"

"Yes, I surely do."

As they moved through the airport both beamed with anticipation about the rest of their reunion. It was clear that they were very happy to see each other. Geri abandoned her hesitation about showing him how she felt. Christian let his feelings pour out onto her as he recognized her readiness.

She had prepared most of their dinner before she left for the airport. The only thing left to do was to sear the salmon and toss the salad. Christian's favorite bottle of wine was chilling in the refrigerator and the scent of jasmine lingered in the air. She purchased candles for each room. She burned them until she left to get him.

When they arrived at her apartment, she took his coat and briefcase and laid them on a chair. He asked where he should put his suitcases and she gestured to the spare bedroom. While he was in the bedroom, Geri re-lit one of the candles. She asked him to open the bottle of wine while she went into her bedroom to change her clothes.

She thought they would spend time catching up, listening to music, and then eat and explore their relationship. As she entered the bedroom though, Christian came in with two glasses of wine and a look of seriousness on his face.

"Now that was fast." She spoke with a questioning smile.

"Sometimes speed is necessary." He smiled back.

Geri walked over to him as he sat the wine glasses down. He pulled her into his arms and they kissed what felt like a lover's kiss. Afterward he lifted her face to him and said, "I know. Not yet". She kissed his cheek as if to confirm that they slow down and then lead him out of the room.

Later they ate, listened to jazz and laughed at each other's stories and her bad jokes. Christian shared how good it was to see his family. He told her that they could not wait to meet her. She thought it a little odd.

"What did you tell them about me?"

"Truthfully, I told them that I thought I was in love with you and that you did not want to be in love with me."

"Christian. Why would you tell them that?" Geri was trying to imagine what they must have thought of her as someone who refused to return his love. The idea that he told them he loved her had not yet registered.

"Wait, you told them that you love me?"

"Yes, I did and I do. You can't be surprised about that."

"Well, I'm not sure. I guess I never thought about it."

Liar, she thought. Of course, I've thought about it. I've thought about it a hundred times.

"If you never thought about it, it was because you were too busy trying not to fall in love with me."

His last statement led to silence. Geri got up from the sofa where they had moved after eating dinner, and walked toward the stereo. She turned it off and began looking through the videos she had picked up earlier that day.

"Do you feel like looking at a movie? We have…" Before she could finish her sentence, he interrupted her.

"Jaz, we can't keep running from this conversation."

She acknowledged his statement by shaking her head. She put the videos down and spoke in an almost inaudible tone, "Christian, I do love you. But you know what? I'm not ready to really trust mine or yours." Before she could turn around completely, his arms were around her. He turned her to face him.

He kissed her gently and said, "Thank you. Thank you for loving me."

"How can you thank me? Didn't you hear the last part of what I said?"

"Yes, I did. But you didn't have to say you love me. The fact that you wanted me to know means we have a chance."

Geri returned his embrace.

"So, you're alright in the spare room?" She asked almost embarrassed that they hadn't talked about where he would sleep beforehand.

"Are you giving me a choice?" He was even more embarrassed for taking it for granted that they would sleep together.

"Not really." She patted his arm and smiled through her embarrassment.

"Okay. Your house, your rules. I guess I'll take the spare room." He backed away from her and then moved towards her again.

"What if we agree that we sleep in the same bed and not do anything?" He smiled broadly and then feigned a brooding expression.

"Seriously? Christian, you know…"

"No. I'm serious. I just want to be next to you, Geri. I just want to hold you." He crossed his heart and lifted his hand as a promise.

"I promise I won't make a move. That is unless you want me to." Smiling still, he took her hand and placed it so she could feel his heart beat.

"Okay. Okay." Shaking her head and smiling she ended with "You got pajamas?"

They spent the next couple of days hopeful about their future. They took walks along Lake Michigan. They talked for hours and made plans for when he returned from Cameroon the following month.

Geri shared more about herself than she had with anyone, even her closet girlfriends. She talked about her father, someone she very rarely thought about. For years she had dealt with the idea that he had abandoned them. Oddly enough, she never thought that he did not love them, but that he just didn't want to be with them. She realized while sharing the story that it was her father that caused her to separate the idea of love from trust. She thought he loved them, but did not trust that it might be okay if he stayed with them.

Clearly her father's anger regarding what he believed about her mother was stronger than the love she believed he may have had for her. Geri also talked about how much she had loved Nathan and would probably continue to hold him in her heart. She asked if he would be able to accept those feelings. Christian's tone was reassuring, but he somehow knew that her holding onto feelings for another man was to protect herself from all she was feeling for him. Geri knew it too. This was different even for her.

The day that he was to fly to Washington, Geri was scheduled to interview with *Today's Writers*, a prestigious literary magazine. Christian planned to stay in her apartment while she was gone. He got up early to prepare for a conference call and make coffee for the two of them. Having had the conversation with Christian about her father before going to sleep that night, Geri dreamed about him and Christian meeting. But the dream seemed to signify that Christian would walk away from her as well.

When Geri woke up and saw she was alone in the bed, her first reaction was that Christian had in fact gone. She called out to him, but he did not answer. Looking around the room, she realized that his being gone was only in her dreams. With a feeling of relief she stretched remembering how happy she was. Her life was filled with love for herself, her family, her friends and now him.

"Hey, what's wrong? I heard you cry out." He sat on the side of the bed and kissed her forehead. It reminded her of how her father used to sit with her before she fell asleep at night. Such sweet memories she had not thought of in years were being brought to the surface. Only this was a morning kiss and not a memory and certainly Christian was not her father.

"I just had a bad dream. It seemed so real." She saw the concern on his face. "But I'm okay. Where were you?" She laid her head against his chest.

"I was in the kitchen making coffee. Do you want a cup?"

"I'd love a cup. Wait, do you make good coffee?" She teased him with the question.

In response, he stretched out with her on the bed and whispered in her ear, "Yes, I make good coffee. Don't you remember? You kept me up all night last Christmas and wouldn't let me lay in your bed…"

Instead of getting up for coffee they moved into each other's arms. They kissed passionately, holding each other tightly. Breathing heavily, Christian whispered "I promised."

As difficult as it was, they both retreated from their passion. He laid on his back as she rested her head on his chest. Still holding each other in the comfort of their love, they fell asleep.

Geri woke up and turned to look at the clock. She saw that she only had a little over an hour to get to her interview. Fortunately, the interview was only a few minutes' drive.

"Good morning. Or did I say that already?" Christian turned over on his side to see her pulling at her face in the mirror.

"What are you doing?" He laughed.

"I think I should get a face lift." She made a silly face. "Good morning back at ya!"

"Geri, you do not need a face lift."

"But look at this big old laugh line. I try to keep my hair pulled back tight to pull it up some. But it's having its own way this morning."

"Come here. I'll fix it." Christian put on his sexy smile and pulled back her side of the covers.

"Get out of here. Your fixing the coffee was enough. Look where that got us. Remember my interview is today?"

"Yes I do, that's why I want to make sure that you're smiling when you leave."

"I'm smiling. Yes, I'm smiling just fine, Ambassador."

As Geri walked out the door, she yelled back to Christian. "See you in a while. Have a good morning."

Christian was in the shower and did not hear to answer, but it was okay. She knew he was there and believed that there would be many mornings like this.

The interview went fabulously. When Geri got back to the apartment, Christian was packed and ready to head for the airport. She offered to drive him, but he declined stating that he would call for a taxi. Geri reluctantly agreed to say good bye in the lobby.

When the taxi came they were already downstairs waiting.

"I left something under your pillow."

"What?" she asked.

"What? It's a surprise. Remember that word *surprise*." Geri laughed remembering what she had said to him at the airport when he arrived and saw her there waiting.

The taxi pulled up before they could talk longer. They kissed lovingly and promised to talk with each other that evening.

"Have a good trip. Don't pick up any more women at the airport." Geri watched the taxi drive away and put her arms around herself feeling happy in love.

Getting on the elevator she found herself already switching gears as to how the rest of her day would be. But the first thing she wanted to do was check to see what Christian left. The second was to call Renee to say, "Hey girl, I did it! Or at least, a lot of it".

She went straight to the bedroom. There was a note on the bedside table from Christian saying 'Look under my pillow.' Running one hand under the pillow and with the intention of calling Leslie at the same time, she picked up the phone with the other. She felt a thin box and pulled it out.

The phone, now perched between her shoulder and ear, began speaking the recording, "If you need further assistance, please hang up and dial…"

Not caring about the recording or Renee at that point, she let the phone fall from her shoulder and tore the paper off the box. Inside was a beautiful double sided silver frame. She opened it and saw pictures of Christian and her from her Christmas party. Renee sent the copies to him per his request. Geri had not seen them. It was a total surprise.

"Wow. These are beautiful." She sat the pictures on the table and thought about the night they were taken. How their relationship had grown. Noticing that a small piece of paper had fallen from the picture frame, Geri picked it up and read what was written.

"This is the revelation, my love."

Geri was immediately taken back to the night of her party when they sat talking for hours. Christian told her that he had a revelation in the midst of speaking about marriage and relationships. He said he was not ready to share, but that he would.

"This is the revelation. He saw us."

The recording on the phone had turned into a loud beep. After a few moments, she got a dial tone and called her friend. Smiling ear to ear she blurted out, "Renee. I'm doing it!"

Chapter 31

Spring was finally on the horizon and Geri was looking forward to what it would bring. Among other things, her mother and Sonia were coming to visit. Her mother would be there the last week in April, Sonia for a couple days in May. She had read Sonia's script and loved it. She couldn't wait to act out one of the scenes with her friend. She wanted to play the foul mouthed sister whose boyfriend was fooling around all the time. Maybe they'd even tape it and put it in a time capsule to pull out when they were old and gray. Geri had just seen a television special on time capsules. She shared the idea with Sonia stating that the bonus would be the recording equipment would probably still be the same, so they could play it back without a hitch.

"Speak for yourself, chick. There ain't a gray hair on this head and won't be anytime soon." Sonia responded as they laughed.

Geri kept it going by saying, "You know I'm right."

Thinking about both visits, she slapped her thigh. It was going to be fun.

This would be her mother's first visit. A couple of months ago Victoria had written a letter to her telling her that she understood what drove her better than she thought. She expressed how proud she was of her. She witnessed Geri overcome a difficult childhood and watched her grow into a wonderful woman of strength and love. She could appreciate that although her daughter sometimes pushed herself so hard, she did it to achieve her dreams. Although she sometimes protested how Geri took on things with such abandon, in her heart she knew it was who she was. Geri reread the letter a couple days ago. She thought of all that she had all of her life, not just now.

Christian was leaving again for Cameroon the same week her mother was coming to Chicago. She had hoped that he could come through to meet her first but he had to leave the day before her mother would arrive. He assured her that there was no need to worry about their meeting. He took the opportunity to also share that he'd told his family he hoped they would have a new member in the family.

She laughed and said "Hey, first you have to pop the question!" She half thought he was joking, but when he didn't laugh, she reconsidered. Was he serious?

Christian could tell that her mind was racing a mile a minute. To interrupt her speeding off a cliff of fear, he asked teasingly "What question?" Even though it had been months, he knew she was still getting used to the idea of them being together. He quickly changed the subject to her mother coming and his regret that he would not have that opportunity to meet her. Still, there was no doubt that he wanted to spend the rest of his life with her. He knew that he would ask her to marry him sooner than she thought, maybe when he returned from Cameroon.

Geri buried the idea that Christian was hinting around about marriage. She did love him, but had not overcome her fear of committing herself to another man. It was easy to stash the idea away while she was fully engrossed in the foundation project. A nagging need to write a children's book had also entered the picture. Her advocacy for children had been majorly replaced by her new career. She remembered the promise she'd made to herself as a child the day she went to the bookstore with her mother and couldn't find a good book to read. She vowed to write books for children, but here she was spending all of her time writing books for adults. It would be challenging, but she could work on both at the same time. The children's books would be short with lots of illustrations, telling stories that would inspire them to love themselves and help them know how much they are loved by the universe. Her guess was that it would take a month or so every now and then to perhaps complete a series of seven.

One thing she had been able to do all along was volunteer at the homeless shelter once a week. A few weeks ago she met a mother and her four children. They had been evicted after the mother lost her job and couldn't find work. Although she was receiving help, it was barely enough to take care of them. With no relatives in the area and no place else to go, the family ended up in the shelter. Two of the children were in elementary school and the other in diapers. Geri would spend time with the older children each time she visited.

There were books for them to read and games for them to play to try to curve the reality of living in a shelter, but nothing to help them feel good about themselves. She kept asking herself, "How could they be empowered in this situation? What kinds of books would empower them?" One night she asked Stephan, the older of the two children. She struggled to frame it for a child's comprehension.

"Stephan, what would make you happier than anything in the world? What would it be?" Geri spoke with her soft voice as she looked lovingly into his eyes. She wished that she could hold his hand, but didn't know his life's circumstances.

"What do you mean?" Stephan answered with a question of his own.

"Well, what if you had ten wishes that could come true. What would some of them be?"

"Wow, ten wishes? Hum. First I'd wish for a big juicy cheeseburger with lots of ketchup that spilled in the plate when I bit it." He looked suspiciously at Geri waiting for her to judge his first wish.

"Then, maybe a play station game. Wait, first I have to get the TV. Okay. Never mind that. Let me think."

Geri wondered why he didn't ask for the TV also, but then understood that he had the foresight to see that he couldn't keep it there.

She could see that Stephan was beginning to put more thought into his answers. He looked over at his sister who was sitting on the bed with their mother and the baby. Putting his head down, he said in a whisper, "I wish my mom didn't cry so much."

"Those are all good wishes. What about the rest of your wishes?" Geri's heart sank as he whispered in her ear.

"Well, I wish that we had a new house with a back yard and a swing. Maybe even two swings. I'd ride on my swing until I could reach the sky and hear all of God's secrets. God's secrets are the ones we need to keep us safe. Yep, that's it. I'd wish for God's secrets."

Stephan looked up at Geri with a proud smile believing that he'd answered her question real good.

"God's secrets, humph? You know what Stephan, that's my wish too. But for right now, what about that big juicy cheeseburger?"

"Really?" Stephan's smile almost hurt her cheeks and it wasn't her face.

"Yes, really." Geri winked.

She left Stephan playing with the toys that the shelter provided for the children and went over to his mother.

"Mary, Stephan would like a big cheeseburger. Is that okay?" Mary smiled at her and said, "Is that boy beggin again?"

"No, he wasn't begging. I asked what he'd like, and one of the things he said was a cheeseburger. That I can get. What about you and you, Miss Susan? What would you like?"

"I'd like one too." Susan responded, but Mary just shrugged and said, "Whatever."

"I'll be right back."

Geri informed the front desk that she was going out to get the family something to eat. She was told that the doors would be locked in an hour, so she had better hurry.

She called ahead to order cheeseburgers, fries and salad from a local diner. On the way back to the shelter she thought about how empowered Stephan might feel if he knew that sometimes all it took was to ask for what you wanted. No, it doesn't happen the way you want it to happen all the time, but if you don't ask, you won't know. Maybe she could let him know that that was one of God's secrets. And maybe God's secrets were available just for the asking.

That experience stayed with her for days after the visit. She thought about the power of words that were used in the right way. Could she use some of those words to write children books, to learn from as well as be entertained by? It wasn't a novel idea, but could she do it? Why not start with God's Secrets?

A few days later she spoke with Patti about the idea.

"What do you think about my sliding in a children's book between now and the month of June?" Geri really didn't know just how long it would take to write the book, but she knew that she operated on deadlines.

"A what?" Patti heard exactly what she said, but wasn't quite sure how to respond. She knew that Geri had a heart for children and that sooner or later the subject would surface. Her only concern was how it might interfere with her finishing the project she was already working on. She also didn't think that the publisher Geri was currently working with would go for it. Patti was a believer of possibilities also and considered that it might be a good idea if she would be willing to write her children's books using a pen name.

"Patti, think about it for a bit before you answer. It would only take a month or so out of my schedule. I need you to maneuver getting it published."

"You're right on both accounts. Let's talk about it in a couple of days."

"Okay. In the meantime I'll send you some of my ideas." 'Oh yeah', Geri thought to herself. The idea felt good, so good that she decided to start working on it that night. She asked herself the question, "Does God really have secrets?"

Chapter 32

The visits by her mother and Sonia were great. They taped one of the acts in Sonia's play and her mother helped her write a couple chapters for the children's book. Talking about the book with her mother and her friend helped to answer the question about God having secrets. Geri confessed that she believed that Christian was one of God's secrets and all she had to do was ask if it was okay to have him. God's answer was a resounding, "Yes."

All was well. Geri felt the excitement of Christian's return rising up in her. The night before he was to leave Cameroon, he called her from an area code she didn't recognize. She noticed it right away and was about to ask where he was when she heard the overseas operator's voice. Instead of calling her from his office it was a transcontinental operator asking if she would accept a collect call from Ambassador Christian Nounkwa. Geri accepted the charges and waited for his voice on the phone.

"Geri. I'm glad I caught you at home." The sound of Christian's voice was muffled.

"Hi my love. Where are you?"

"I think I'm going to have to delay my flight home to Cameroon for a day or so. I'm sorry, babe." Christian continued by sharing that he had to meet someone outside of Cameroon, but would be traveling back there to fly to Chicago. He told her that the weather was bad and he would need to layover where he was staying until the morning. This would most likely delay his return to her for a few days.

"What happened? I thought all of your time was going to be spent with your family. How are they?"

"They're fine. And I did spend a lot of time with them, but I had something really important to take care of outside of Cameroon. That's where I am now. The weather's really bad. I'm disappointed too."

He sounded genuinely disappointed and just as mysterious. Geri hoped that everything was okay.

"I think you'll be happy with what I have to bring you, everything I have to bring you." He continued, "Don't worry. Nothing's wrong. I can hear the questions running through your mind."

She could only sigh. He had not left any room for more questions.

"Okay. I understand. Actually, I don't understand. But it's okay. Just bring me you, Mr. Ambassador. I'll be here waiting." Geri felt nervous. She wasn't quite sure why the feeling was so strong after he had reassured her that everything was okay. There was something about the tone of his voice.

"See you in a few days."

She hung up the phone. The feeling that she had while talking with him lingered. She had prepared for his arrival by hanging a couple of new art pieces she brought one afternoon during one of their gallery browses. The colors in the largest piece was vibrant like those in the throw he sent to her months ago. The eleven roses she received from him the day before were in the center of her dining room table, the card leaning against the vase. She did all of this thinking that she would see him within a couple of days. But now she sat quietly on the sofa holding the throw under her chin uncertain about how to feel.

She began to pray. "Lord, I do love this man. Thank you for bringing him into my life. Thank you for revealing the secret. Please don't keep another one from me."

With every effort to stifle the nagging concern that something was wrong she wrote a few pages in her book. The protagonist she now thought of as 'their' Jasmine had become a suspect of espionage by the government. To try and remove the suspicion, her lover asks her to marry him. He shares that it would make them seem like a normal couple . She refuses and tells him that she cannot see him again.

At that moment two government officials knock on her door to arrest her. Her lover forcibly takes one of their weapons and tells her to run. Once she leaves he is overpowered and shot.

It was now 2:00 a.m. Geri was tired, but afraid to go to sleep. Had her storyline provoked her continued concern about him or had her concern about Christian allowed the story line to unfold? Before falling asleep she reached under her pillow and held on to the double framed pictures that he left the last time he was there.

Geri had replaced the closed frame under the pillow each time she made the bed. His gesture had touched her heart as much as the gift itself. He was on one side and she was on the other, but they were still connected. It was sort of how she felt that night. After searching his face, she held on to the frame falling asleep with his smile on her mind. That night she wished they had made love. What if she never got the chance to be with him again?

Her dreams were more upsetting than they had been in a while. Although she had not been thinking about Nathan, she could see his and Christian's faces moving in a deep fog. The fog became a blanket of snow covering only them, not their surroundings. Both men were looking at her with sad eyes and then Christian smiled and said, "I love you, Jaz." As he spoke the words, he faded deeper into the fog and snow. She could see footprints in the snow that she somehow knew were Christian's and not Nathan's. There were rose petals strewn across the footprints. They were the color of crimson. Suddenly they blew away. Eventually all that was left was a shadow of the face she sensed was Nathan's and one petal.

"Christian!" Geri awakened startled and cried out.

Sweat drenched her nightgown. She sat up in the bed still seeing the snow in her mind's eye. It was now all around her. Feeling a pressing sensation of loss piercing her body, she laid back down. She could hardly breathe. Tears streamed heavily from her eyes, but no sobs came from her throat.

"It's just a dream, Geri. Go back to sleep." As she held on to her pillow, she smelled the scent of jasmine replacing the light lavender and vanilla that she often sprayed on her linen. The smell calmed her and she drift into a peaceful sleep. This time she dreamed that Christian was sitting on a grassy hill looking out over a field covered with wild flowers. She called out to him and he turned to her and smiled. She couldn't hear him speaking, but she could read his lips as he spoke,

"Hello, Jaz. I've been waiting…"

Before she could read the last words from his lips he vanished. The hill and the flowers were still there, but Christian was not. Sorrow came over her in her dream and as if she was awake sensing it all, her sleep filled body shuttered as tears ran down the sides of her face.

Geri woke up in inexplicable peace. She tried to fi out her dream. She waited anxiously to hear from Christian all morning. Her attempts to call him at home were in vain. There was no answer. After getting no answer at his office she thought again about "God's Secrets." She had the strange feeling that God had a secret about her and Christian. It made her think about the children who had inspired the children's book she just completed. Her mind traced back to the morning that she met the Chaves children - Angela and Juan. She thought about Stephan, the little boy in the homeless shelter. She wondered how they were. Geri frequently thought of them, but asked herself 'why so much today?'

As a distraction, she started jotting down different names for her children's book. The publisher generally had the final say, but the book meant enough to her to press the issue. She decided that she would not write using a pen name so that sizable percentage of the royalties could be donated to her favorite children's charities. The dedication would read "To all of my children and to the one who set the child in me free, C. N."

The diversion worked. She was able to refocus her energy. Nonetheless a foreboding prevailed in her spirit. Each time it resurfaced she talked herself out of paying it any attention.

Later that day Geri tried calling Christian's office again. Finally she got through. There was heaviness in the greeting on the other end.

The person answered in English, not French. She didn't recognize the voice. She asked for Christian in a more formal manner than usual. "Hello. Can I speak with Ambassador Nounkwa?" She waited during prolonged silence.

"May I inquire as to whom is calling?" He asked ceremonially.

"This is Geri Michaels. I am a close friend of the Ambassador's." For some reason she felt compelled to state their connection.

"Madame, the Ambassador is not here. Can I help you?"

"No. I said I am a close friend. I need to speak with him!"

Impatience rang in her tone, but it was really the fear of what he would say next. The pit of her stomach was dropping to her feet and she couldn't catch it. Holding her breath to the point of dizziness, she grasped the phone tightly like it was a life preserver. And then she heard his words.

"Madame Michaels, I am sorry. Ambassador Nounkwa was killed last night in a plane crash."

The phone slipped from her hand. A silent scream pounded in her head as she collapsed to the floor. She rocked and cried as if to let the pain pour through the tears. She could hear the voice on the other end calling her.

"Madame Michaels. Madame Michaels. Are you alright?"

Geri managed to click the phone off as she moved from the floor to the sofa. Christian's gift laid across the arm of the chair. She pulled it around her shoulders and sunk deeply into the chair the way she did the night he sat there with her. Numbness began taking over her mind and body as she repeated, "No secrets. No secrets." Her chanting subsiding, she stretched out fully and floated off into an oddly peaceful sleep.

Chapter 33

Months had gone by since Christian was reported dead. Geri was lost in a deep depression during much of that time. She couldn't remember exactly what brought her out of it, but when she emerged it was with the resolve to finish writing the book. The story was somewhere lodged between what still seemed so surreal and the reality that he was gone. She was determined to find it, write it and celebrate it as if he was right beside her.

It was a cloudy and damp afternoon, good for staying in, reading a book or watching T.V. As was nowadays so often the case she'd turned down the volume on her phone low enough for her not to hear if it rang. She sat in the living room chair with her legs thrown over its arm, staring blankly out the window. After several minutes of contemplating whether to read or turn on the television, she sat up. Her elbows resting on her knees, Geri placed her hands under her chin thoughtfully. She would not read or watch a movie. It was time for her to give new life to her new story. Smiling at the sense of confident that was welling up inside her, she went to her office to gather her old notes and the laptop computer then headed for the kitchen.

She arranged everything on the kitchen table in her familiar working fashion and turned on her CD player. Before sitting down, she got a bag of chips, M&M's and two bottles of water. Going over her notes she saw where she had written the name 'Jasmine' in the center of a blank page. She recalled writing it one night after she and Christian had spoken over the phone. She smiled broadly and rubbed the page with her hand. Jasmine was becoming her new and favorite heroine. After reviewing a few of her notes, she pushed them aside and began writing. Words came easily, fluidly moving from her mind until suddenly they just stopped.

Massaging the back of her neck Geri glanced at the clock on the wall. It was much later than she thought, but she was not surprised. She was in her writing zone and until now had not paid attention to the ache in her neck, a sign that she had been sitting too long. The music streaming softly through the room had been mimicking the words on her computer. Signifying how love felt when it had no place to go, it was a perfect soundtrack for the love turned upside down storyline unfolding on the screen. Suddenly, she was more conscious of the rain pelting hard against the window as if it was part of the story's drama. Too bad she wasn't writing a screen play, she'd use it all. The atmosphere was one to be appreciated. Feeling the music she turned up the volume. Fingers tapping lightly on the table she scrolled to the top of the page with the other hand.

"Shoot. I can't believe I did this." The declaration fell out of her mouth in a whisper as if someone else was in the room and she didn't want them to hear. The mood was broken by what was on the computer screen. The rhythm of her writing had taken her some place she did not want to go, subconsciously transposing part of the last chapter of her life onto what was supposed to be purely fictional. Personal experience was how she often developed a story, but she did not want to expose herself this time. Clicking the remote to turn off the music, she wondered how much she would need to rewrite. "Shoot," she said again and let out a sigh in anticipation of all she would have to delete. Geri leaned closer to the computer as she read.

"Humph." It was a surprisingly good read. The piece of her story that slipped through fit perfectly well. It intensified the character's story in a way that intrigued even her. Dr. Jasmine Moudime was indeed her new and favorite protagonist. The strength of the character was not unlike the other women she wrote about in her novels. It came through by the way she loved and her passion for righting wrongs - exactly what the Goddard Foundation wanted. Jasmine was coveting and acting out her creator's persona like it was her own.

The first few lines on the page sent chills through Geri's body. Her subconscious was trying to speak through her writing in a way that she had been unable to do since losing the love of her life almost a year to the day. She wondered when and how she had become the writer who could give up so much control. In the midst of feeling the need for utter privacy about what she was going through, she had allowed her character the freedom to be in her shoes. Jasmine had taken what Geri called 'character authority'.

With unexpected approval Geri relaxed in the chair and continued reading. The tension in her neck was easing. She had not noticed that the rain had stopped, but now the quiet in the room was broken by the sound. The rain was now rolling down the window again like streams of tears, similar to the ones that were coming from her eyes. She started reading from the top.

What do you do when the end comes and you're not ready? ... grace had somehow put her pain to rest. Grace had kept her from losing her mind. Grace had become her closest friend and tonight "Grace" was still there. She turned out the light believing that someday it might all make sense, but for now...

Chapter 34

Its funny how your search for an ending or to get closure and something brings you back to where everything began. Sometimes the beginning is not a place where you have actually been, but instead a place in your heart where you know you once belonged. When she arrived in Douala, her life journey engulfed her senses. She found herself listening to every sound and smelling every astonishingly familiar fragrance with an intensity that had lain dormant in her since she lost Christian. She inhaled the light scent of the jasmine that bloomed all around her. It mingled with the warm wind that could very well take your breath away if you let it. Christian had done that and named her after the flower that she now understood to be the one that grew all around him as little boy. She stood fascinated as she could almost taste the wind. It was not a dusty taste that you might expect as she watched a patch of dry dirt raise up in a mini cloud on the unpaved road, but a sweetness that seemed to personify life her life, the voices of the people who spoke in diverse dialects echoed around her. The more she took in the more she thought about the one taken from her. This was the land where birth was given to him. Cameroon was giving her the gift of knowing that with all its losses and pain, life was still sweet.

It was a place like this that had given birth to her spirit the way a strong and beautiful flower grows in a garden with rich soil. She believed that if she pressed her ear firmly to the ground, she would hear the ancestors saying, "Welcome home." She was there. There, in this place that her heart had unknowingly dreamed of and where her love had lost its trail. It was the beginning and the end connecting in a way that was unsettling and comforting at the same time. She was beginning to consider that the closure she so desired was too elusive for comfort, yet absolutely comforting because she felt a strange sense of hope.

The long awaited day had finally arrived. She had opted not to come before now to do any research. She believed that holding Christian in her heart was all she needed to understand his people. They would hear her heart as she read excerpts from *Sometimes in December* a story of love's unexpected blessings and extraordinary losses. Carine Nounkwa, the young woman she met at the Wright-Goddard Foundation who turned out to be Christian's niece, would stand beside her as her anchor.

The foundation had arranged for the visit through the Nounkwa family. As Geri would discover, it was because of their son that she received the fellowship. It had not dawned on her that Christian might have been the one to nominate her. She had never even suspected. She had yet to meet him before he fell in love with her writing, a love that ultimately became his reality.

Her mind drifted as she sat drinking her coffee and going over what she would say before reading excerpts from her book. How had she gotten here? She had not given it this much thought for a while. It seemed an eternity since she was informed about Christian's death and she still knew nothing of Nathan's whereabouts. Perhaps he too was dead. She asked God "How could any of this happen?" Had God been in this with her all along? Had God understood the foolishness of her prayer and sent Nathan to her until she knew better?

Grasping the book in her hand she remembered how it seemed that Jasmine's story died with the death of beloved Christian. The truth be told though, it wasn't Jasmine's story that withered away, but her own. There was silence until the ghostlike Jasmine herself, the one who Christian named and Geri gave birth to, chose to speak to her one night. As she rested her head on her kitchen table reminiscing about the Christmas party that seemed so long ago, she heard what sounded like a sweet whisper.

"Geri. It's time to set me free." As crazy as it might sound to others, Geri knew it was Jasmine – or more precisely, her heart using Jasmine to speak through.

The story took little time to complete after her encounter with the leading lady. They actually became good friends. For Geri, remembering her feelings for Nathan and Christian became part of the storytelling process. Those feelings were as innately different as they were richly the same. Both led her to understand that sometimes we must lose to gain. Dr. Jasmine Moudime imparted this vital lesson as the story unfolded. Geri was able to write about healing and recovery of what she had lost through this one that Christian named.

At the end, Jasmine and her family were out of harm's way. She returned to the United States to become the professor of History she so desired. The family eventually joined her. It was a powerful story. As Geri thought about it today, her heart smiled.

The Wright-Goddard Foundation loved the story. Since its setting was in Cameroon, they wanted to share it with the community where Christian Nounkwa grew up. She still laughed every time she was reminded that Christian was the one to submit her name for the fellowship.

"Geri, are you ready to go? I'll ring the elevator." Carine knocked on Geri's door as she spoke then walked across the hall towards the elevator.

"Yes I am. I'll be right out." Geri turned to take a last look in the mirror and smiled at herself because she was actually pleased with what she saw. "I feel good this morning. And I look good, too."

They rode down to the lobby in silence. Carine understood that Geri was a little nervous about the event and decided to give her the silent space she sensed she needed.

She had agreed to be her translator while she traveled through out the West Coast of Africa because she spoke French and knew some of the other dialects. Much more than being a translator she agreed to travel with her because they had a common love.

Getting off the elevator Carine suggested that Geri wait until she made sure the car was out front.

"Good idea." She watched her walk out the front door and thought how happy she was that she was with her. A representative from the European division of the Wright-Goddard foundation would meet them at the auditorium, but Carine's presence was personal. Watching for the signal to come out to the car, Geri suddenly felt someone standing behind her.

"I have been waiting for you all my life." As she turned to meet the softness of the voice that breathed and whispered so closely from behind into her ear, her heart pounded as if it would implode. She felt all reality drain from her eyes, her lips, and even her fingertips, her whole being. She knew that she was still breathing, but could not understand how. It was his voice. The one she promised always to recognize and never to forget. Geri turned as carefully as her body would allow.

"Oh my God." Her words almost caught in her throat. She was not sure if even he heard them. "I thought you were…"

Before she could continue, Nathan spoke from his nervous smile.

"You thought I was dead."

"Yes. Dead." The words barely escaped from her mouth as tears streamed down the curve of her cheek the way he used to touch her face.

"I thought I would never see you again." Geri managed to speak then threw her arms around him.

He responded with all of his strength, holding her as though trying to stop her from falling. He kissed her eyes, forehead, mouth, and chin. As the tears rolled down his face, he spoke with words that seemed to drift into the air.

"Geri, I have dreamed of you every night. I knew that this day would come. With everything that I've lost, I knew that from the moment I saw you, we were to be together."

Geri could not believe that it was his voice that she heard. Not knowing what to say she let him take her hands into his as he raised them gently to his lips. Still trying to reconcile the moment, she heard her inner voice recalling, "The universe gives us things…"

Nathan interrupted her thought with, "Do you have a few minutes before you have to go?"

"Yes, I think so." She walked with him towards the sitting area in the lobby. He held on to her hand afraid that she might otherwise run. They both sat slowly and quietly as their minds raced with the excitement of life that allowed them to reunite, but the fear that perhaps it was not real. Neither had any understanding of the mystery that haunted their lives while they were apart and they did not know just how to proceed with trying to understand.

"Where do I start?" He looked into the space of the room as if trying to collect the memories of what had occurred over the past years. He looked older and more peaceful than she had remembered. His clean shaven head was now covered with coarse black hair that grayed at the temples. How distinguished he looked. She was at once happy that he was all right, but saddened by the idea that he had been alive all this time and she did not know. What had he been through?

"Where have you been? How did you know I would be here? Why did you let me believe you were dead?" All of Geri's questions began to punch at one another. She was overwhelmed by a rush of feelings that included elation and bewilderment. She tried to calm herself as he answered.

"I was told that there was a man, an Ambassador from West Africa who came to my country to find out about me. I understand that he met with a high official in my country and persuaded them to find me. I was in prison being held for a trial that I believed would never happen. In fact, it did not. The man, Nounkwa was his name, arranged for my release." Nathan turned back to Geri and saw the fresh tears fall from her eyes.

"Christian Nounkwa. Ambassador from Cameroon." She spoke softly, carefully pronouncing each word as she placed her hand over her heart.

"You knew him?" He was surprised by her reaction.

"Yes. We were close. He was killed in a plane accident. I plan to meet his family while I'm here."

"Geri, it was not an accident. The thought that someone else had chartered the plane. Nounkwa was trying to get home and persuaded the pilot to give him a lift back to Cameroon. Now I believe he was trying to get home to you." Nathan spoke perceptively.

Her heart began to pound wildly, but she felt herself calming down as she thought about Christian's act of love. She placed her finger to Nathan's lips. "I don't want to hear anymore."

"Geri, we've got to go." Carine walked over to them and stated that the car was waiting. She had seen pictures of Nathan and had an idea about their meeting, but they did have an appointment to keep. It was an appointment that they had been looking forward to for months. It was the day that she would finally get to visit the village where Christian grew up and talk directly to his people. It was his home. This was his time with her.

"Carine, I'm coming. Nathan, where are you staying? Can we talk later?"

"Yes. I am checking in here. I just arrived and came directly to see you. I know that you need to go. Nounkwa would be pleased by what you are doing."

They hugged and walked out together. Carine waited by the car door and greeted Nathan with a polite nod as he walked away.

"That was Nathan." This was all that she could say as they climbed into the car.

Carine smiled as her thought about who Geri was speaking with was confirmed. She looked at Geri and said, "It is a beautiful day, my friend."

Geri exhaled and reached for the compact mirror in her purse. She touched up her makeup and said, "I want to be my very best for my Cameroon audience, Carine. And I especially want to be my very best when I meet your family."

Cameroon was Geri's final stop. She considered that it was the most important stop on any of her book tours. In fact she was convinced that it was the most important stop on her life journey thus far. Even though she was so close, she had purposefully decided against traveling to Nathan's home. It all seemed so ironic now. She had no idea that he was alive. Seeing him was like a miracle sprinkled across what she knew would be a magnificent day. The little that Nathan had shared with her helped her to put the pieces together about her last conversation with Christian. The extended assignment that he told her about involved looking for someone he knew was so dear to her that he would take the chance of losing her should he be found. Christian was coming back to her with the news that Nathan was still alive and would be released from prison soon. His haste to get back to her, though, caused him to take the plane that had been designated for another passenger, another person's demise. Christian was not the target but suffered because of his love for her.

She contemplated on how God had been silent in her waking hours, but had talked constantly to her as she slept. If the truth had been known it would have been too overwhelming. She wondered how life could trade one love for another, letting death reap the benefits. What was the path that she was to take after all? As the car moved along all of these thoughts moved profoundly through her mind. What was the connection?

When Geri stepped from the car, Christian's mother embraced her. She recognized her from the copy of her first novel and the picture on the back cover. Christian had sent a signed copy to his mother.

Geri had not expected Mrs. Nounkwa to be there to greet her. Carine looked at Geri and winked.

"Welcome, my daughter." Christian's mother was both warm and strong. She looked just as Christian had described her, but more significant was the resemblance between her and him, especially the dimples.

"Thank you, Mrs. Nounkwa. I am so very happy to be here." She spoke trying to hold back the tears that formed in her eyes. She was actually glad that Carine didn't tell her that the family would be there for that part of the day. She might have been too nervous about meeting them in public.

The conversation she had with Christian the day he told her he shared with his mother that he loved her raced quickly through her mind. Geri wondered what his mother thought of her then, but now it seemed even more important. Did she know how much she loved her son? Geri wanted to hug her closely as if to feel the essence of Christian and say, "Oh, I love him so." As if able to see all of that in her face, Mrs. Nounkwa looked at Geri with love filled gentleness.

"It is alright." She took Geri by the hand and led her up a narrow path to the building.

Geri felt a sense of having come home for sure, not just to that land, but in an odd way she felt that she had come home to herself. She remembered how Christian spoke about going home when he left for Cameroon, and about coming home when he planned to head back her. At that moment she realized that home was where you were in relationship with those you love and who love you. Home was in your heart. Home is where your heart is, is a true saying. Coming home had caused the peace that she could not understand.

The event was wonderful. She witnessed a confidence and regality in Carine that she had not seen before. Geri was proud to represent the foundation that cared so well for her. She was impressed by how she captured her words in a lyrical way that let her know the translation was perfect. When she said the name Dr. Jasmine Moudime and heard Carine repeat it, her heart leaped so she wondered if anyone heard the thump.

From the lecture hall they went to the Nounkwa home. The family insisted that Geri ride with them. The visit was nothing short of one of those things you consider with gratitude. How she wished he had been there as well. While sharing about his son with her, his father confirmed that Carine had read Geri's first book and pressed Christian to use his Ambassador status to arrange a meeting between the two of them.

Although he refused, her enthusiasm prompted Christian to read the book himself. Accepting the invitation for Geri's book signing was not a coincidence. Christian liked what he read in the story and what he read about Geri. His niece was to have accompanied him at the signing, but had gotten ill the night before. Geri was grateful for the stories they shared about Christian and was soothed by the laughter that accompanied the stories. She was humbled and pleased by the way the family welcomed her before leaving their home Geri vowed to stay in contact with them. Convinced that her sought after closure was unattainable, she was happy to let the cycle of life continue through her new extended family. As the car pulled up to the hotel, she began to shift gears. Her thoughts about closure and continuity had become the grace she wrote about in her first novel. It was not fiction, it was her life.

There was a message awaiting her from Nathan giving his room number and the request that she call him when she returned. Geri was not sure if she was ready to see him and decided to give herself the option of taking a shower and just going to bed. When she got in her room, however, she knew that she could not rest. She called.

It wasn't very late, but the lounge was almost empty. They sat at a table that offered privacy, but did not scream of a clandestine meeting. Geri was conscious of being in Christian's home and even more, she was determined to have any meeting with him out in the open. When the waitress came over to them, they looked at each other as if to confirm that they both had a flashback of times passed.

"Good evening. What can I get for you?"

Geri ordered a club soda and Nathan ordered a beer. At least that part of them hadn't changed.

"How was your day?"

Geri answered with, "It was actually wonderful. I feel blessed to have experienced it." It was nice to hear his voice. "How was yours?"

"It was good." He answered in a small talk tone.

There just didn't seem to be anything to say. Their silence spoke volumes.

"I know. There is so much to say and talk about that it's hard to figure out where to begin." Geri spoke as she struggled with the reality of his sitting right across from her.

"Are you tired?" Accepting that the night would not render any real discussion, Nathan said he would wait as long as it took for her to feel more comfortable about talking with him.

"Yes. I think I do need to get some rest."

He gestured for the waitress. After paying they walked toward the elevator. He offered to walk her to her room. He took her hand, but said nothing. She politely pulled it back and smiled at him. She felt silly pulling her hand away. But when he touched her, she felt his love and the uncertainty about hers. When they got to her room, he asked if he could give her a hug.

"Yes." She responded believing that she would be able to give him a good night hug without a problem.

The hug led to a kiss. Afterwards they held on as though each was afraid to let the other go. The kiss took Geri back to a time when everything seemed possible with love. How she had longed for another moment like that, and here it was.

"I love you. I still love you so much. Let me love you." His words broke into the present moment.

Geri was not sure what he meant by "Let me love you." She knew that her love had not faded, but it was different. She believed, however, that something might be rekindled in a moment of passion. But she also knew that the moment of passion would have been just that. Yes, she still cared for him. But she did not want his being alive to serve as compensation for Christian's death. If it was up to her, it would be Christian's arms that she would be in.

"Nathan." She hesitated. "Are you free to spend the day with me tomorrow?"

"I am free."

Geri smiled remembering those words from before.

"I will see you in the morning." Again, she paused before saying,

"Nathan, I have never stopped caring about you." She wanted to say more about what that looked like now, but decided to wait until the light of day.

They said their 'good nights' and Geri went into her room. Closing the door behind her, she put her hand to her head as if to hold in the thoughts that she believed he could somehow hear. She said no to him, and no to her heart, but that didn't mean that she hadn't wanted to be held and loved by him. Maybe more than ever before in the hope that it would help her make some sense of what had happened over the last two years. Was he spared because he was who she was to be with? Or was it just that the day spent with Christian's family and experiencing his absence in its truest sense had heightened her need to be held. Could he caress her loss away? What if he knocked on the door after she was in the bed? Would he do that? Geri was not sure. She was also not sure what she would do if he did.

Chapter 35

Sleep came swiftly. No dreams. The peace that she experienced was something she had not had for months, perhaps years. She was not awakened by an alarm clock that dictated the time of her getting up or by an alarming notion that she had no control over her life. That morning was filled with new possibilities. She was thankful for everything that brought her to that point in her life. She was consciously grateful for life itself. There had been pain, but the love and joy she'd experienced far outweighed it. She embraced the comprehension that it was not always necessary to comprehend. Certainly her being in Cameroon without Christian fell into that category. But she did have choices, one of which loomed in front of her.

She leaned over for the phone at her bedside. She felt in full control as she dialed his room number.

"Good morning." Her voice was clear and deliberate.

"Good morning. How did you sleep?" He seemed surprised that she called.

"I actually slept very well. Are you up? Can we meet downstairs in about half an hour for breakfast?" She was now sitting up on the bed in a purposeful and upright position.

"Yes. I'll see you in the lobby?" "Okay."

Geri was a few minutes late after taking a call from Carine and the foundation person she met the day before. He complimented her on how she captured the audience and wished her a good trip back to the States. When she arrived in the lobby, Nathan was at the front desk checking out. She walked up and stood to his right. It amused her that she actually gave thought to how to approach him from the back or to the side.

"Hey. Sorry I'm late. I had a couple of phone calls come in." She stood close to him and leaned slightly on the counter with her right arm.

"No problem. Are you hungry?"

"I sure am."

Nathan finished the paperwork as Geri tapped gently on the counter. She didn't know if she was nervous or just really relaxed. The tapping was a signal of both. It was one of her little quirks that she hadn't noticed for a long time. But he did.

"Are you nervous and happy?"

Geri smiled at him and began moving towards the dining room. He was just behind her and reached out to take her elbow.

"So, you're checking out? Where do you go from here?"

"To breakfast." Nathan laughed and said, "You are happy, aren't you?"

"That I am." For the first time in a long time that answer was absolutely true. There were no qualifiers or quantifiers. She was happy.

After breakfast she suggested that they go back to her room to talk. She had asked the maid to clean the room when she saw her in the hallway before going down to meet Nathan. Going into the room with the bed unmade may have been too tempting. Fortunately, the maid had enough time and left the room freshly cleaned. They sat on the loveseat. He held her closely. It felt nice and normal. But then it always had.

"So, tell me what happened." Geri looked into Nathan's eyes with a seriousness that came out of all of her life experiences. He told her how he had been taken into custody almost as soon as he arrived in his country. He was tortured physically and emotionally as the police taunted him by telling what they had done or would do to his family. He did not find out that they were not harmed until he was in prison for several months. A guard finally told him that his family was informed that he was dead and they relocated to another African country. Nathan was not sure how the guard knew this until he shared that a prominent man had been inquiring about him, and he believed that the man eventually spoke with the General to have him released. During the time that this man was inquiring several bits of information began to circulate about Nathan and his situation.

Nathan shared that through it all he held on to his belief that everything was working together with purpose. He told her that although he felt helpless in many ways, he prayed for his family's safety night and day. He also prayed that she would have a happy and safe life. One night he was awakened from a nightmare about her being in danger. As he recalled the dream, he told her about how he could see her crashing her car against a wall of some type. On that night, he prayed for her safety. He said he called out to her as he poured out the love he had for her and hoped that she was okay. Geri remembered how she had seen his face the night of her accident, but she did not speak about it. This was her time to just listen. He was in prison for almost a year before being released.

Afterwards, his time was spent trying to locate his family. As he told his story, Geri remembered what he shared with her in her apartment that first evening. She thought about all he had been through and was grateful for the opportunity to sit with him again, no matter what would happen from that point. She listened intently as he continued to share.

"When I found my family, my child's mother had married thinking that I was dead. I didn't need to tell her about you, but I did because I still loved you and wanted to get back to you, to marry you. Geri I wanted to get back to you."

His life had turned so many corners, many of which he had not anticipated. When he and Geri met he'd still intended to bring his daughter and her mother to the United States. They planned to marry. Because of Geri, his feelings had changed. And now, everything had changed.

"When and where did I begin to fit into the picture again?" Geri wanted to cut to the chase. She did not want to seem insensitive, but the truth be told she could feel her emotions moving from sensitivity to a bit indignant.

"Ah Geri, you were never out of the picture. What I felt for you was and still is real. It just wasn't right yet. I am free. I am free to be with you. I want to be with you."

Geri got up from the sofa and stood at the window looking at the grounds. "This is so beautiful." She breathed deeply as if to smell the warm air through the closed windows. Breathing consciously and pointedly was what she needed in situations she felt might get away from her.

"How did you know I was here?" Her thoughts were once again cleared.

"I have been following your journey. I read both of your books. I knew that you would be here because I have been waiting for the right time to approach you. I believed that this was the time. I'm not sure why, I just did."

"What did you want or think would happen, though?"

"I wanted to clear some things up here, and then come back to you."

"Humph." It was all she could say.

"Geri, you know I will not try to force you or trick you. I understand why you're saying what you're saying. But I can't pretend. I want you."

"I'm leaving tomorrow. I'm leaving to begin the rest of my life, Nathan. Where do you fit? I'm not sure you do fit."

Walking back to the sofa she gestured for him to stand up. She smiled and kissed him lightly on the cheek. He pulled her closer, but she pushed away. She knew that if they spent one more minute in the room, she might give in to his touch. The love she had for him was in many ways still there. There was nothing separating them any longer. They were both 'free'.

"Right now I would just like to have a good day. Let's go to the market place."

"Okay. If that's what you want." He moved away from her.

"I need to let Carine know. Do you know where it is?" She spoke capriciously, feeling good about his being alive and glad that she discovered it while in Cameroon. Somehow the combination of events made her stronger and more determined to grasp all the brass rings in her life. The mantra that her grandmother and mother spoke to her as a little girl came back with new clarity. "When you are strong, you can afford to have a good heart. Make sure one evens the other." Indeed, it was true.

The day was in fact wonderful. They laughed like old times. Whenever there was a moment of melancholy for one, the other would endearingly pull them out. She told him about Christian, sharing that she believed they would have married if he had not been killed.

"He must have really loved you."

"Yes, he did. And he was so patient with me. It just seems too crazy that as soon as I came around, he was taken from me."

Nathan hugged her gently. He could understand how Ambassador Nounkwa loved this woman so deeply that he would risk saving the man that she loved first if it would make her happy.

That evening they dined at a nearby restaurant. Later they walked silently back to the hotel. When they reached her room, he asked if he could kiss her. She looked at him, searching his face to see if he was still the man she fell in love with. Feeling that to be the case, she kissed him. It was a good night kiss that was oddly sweet, instead of passionate. Maybe it was the reconciliation she experienced the past couple of days knowing that he was alive, and that she was ready to begin her life from a place of recovery. Mourning Christian in the midst of it all helped her understand the loss was to be a beginning. She got it.

During dinner it was decided that Nathan would accompany her to the airport the next morning. She could not imagine boarding the plane without his face being one of the last that she would see in this place.

Geri, Nathan, and Carine rode in the same car to the airport. The three of them talked about the beauty of the countryside. They laughed as a group of goats stood on the road not allowing the car to pass. When the car moved on to the highway, however, there was silence. It was as if the road brought them back to another place, a place of goodbyes and hellos that could lead almost anywhere. Carine was about to board a separate plane that would end their current journey together. Geri would miss her.

When they arrived at the airport, Geri spoke privately with Carine as Nathan waited. They embraced and expressed how much they meant to each other, then promised to keep in touch. As Carine walked away, Geri turned to Nathan and exhaled.

"This is still so amazing to me." Her heart was full with emotion.

She walked towards him feeling strangely torn between leaving and wanting to spend more time with him.

"Geri, I can only say that I love you still. I have the same understanding that I always had, believing that what is to happen, will."

As she was about to respond, the call to board her plane came over the speaker. There was a hint of sadness in the smiles they exchanged. They hugged for what might really be the last time.

"Talk to you." Geri spoke softly. The words that Nathan had spoken so many times, leaving her uncertain about when she would hear from and see him again, were now hers.

"I love you."

Nathan responded, "Me too."

He watched as she walked up the ramp and boarded the plane. She settled in her seat and exhaled as she had when Carine left to board her flight. "Everybody has to leave at some point. Even me." Her words were quietly deliberate.

Out of nowhere she remembered that it was December 22. She would get back in time for Christmas. She closed her eyes and reclined the chair. They would fly through the night. She would hopefully sleep for hours. She prayed silently that God would give them traveling mercies.

Chapter 36

Night flying was boring to her. All you could see outside the window were the lights on the wings in pitch dark. She fell asleep almost immediately and as she often did on a long flight, lapsed into a full dream. There was certainly much to dream about and the first scene came readily.

In front of her building was a shiny new yellow bus waiting for her. The driver had a sign that said, "Yes. I am waiting for you." She smirked and said nothing, then got on the bus. Suddenly they were at the bookstore.

"Ms. Michaels, we have you set up over there. Is that okay?" The bookstore manager wanted to make certain that everything was just right. He admired her work and wanted that sentiment to be as evident as possible. *He moved around the space where she would sign her books like a busy little bee. Yes, he did sort of resemble a bee. He had big eyes and what looked like a yellow stripe that circled around his head. She was tempted to say to him "Please calm down. Everything will be just fine. Everything is just fine. My goodness!"* Instead, she replied, "Yes, this is fine. Do you have any water?"

She was extremely thirsty. This generally happened when she was nervous or just warm. Maybe it was because the warmth of spring had come out of nowhere and she was still dressed for cool weather. Having done so many of these book signings she couldn't understand why she was so nervous about this one especially since her return to the United States found her basking in the success of the novel. "Home Is Where You Are" had taken the literary circuit by storm and was currently on the New York Times Best Sellers list.

It was the best book tour ever. Her last event was in Chicago, the place she now considered home. She was really excited because many of her friends said they would drop by to see her. Glancing at her watch, she timed that she should be through by 1:00 and lay out on her sofa by 2:00.

"Oh, thank you." She received the water from the manager and began to get settled at the table.

The book signing table seemed extremely long. Maybe it was because the bumblebee like store manager wanted to make a big impression on her. As the line started to form with anxious and patient customers alike, she looked up and cast her best smile on her first purchaser of the day. Then suddenly it was Nathan standing over her smiling the smile she had missed for so long.

"Oh my God." It was him. *The beat of her heart was so loud in her ears that she believed it could be heard above the music playing in the store. She covered her ears thinking it would drown out the sound.*

She stood up and Nathan met her at the end of the long table. She threw her arms around his neck as he lifted her off her feet. She began to cry and laugh at the same time. They both laughed with the joy of seeing and holding each other. They cried with the same joy knowing that their love had lasted. The woman who she thought was her first customer was now behind him still waiting to get her book signed. She was laughing and crying with them as others clapped. The manager came over to see what was going on. He turned from the two of them and said to one of customers, "So, home is where you are!"

"Hello, Geri." Nathan finally spoke.

"Hello, Nathan." She wiped the tears from her eyes.

After composing themselves, she asked him to meet her at her apartment later that afternoon. His response was,

"I cannot do that. I want to stay right here with you. Home is where you are and this is where I want to be. I will wait right here as long as it takes."

And wait he did. Geri moved through the book signing anxiously awaiting the end so that they could begin. "Ah, life is a cycle!" was playing like a melody in her head. She looked up and somehow Nathan was now in the parking lot calling out at her,

"It is a good day. Do you know why it's a good day?"

She could only mouth back. "No, Nathan, why is it a good day?"

He laughed loudly and said, "It's my birthday".

"Get out of here man! Your birthday is in…"

Before she could get the words out, he was back in front of her. He lifted her face to his and said, "Will you come anyway with me now? Marry me, Geri. Marry me before it's too late."

She was trying to answer, but she couldn't open her mouth. Nathan was shaking her gently, repeating her name.

"Geri, Geri"

"Ms. Michaels. Ms. Michaels." The Flight Attendant was touching Geri's shoulder lightly and calling her name.

"Ms. Michaels, I'm sorry to have to wake you. You were sleeping so peacefully. But we'll be landing in 20 minutes. I need you to bring your seat back up and make sure that your seatbelt is secure." She opened her eyes realizing that she had been dreaming. As she sat up, she pulled her thoughts back to reality. She looked out of the window wondering whether the dream had spoken to a desire to have him back in her life.

Shaking her head in an effort to remove the thought from her mind, Geri stared at the clouds that she loved so much. It was daylight and they were touching the wings of the plane. Was the plan for her life going to remain constant like the clouds no matter how circumstances change? Is that why Nathan resurfaced? She thought about the clouds she had painted on the walls of A Haven for My Children. She may not be there, but would it always be there for the children?

She felt someone near and looked up into the pretty face of the Flight Attendant.

"We're about to land. Hopefully you won't get caught in a long line for Customs so you can get home and continue your rest. You were sleeping so soundly."

She thanked the attendant and agreed. She wasn't really tired, but just wanted to get home. She looked at her watch to see the time. While in Africa, she used a different watch. The one she wore today was still set at Chicago time. It was 2:00 P.M. After sleeping for most of the flight she was rested and thinking about what she had to do when she got in.

As passengers deplaned, Geri wished that she had asked someone to meet her. But all that was waiting was the car service. It was a different service from her usual, so the driver would not be familiar. She sighed as she moved down the aisle of the plane.

"Goodbye, Ms. Michaels. Thank you for flying with us. We hope to see you again." The pleasantries of the flight crew were a little reminiscent of the people she had met in Cameroon. She considered that some of them were Cameroonian, and without thinking, she said goodbye and thank you in a native dialect. They responded with a warm smile.

As she walked to the Baggage Claim area she thought about her dream. She could not believe that it was so vivid and realistic, while at the same time crazy. Maybe it had manifested out of her subconsciously hoping it would happen. It would be a way to close the chapter on her relationship with Nathan. Or would it? She recalled that she didn't answer him.

'Next chapter, please.' She reasoned.

"Oh, man. Look at this line." Her attention was diverted to the Customs lines that seemed to go on for miles.

The wait in the line was not as bad as it could have been. After making her way through the airport channels, Geri saw the white cardboard sign with her name. She waved to the driver and motioned for him to come over.

"Ms. Michaels?" The driver approached her politely.

"Yes. I'm Geri Michaels. How are you?"

"Fine, Ma'am. How are you and how was your flight?"

Now feeling that she didn't want to have any more conversation, she smiled and nodded to indicate that it was okay.

"Let me get a Baggage Handler, Ms. Michaels. I'll be right back." The driver spoke as if he could read her mind.

"Thank you." She exhaled and looked around the familiar airport. Her trip was wonderful, but it was good to be home.

The driver came right back with someone to load up her luggage. She had been gone for a while and had six pieces of luggage, including a trunk filled with gifts that by the grace of God were not confiscated by Customs. She considered that it was because a lot of it was material and clothing.

The carved wood pieces she sent by mail and had placed her purchased jewelry in with her regular pieces. The one thing she carried on the plane was the box that Christian's mother had put together for her. In it were gifts from her and his father along with a bust of an African woman that was in Christian's bedroom. She had admired it, but was not aware that it was being packed while they were having tea. At the end of the visit, both of his parents presented the gift box to her with a hug and a word of blessing.

It was December 23. What did that mean for her Christmas? She decided that it didn't really mean anything. She had been given the gift of reclaimed and newly presented love. What more could she ask for? She was eager to talk with her family and friends.

"Hi mom, I'm back." She called her from the car so that she would not forget when she started to unpack or get distracted in some other way.

"How was your flight?"

"It was good. How's everything?" Geri had spoken with her mother several times while away, so questions about the trip had for the most part been answered. She wasn't sure if she even wanted to share the last day's events.

The traffic was not bad during that time of day. The ride was steady even though a light snow was beginning to fall. Geri began to think about her trip and all that happened. She thought about Christian and what he did to find Nathan. He impressed her even in his death. What kind of man would do what he did? She picked at it for a moment and realized that it was who Christian was.

He loved her. He wanted to be with her, but not as a consolation prize. He wanted to have her because of her love, not because of her loss. Geri tried to imagine what would have happened if Christian had lived and she had to make a choice between the two men. She loved them both so, but in different ways. Even though she thought she no longer felt the same way about Nathan before seeing him again, the sheer irony was that she believed she was also 'in love' with both of them. Would that have changed if she saw them standing side by side?

"Christian." She sighed and closed her eyes.

"Excuse me, Ms?" The driver thought she was talking to him.

"Oh, I'm sorry. I was talking to myself. It was a long flight you know." Geri laughed as he smiled through the rearview mirror a little embarrassed.

Finally, we're here. Geri looked around the grounds of her building as the driver moved to the trunk of the car to get her luggage. Carl, the Doorman came out with a baggage pulley. 'Efficient as ever' she thought as he came towards her with a big smile.

"Welcome back, Ms. Michaels. We missed you!"

"Thank you. I missed you too!"

As the two men handled her luggage, Geri headed to the building. There was a chill in the air that reminded her once again that it was winter in Chicago. Christmas was just two days away, but it did not seem to bare any significance in her life at the moment. There was no book to push or soirées to attend. She expected that her only company would be her thoughts while she soaked herself in a hot bubble bath, made a good cup of coffee and selected someone else's book to read.

She had arranged for her mail delivery to stop until a week ago. This week's was stacked in her mailbox. The rest she would get from the post office in a few days. There was absolutely no hurry. Carl informed her that a couple of UPS packages were left at the lobby desk. Knowing that he would bring her luggage up himself, she asked if he would include the packages.

Carl knocked on the door just moments after she entered her apartment. He had her suitcases and packages on the cart.

"Where would you like me to place these, Ms. Michaels?" With warm politeness and familiar efficiency, he smiled at Geri. She smiled back and pointed him to the alcove next to her bedroom.

"Thank you, sir." She smiled at him again as she placed a folded fifty dollar bill in his hand.

"This is for taking such good care of me. And Merry Christmas by the way!"

"Thank you, Ms. Michaels. Welcome back again." Carl knew her generosity; he did not look in his hand.

As he walked towards the door, Geri moved behind him impatiently, wanting him to leave so she could be alone. When she shut the door, she stood looking around her living room and saw that everything was just as she had left it. Her cleaning person had come the day before as they had agreed, so there was freshness in the air. She could even smell the hint of jasmine that rested in her candle holders.

Geri flopped down on the sofa as if she weighed a ton. She was relieved to be home, but she also felt a little sad. A sense of melancholy fell over her. Suddenly she felt really tired and wanted to sleep. Perhaps she was not quite ready to face her holiday alone, sleep would postpone it at least for a little while longer. She stretched out on her sofa with her coat still on.

Chapter 37

For the first time in her life Geri spent the Christmas holidays alone. She talked for hours with family and friends, mostly sharing her experience in Cameroon. No one could believe that Nathan was still alive. They were happy for him, but concerned for her. Everybody changed the subject after a few minutes of talking about him. They laughed a lot about silly things and talked about what was going on in their lives. Each conversation ended with the promise to do better about keeping in touch more frequently in the coming year.

Geri declined the offer from friends to join them for New Year's Eve. The need to continue her solitude until she figured some things out was still pressing. She found herself thinking about what she really felt for Nathan. She knew she wouldn't act on getting back with him under any circumstances, but she needed to close the chapter without any lingering doubt. Nathan wasn't the only source for reflection. With all that she'd been through over the last couple of years – good and bad – she wanted to take time to find out what next. So far she decided to take a break from writing for a month or so. It would be a good time to visit her family. But for now, she wanted to be alone with herself the person she'd come to know, love and trust more than anyone.

Christmas passed. She was proud of herself for being able to spend it alone celebrating and not depressed. She went out a couple of days later to mail some packages and pick up a few things from the Seven Eleven around the corner. Food had been the last thing on her mind since she got home. She ate tuna and a couple of frozen dinners. Tired of drinking black coffee she wanted to get cream. Her house cleaner had thrown out a brand new container she'd bought just before she left. She probably read the expiration date and thought she was doing the right thing. Geri knew she could have gotten a couple more days out of it. She left a note to tell her not to throw anything out unless it was molded or black when it should be yellow. Talking with Patti earlier that morning she tried to convince her to overnight a batch of Zemmels. It would be really nice to have some to go with her coffee.

"Come on Patti. When's the last time I asked you for anything?" Waiting for her all too blunt response, Geri was nonetheless hopeful that she might surprise her by saying, "Okay." But the response didn't even resemble that word.

"Geri, I believe that you left part of your mind over in Cameroon." Patti laughed and admonished her for not having sent out to the grocery store to have food delivered to her.

"But I don't want food. I want Zemmels." There was an exaggerated frown on her face.

"Sounds real personal to me, my love. And the crazy little expression that I know you have on your face right now don't make a difference."

Geri relented with laughter. They said, "Happy New Year!" and hung up.

"So Ms. Geri, what about New Year's Eve? It's just a day away. What are you going to do with yourself?" She spoke aloud to herself with honest concern.

After talking with Patti she felt a little lonely. Trying not to think about the last holiday when she was with her friends, she closed her eyes and lifted a word of thanksgiving for all she had been blessed with since that time. So, how would she celebrate? She thought about fixing herself a lavish dinner since she knew she needed to go grocery shopping, but decided against it. The idea about just going to the convenience store vanished as she thought about what she would really like to eat. The more she thought about New Year's Eve, she was reminded of her superstitions about going into a new year with dirty clothes in the hamper, an unmade bed and an empty refrigerator. With all of that, fixing a meal was taken off the drawing board. Pondering it further she thought, 'Umh. Popcorn - caramel and cheese, with a champagne chaser.' She laughed at herself and said, "Why not?"

Deciding she would get it now and save some for New Year's Eve, Geri grabbed her coat from the closet and headed downtown to Garrett's, her favorite popcorn store. As she glanced at her watch and realized that it was 5:15, she hoped that the store would still be open. It would take her at least twenty minutes to get there. The thought of calling ahead didn't enter her mind until she got into her car. Then she didn't want to pay the information charge to get the phone number on her cell. "I can't believe it would close this early though."

She was in luck. The store was still open, but the line of customers was actually extended onto the cold pavement. Thinking that it wasn't that serious, she drove on to the grocery store. The lines might be long there too, but that was a different story.

Anyway, she could really do without the popcorn. Especially since what she was really craving were those damned Zemmels. Maybe she could find something similar in the store.

"How am I living?" she mused.

Pulling up in the grocery store parking lot she could see that several people were there still shopping. Geri rushed to the door and saw the sign indicating that the store closed at 6:30. It was 6:10.

"Okay. That's what I get for waiting." She chided herself mildly as she entered and pulled a shopping cart from a bunch in front of the store.

Unsure of what she even wanted, she threw some staples in the cart and pulled all the sweets she thought she might want off the shelf.

"Frozen pizza?" She asked herself. "No." She answered.

"Champaign…or something like it?" The next question. "Yes." She answered and moved hastily to the wine aisle.

After selecting the best champagne they had, she headed for the checkout counter. On her way she saw the refrigerated flower case and was drawn almost magnetically to it. She hesitated for a moment, then opened the case.

Geri left the store with two bags of groceries that she would not have been able to identify if asked before she placed them in her car, two not so great bottles of champagne and flowers.

Finally home from her mini shopping excursion, she settled in for the night.

"Happy holidays. Happy New Years. Oh, and a belated Merry Christmas!" She spoke mockingly as she made herself a turkey sandwich.

Purposefully ignoring the flowers that she laid on the kitchen table when she came in, she popped open the bottle of champagne and poured herself a glass. She was surprised that she was pretty much feeling okay.

All around her were things that reminded her of the love she experienced in her life. Family pictures, African and African American art she'd painstakingly decided to buy although pricey, the Cezanne still life she received as a present from Renee's trip to Paris and the brightly colored throw that Christian had sent to her before he was taken from her. She watched a couple of her favorite movies as she snuggled under the throw that she kept on her sofa. She had convinced herself that Christian's scent was still lingering from the last time they laid under it together. No, she had not cleaned it since then and didn't think she ever would.

Before the second movie ended, she had toasted to her life and the lives of those she loved, and felt a bit tipsy from drinking almost half a bottle of champagne.

She got in the most comfortable position on the sofa determined for some reason not to go to bed. She remembered how her mother used to sleep on the sofa waiting for Christmas Eve to make sure that she and her sister didn't sneak under the tree to open their presents. She also remembered how her mother would sleep on the sofa waiting for her to come home on the nights that she would be out with friends while home on vacation from college. Good memories they were. But what meaning did they have to her this night? Deciding to turn off her mind, she gave into the champagne's effect and drifted off to sleep.

The special ring on her phone was from the front desk. She reached for it on the table but realized that it was on the floor. She scrambled to pick it up before the call was lost.

"Hello." Her voice was a little hoarse.

"Ms. Michaels, there's someone here to see you. He wants to speak with you. Is that okay?" Carl's voice had a strange question mark in it.

"Okay, Carl. Wait. Who is it?"

The other voice was on the line, "Geri?"

She sat up trying to catch her breath and silently clear her throat at the same time. She recognized the smooth tone of his voice, but considered that she was dreaming. She shook her head to clear the dream and wake up.

"Yes." She repeated. "Yes." If it was a dream, she was angry with what seemed to be a cruel intention. But as her head cleared and she realized that she was not dreaming, she placed her hand to her chest as if trying to hold her heart inside. She felt that her body had been suspended in air. She had indeed dreamed of this, but like her dreams about snow, she just considered them to be sleep filled moments of comfort that she could not get when awake. The snowflakes would melt as she kissed them.

For a moment there was silence. Not hearing his words or saying anything herself, her mind flashed back to the dream about the bus and the sign that she could never read. The sound of the bus whizzing by seemed to open her ears as she heard him calling her name.

She answered again, "Yes."

As she answered this time she saw the yellow sign that moved alongside the bus. It stopped and stood still for a moment as she heard it speak into her spirit, "Sometimes in December life springs from the ground. It is a gift. Embrace and believe."

"Geri?" He breathed deeply after speaking her name again. Holding back the desire to say anything else, he waited for her response.

"Yes." She said softly, "Yes. Please come up."

She walked slowly to the door and opened it as she let out the breath that allowed her to believe in this miracle. Standing, waiting in the doorway, she realized that it was holding her breath that had made her feel dizzy and not what was actually happening.

The elevator bell rang in the quietness of the hallway. He stepped off the elevator. Her heart raced as she looked into his very lean, but wonderful face. She felt his presence as if he was one of the gifts he'd sent so many times when he'd traveled home. But this time he was the best gift of all, and her memories of all that had been, was now again. He was home.

Chapter 38

Geri watched him walk from the elevator towards her. She could not hear above the voice that kept whispering in her ear.

"Can this be true? Can this be true?"

It was a whisper that was almost inaudible, but its cadence moved with the beat of her heart drowning out all else until she heard his voice and felt his breath on her ear. When they embraced she could hear the question that began as a whisper getting louder and louder and her heart answered, "Yes." Christian had returned to her. It was now clear why she felt so much peace in the midst of the pain when she'd thought about him every day.

She could not move, but he stepped towards her with his hand out as if he was beckoning her to get off the bus that had haunted her dreams for so many years. She reached out her hand and moved towards him. Pulling her closer, he hugged her as if she was a life raft that would keep him from drowning. Geri returned the strength of his hold. She heard the softness of the sound that she had longed for and had unknowingly waited for that night.

They eased their embrace and stepped back enough to see the other completely. It was as if time had stood still. Christian was a bit leaner, but handsome as ever. Her heart leaped when she took in his familiar smile. He smiled and shook his head in admiration. She looked as he had remembered. He pulled her close again. His lips brushed her cheek as his mouth moved to her ear.

"I've missed you so, Jaz."

Geri breathed deeply then blew out as she spoke through her tears.

"Oh my love."

Chapter 39

As wonderful as he looked, Geri could tell that Christian was tired. Soon after getting inside the apartment he asked if he could lay down. Geri recalled that clothes were left strewn across her bed from earlier that day. She went to her bedroom to clear her clutter and make things as comfortable as she could for him. She was so glad that mementos from him and about them were strategically placed around the room. The double frame pictures of them remained under his pillow from the moment he placed them there.

They held each other through the night allowing sweet intervals of sleep to weave gently between their expressions of love. Geri was afraid that if they let go of each other, she would discover that it was just a dream. At one point, she opened her eyes after dozing and exhaled with relief. The two of them were not a dream.

The cold of winter's snow had melted and they were surrounded by a beautiful turquoise sea. The blanket of snow had turned into foamy white waves rocking them into a peace that was unspeakable. The water flowed to nourish the earth but it no longer separated them. They were together. Their love sprang from the ground like the jasmine he'd spoken of, the scent she smelled in his family's garden. Winter had been transformed.

Now fully awake, and witnessing the sun rising, Geri listened intently to Christian telling what took place before he was considered missing. At first reluctant to begin with the mention of Nathan's name, Christian recognized that there was no other place to begin the story. Choosing his words carefully, he told her how he had arranged to get Nathan out of prison. He shared admittedly that his motivation for wanting to locate her friend was mixed. True, he wanted to do it for her because he had fallen in love with her and wanted to give her that gift. His other motive was selfish. He was concerned that she would continue to mourn over or love Nathan in a way that might stop her from opening her heart to him. The latter may have been a bit irrational, but it was how he felt.

At no point during his sharing did Christian look at Geri. He was afraid of how her expressions might deter him from telling the story just as it occurred. Still, he was surprised by her silence. He paused after a couple of revealing statements to give her time to react. But she did not.

Christian continued by sharing how the more information he received about Nathan's circumstances, his motivation changed from strictly personal to one of justice.

"Weeks before my trip to Cameroon, I contacted my old college friend, Kristopher. At the time he was a big shot government official in Nathan's country."

Christian continued. "We trust each other like brothers."

He explained that their most recent communication had been about his friend's desire to leave his country. Like Nathan, he had been privy to information that placed him in jeopardy if he tried to leave. Decidedly, Kristopher wanted diplomatic sanctuary in the United States. Christian agreed to quietly look into it. He was already on the case when the concern about Nathan came up. In their last conversation he asked his friend to find out what happened to Ntheba Nathan Muafumba. Christian shared why, knowing that he would understand. It was ironic how the two situations, Kristopher's and Nathan's, were in some ways similar. Half expecting otherwise, just days before he was to head back to Chicago he was informed by his friend that Nathan was alive. Thinking back he recalled the conversation.

"Hey, my brother. I have news for you." Kristopher's tone was muted, but with urgency. "Mr. Muafumba is alive in detention. Here's the plan."

"Ok. Let's have it." Christian replied.

Hesitating to go on, he looked at Geri. She knew he was asking whether he should proceed. Geri shook her head, taking his hand as he took in a deep breath and continued.

The story unfolded. Nathan had been detained for over a year for what was supposed to be questioning. He did not disclose this part to Geri, but it had not initially been his intention to rescue him. He hadn't considered that it was even a possibility. He wanted to be able to let Geri know what happened so she would no longer have to wonder. Now knowing, what would this mean for everyone? What were the real risks there and abroad? What would he tell Geri one way or the other? Neither of his questions had time to marinate. They moved quickly.

Kristopher's official status served to minimize some of the danger associated with releasing Nathan. Getting him out of Angola was another thing entirely. He would have to travel secretly. Christian ruminated over how it would be Nathan's second experience with leaving the country in that manner. He managed to convince the Cameroonian government to let him enter the country and stay there until there was a more permanent solution. Each movement would occur separately. They would not travel together and Christian did not know what communications would occur afterrwards. Nathan might never know who arranged for his release.

The weight of it all was in Christian's voice when he last spoke with Geri. Detecting that something was wrong, she inquired why he sounded so serious.

He responded by saying, "I'm just exhausted and can't wait to get back to you."

Listening to his story took her back to that conversation. It was now clear what was going on and clearer that she was right in being concerned. Trying not to allow her expressions to show all that was going on inside her, she laid her head on his shoulder so he could not see her face.

3. and lifted her chin up to him. She sat up straight now looking in his eyes. He knew she was ready to ask questions or just share how she was feeling about all that he'd shared so far.

He spoke first "I was not certain how any of it would turn out. For the sake of secrecy outside the necessary parties, I could not share any of it, even with you."

"But why didn't you tell me what you were trying to do? You could have trusted me." Geri asked. Her frustration was now apparent.

"It wasn't just about the secrecy. I didn't want to get your hopes up. I wasn't even sure that I would go through with it." Christian responded. "I know this is a lot, Jaz. Do you need a break?"

"No. I want to hear it all, Christian. There's more I want to ask and even tell you, but please, tell me everything." As the words came out of her mouth she was considering how she would tell him that she'd seen Nathan.

"Well, it was all arranged. I couldn't wait to see the expression on your face. More than that, I couldn't wait to get back to you. I'd been away from you too long." He sighed heavily.

Contrary to his government's initial suspicions and the international media reports, his plane was not attacked.

Geri shared how it was immediately suspected that the reason for the plane crash was political. The media sensationalized the possibility for months without any evidence that it was in fact the case. Even after the government officials in Cameroon ruled it out, there was a period when the media would not let it rest.

He could only imagine what she was thinking through it all. It was true that he had some concern about retribution from Nathan's government, particularly where his friend was concerned. Kristopher's connections and a deal with one of the prison personnel made it happen.

"Have you heard from him? Kristopher I mean?" It was the first time she had heard his name and was curious about what happened to him.

"No. I will look into his situation as soon as I can." It was odd to him that she would ask about his friend in the midst of his sharing the chain of events and not about Nathan.

"You haven't asked about Nathan." Christian made the statement, but it was mostly a question.

"I will. I just never heard you speak of your friend before." That was another reason, but she did not want to talk about Nathan until he finished telling his story. She immediately regretted her interruption. Christian looked at her suspiciously. She took his hand again.

"Before we took off from Angola, the pilot told me there might be problems flying into Cameroon because of the storm brewing along the coast. He assured me that we could still make it if we left within the hour. I believed him. More than that, I wanted to get out of there as soon as possible."

Sensing his anxiety rising and knowing that hers was as well, she all but held her breath as he continued talking.

"There was another passenger on the plane with me who was not part of my plan." His voice lowered. "He was the prison officer that arranged for Nathan's freedom. It was safe to say that he would have been in danger had he remained in Angola. The plane went down when lightning struck and tore off one of its wings." Christian's heart was beating rapidly.

"The pilot and the officer were killed in the crash. The bodies were burned beyond recognition."

Geri put her hand to his chest to help calm the feelings that were now so obvious in his voice and posture. The other passenger's presence was undisclosed. The authorities concluded that the bodies were the pilot's and Christian's.

"Jaz, maybe it was your love or even God that spared me. I was miraculously thrown from the plane into an embankment of heavy brush."

He smiled resolutely when he heard himself speak of God the way she had on so many occasions. He considered that the chain of events had increased his belief and understanding tenfold.

"I remained unconscious until a group of children from a nearby village found me." Tears welled up in his eyes. "The authorities had no reason to search since they found two bodies."

It was a story that you see in the movies. She couldn't recall ever reading or hearing about anything like it in real life. But if things like this never happened in real life, there would be no basis for it on the screen. As she listened to the words and saw the expressions on his face, flashes of Nathan's story could not help but surface. His storyline was unspoken. Regardless of how miraculous, it had no glory or grandeur attached. He was just a man trying to survive, trying to protect his family. She wondered how Christian's story would now be presented to the world.

"My God, Christian." She kissed him tenderly. They sat embracing each other in silence, trying to find out what to say or do next. Geri knew it was her turn to share.

"I guess it's my turn." She looked at him and saw the quizzical look on his face. "Where do I start?"

"I know that question all too well. At the beginning." Christian responded rhetorically.

Geri began by recounting what happened with the book, then fast forwarded to her trip to Cameroon. She shared how gracious and loving his family had been to her. And then she began telling him about her encounter with Nathan.

"Seriously?" Christian asked surprised.

"Yes. Seriously." She answered placing her hand over her heart as if to stop it from jumping out of her chest.

She shared every detail, including her having to consider what she still felt for Nathan. "You can't imagine how shocked I was to see him. I thought that he was also dead." She spoke like she was reading from one of her novels.

"Nathan had found out about your intervention and shared it with me not knowing anything about us. He seemed to be as shocked about you and me as I was about his being alive."

It was Christian's turn to be silent. He rested on his back as she sat with her legs folded facing him.

From start to finish, sometimes animated and other times solemn, Geri talked about her encounter with Nathan answering all of Christian's unspoken questions.

When she was through, a comforting calm entered the room. The worst had passed and now a new and different life could begin. There was no need to clarify or bear witness to anything else accept their love.

"How about something to eat?" Geri broke the silence with a whisper.

"You know what? That sounds like a good idea." Christian bit her hand gently and smiled.

"Actually, I am hungry."

"Ok. Stay right here. I'll be right back!" She leaped from the bed with energy she did not know she had.

"I'll be right here." Christian answered.

When she entered the kitchen she saw that the flowers she bought in the market were on the kitchen table where she left them hours ago. She had forgotten about them. How appropriate it would be to place one on their breakfast tray. She made omelets and toast as she picked at the cheese to quiet the growling in her stomach. She would not allow herself to mull over anything that was just said in fear that she might break down in a bath of tears. Each time one would present itself, she wiped it away swiftly. Fittingly she hummed a new melody to the words. taught to her by her grandmother and sung so sweetly by her mother.

Arranging everything on her largest tray, including the single rose, she added a couple of snacks for later. On her way out of the kitchen she noticed her children's book on the counter. She stopped and smiled back at the face of a little boy smiling with his hands cropping his chin. His face was golden brown and that morning his cheeks seemed to glisten. The little boy's name was Stephan. The title God's Treasures Are Little Ones crowned the top of his head. Little Ones, pointed to how even the smallest of blessings are huge at their core. Geri placed the book on the tray.

"How's this for service?" She asked blithely. Christian sat up as she placed the tray on the bed. Before she could hand a plate to him, he took the book from the tray. She felt so much love in her heart at that moment, she leaned over and kissed him before he could finish what he was about to say.

"What's this?" Christian pointed to the book.

"It's a gift." Geri responded with delight in her voice.

"A gift for me?" He asked seeing that it was a children's book.

"Yes. Open it." She almost bounced on the bed. Christian opened the book. It fell immediately to the dedication page.

"To Christian always, with love Jaz." The words were inscribed in raised black type. He ran his fingers across them. He put the book on the bed and touched the side of her face with his hand. He kissed her gently, speaking at the same time.

"Thank you."

"You are so welcome." She responded with kiss filled words then placed the book on the night table.

"You have got to eat. I'll read the book to you later."

"I always knew you were bossy!" He teased.

"Me. No way!" She teased back.

"We can't live on love alone." Pointing to the tray of food, she asked, "What do you think?"

Along with their breakfast, there were cups of coffee and orange juice, chips, M&Ms, apples and two bottles of water. He smiled and took the plate from the tray.

"Some buffet. I'm surprised you fit all of this on one tray."

"Practice." Geri said with a smile. It was the way she filled her tray with snacks for writing.

Taking her plate and coffee off the tray, she moved to the other side of the bed. Christian waited for her to get settled. Before they started eating they prayed together thanking God for the meal, but mostly for their reunion. They ate everything except the apples and a few M&Ms.

"I guess we were hungry!" Christian laughed.

"You think?" Geri laughed too and put the tray on the floor.

"Tell me more about the children's book." He knew she loved children, but she was an adult novelist.

"What made you write God's Treasures Are Little Ones?" He hoped that his question did not sound imperceptive.

On the contrary, Geri was happy and impressed that he asked.

"To tell the truth, a lot of things. But, mostly because of a little boy I met in a homeless shelter." She replied looking at the book cover, then sighed.

"His name is Stephan. Stephan was living in the shelter with his mother and younger siblings. Christian, he was this amazing little boy who believed that God had the secrets to his family's safety. We talked for a while about what he wished he could have."

"How old was he?" Christian was intrigued.

"Eight. He would have turned nine last spring." A warm feeling came over her as she thought about him.

"He talked about God's secrets and how he believed that if we could just find out what they were, we would all be okay. So, since I didn't want to name the book using Stephan's quote - God's Secrets - I turned it inside out to tell one of the secrets."

"Clever. I like it. So one of the secrets is that God's treasures are little ones? What? Little children? Little blessings? Little things?" Christian was intrigued by the whole idea and could see how Geri lit up when she was explaining the book to him.

"All of it. The feeling led to the first short story in the book Corey's Secret. When you read it and you will, right?" She gave him the eye.

"Of course I'll read it. Wait, didn't you say you would read it to me?"

"It's about a little boy named Corey living in a homeless shelter with his parents and baby sister. The plant where his parents worked closed down, they lost their jobs. Anyway, Corey has a dream where he meets a stranger that reminds him of his grandfather who he never met, but saw his pictures. Poppa Jim - that's the family's name for him - tells Corey a secret about what's going to happen for him and his family." Geri stopped there not wanting to tell Christian the whole story.

"And? What happens? What's the secret?" Christian couldn't believe she stopped, leaving him hanging.

"I don't want to tell you all of it! Then you won't need to read the story."

"Well, is it good at the end?"

"Oh yea. It's good. And it goes back to my story about Stephan. God really does have secrets about our safety. The secrets are always revealed through the ones who can help us be safe. Doesn't that make you want to just smile? I mean smile big?" She grabbed a handful of M&Ms from the tray and put them in his mouth.

"All in your mouth and not in your hands." She laughed at his expression. She forgot he was not from the U.S. and had no idea about the M&M commercial.

"You want more?" She said playfully and kissed him. "No. I'm good." He mumbled. His mouth was almost full.

"Okay. I'm sorry. I couldn't resist it." She laughed and laid back on the bed.

"You are amazing. Your heart is amazing. And that is no secret!"

Christian felt pride filled with the love that he had for her. "You think so?" She couldn't contain her grin.

"Yes, I do."He picked up the rose and smiled at the gesture. The last time he had only sent eleven to her believing that he would deliver the twelfth as before.

"Well, thank you sir."

Feeling the need to get up and move around, she removed the tray from the floor and placed it on the dresser. She took sweats out of a drawer and laid them on her arm.

"I'm going to take a shower. Want to come?" She turned to him, but could see that he was dozing off. Deciding not to disturb him, she went into the bathroom and quietly shut the door. As the water ran down her back in the shower, she could feel the hot tears roll down her face.

'More tears?' she thought. They were tears of joy for his return and tears of pain when she considered all he'd been through.

The tears would probably come and go for a while. Her emotions included the idea that it all happened as a result of him ultimately trying to free the man whom she once loved.

"What kind of man does something like this for the woman that he loves?" She repeated the question quietly to herself and answered it in her heart.

"The kind of man that God has given to me. One of God's secrets."

Chapter 40

"What are you doing over there?" His voice was deep and raspy.
"Watching you."
"Come here." He turned on his side and patted the bed.
Geri walked over to the bed and pushed him gently onto his back. Lying on top of him she rested her elbows on each side of his head. "I like it better here."
"In that case, I think I need to take a shower too so I can smell as good as you."
Teasingly, Geri answered. "You know what? I think that's about right."
"Oh, so that's how you gonna talk about me." Christian laughed as he gestured to let her know he was getting up.
While he was in the shower she made the bed. Humming softly she took the tray to the kitchen and emptied the dishes in the sink. She looked around and thought 'What a mess', but had no intention of doing anything about it right then. Still humming, she sauntered back into the bedroom with a big grin on her face. Life was good.
Christian was standing at the window when she returned. Hearing her and without turning around he continued to tell his story. The first words dissolved her grin. "I was cared for by the elder women of the village. You know, if those children had not found me I would have either died from my wounds or been killed by animals."
Geri sat on the bed. She wanted to ask more about the children, but did not interrupt. He shared that it took weeks for him to gain back his strength. For a while he couldn't remember anything, not even his native dialect that the people who cared for him spoke. He had learned it as a child, but hadn't spoken it in years. The village was in the mountains and there were no hospitals in the vicinity. The village elder took him in like a son. He was nurtured back to good health and strength with medicines concocted from local herbs. He had not anticipated that it would be so long. Perhaps it was not only his health that kept him there.
Christian joined her on the bed.
"I know it doesn't make sense to you. It doesn't really make sense to me. But, I felt compelled to just stay there. Maybe I was just tired and didn't want to face coming back into the 'rat race'. When I think about it now, maybe I was afraid that you and Nathan had reunited and I just couldn't handle that. I know it's strange for me to say that, especially when I went over there to get him. What was I thinking?" Christian gave an exaggerated frown.
"You were thinking about me. You were being your compassionate self. I don't know of another man who would have done what you did."
Geri could not express the profound affect that it would have on

her for the rest of her life.

"Maybe I wanted to be your hero or prove that I could make you forget about him if you had a choice between the two of us."

She did not respond.

"As soon as my memory came back, I thought about you every day. I actually thought it best to stay out of your life. I thought it was some kind of fate that allowed me to get Nathan out of prison and then end up in a plane crash. I thought…"

Christian paused. "I thought maybe it was how it was supposed to be. Maybe she is to be with him and I am just the facilitator - the damned diplomat!"

"No. I am to be with you. I am to be with you. This is the fate. Our love."

Geri looked into his eyes. She was struck by his words. Her heart was deeply saddened by the look on his face and she was concerned that his emotional state had taken its toll, taken away the confidence and lightheartedness in him that she remembered. Had he been pretending how he was feeling since they reunited?

"Christian, I told you. I have seen Nathan. He shared what he understood happened. He's so grateful to you." Geri began telling her story again, "Yes. I saw him. Strangely enough I was in Cameroon. I was there to celebrate my book and your life. We thought you were gone. I was happy that he was alive. I had some mixed emotions. They followed me when I got back home. But, my love, once I returned I knew that I loved only you."

"Why are you crying?"

He wiped the tears from her face so gently that it did not seem that he was touching her.

"I don't know. I'm just so full. I can't tell you how much it hurt when I thought I had lost you."

She held his hand to her face and continued to speak as if to will him to physically feel the words as they came from her mouth. It seemed everything they held in till that moment was exploding. Maybe it was because they were now settled in and rested. Maybe it was because the shock of his return and the over exhilaration of her being there to receive him had worn off.

"I heard what you said before about my love for Nathan blocking my ability to love you. But trust me. I love you even more knowing what you did for him."

She looked at him wanting him to say something. After what seemed like a forever pause and trying not to read into his silence, she continued.

"Nathan came into my life for whatever I needed then. More than anything he helped me make room for you. Does that make sense?"

She moved closer to look into his eyes. She could see his relief. It was a look of assurance that nothing in the past mattered. It was all about that moment. It was all about their future.

"Jaz, I love you. Please forgive me for taking so long to come home."

Christian kissed her gently then held her in his arms.

After a few minutes passed, Geri began telling him about the foundation fellowship. She thanked him for nominating her. She clapped her hands joyfully as she shared her experience in Cameroon, meeting his family and finding out more about his culture. A copy of her book was in the nightstand drawer. She finally pulled it out and showed him what he had helped to inspire.

"Jasmine. I called her Jasmine. See how you influenced me?"

Geri finished her story and wanted to get back to his. She wondered how his family felt about him leaving Cameroon so quickly. He had spent only a short time with them before coming to her. She remembered the love that emanated from his mother to all that were in her presence. She could imagine how happy she was to know that her son was still alive. Oh, how happy she must have been to see his face.

Epilogue

Now that Christian had returned to the United States the full story would be disclosed to the public. Unlike Nathan's story and the story of the young man that died in the plane crash, the Ambassador's story would be of interest. The public loves stories about politicians and celebrities. The other men would be mentioned, but not celebrated. The media would put a spin on how Ambassador Nounkwa "returned from the dead". How would it be reported on Good Morning America and the Today Show?

Aside from all of that, who would be the first to hear the story from her? Geri's family and friends believed that Christian was dead. One of those charred bodies was supposed to have been his. This was not a coming back from the dead story. It was a story of life, love, hope and promise. Sometimes wonderful things did happen. This was like spring overriding winter and flowers blooming in the most unlikely place. This was life doing what it wants to do and this time it was good.

Geri understood that had she never believed that there was more to life than what was seen, her own personal hopes and dreams may never have come true. Now she was experiencing more than she could ever have hoped or dreamed would be true. They spent much of the day in each other's arms unwilling to separate and unable to say much more than that which comes out of love and passion.

Finally deciding to leave the bedroom they headed for the kitchen. She caught a glimpse of the fullest moon she had ever seen peeping through her window. She saw the soft flakes of snow falling in the moonlight as if they had no place to go or nothing to do except drift in the air. Without saying anything to Christian, she squeezed his hand and smiled. He looked at her and smiled back thinking about the first time he was in her kitchen. They stopped and gazed out of the window, her back turned to him and his chin resting on the top of her head, with his arms around her waist.

"Christian?"
"Yes."
"Did I ever tell you that my favorite poet is Nikki Giovanni?"
"No you didn't. But I'm not surprised."
"Can I share the words of one of her poems that I like best?"
"You know it by heart?"
"I do."

Geri turned her head to look up at his face and then turned back to gaze out of the window. Still in his arms, she pressed Christian's hands against her stomach. At that moment everything she was feeling was coming from the place you can feel centered in your belly. It was strength in her being that she had not felt in a while.

Staring intently at the snow falling outside her window, she started reciting, "Once a snowflake fell on my brow and I loved it so much and I kissed it and it was happy and called its cousins and brothers and a web of snow engulfed me then I reached to love them all and I squeezed them and they became a spring rain and I stood perfectly still and was a flower."

Christian's face glowed from the light outside the window and joy that he felt in his heart. Like Geri, it rose from the very pit of his stomach. It was almost an ache. He turned her around to face him. Before asking her the question he believed he'd been waiting to ask from the moment he saw her, he displayed a playful eagerness in the leading question.

"So Jaz, you've always known that you were a flower?"

"Well, I guess I have." Amused, Geri added, "And to think you knew too."

"More than you know. I knew that you were a gift of sheer beauty to the world. Sounds corny and not deep like Nikki, but this is me trying to be poetic. This is me letting you know how precious you are to me."

He paused and took her hands to his heart. It was pounding.

"Jaz?" His expression was now serious.

"Yesss?" Recognizing his seriousness, she tried to lighten the moment by stretching the word out playfully.

He stepped back to get a full view of her face then asked,

"Will you marry me?"

At first she did not respond. A hint of concern washed over his face. He could tell that the question had taken her by surprise.

Then she shouted, "Yes!" and threw her arms around his neck.

Words could not describe how she felt in that moment. Peace and joy and all things good swooped her up. She stood back to look at him. As she looked in his eyes she was grateful that she believed that God had dismissed her misguided prayer. She put her head on his chest and closed her eyes letting the stroke of his hand caress her head. Their breathing was syncopated.

Christian looked out the window and noticed that the snow had stopped falling. He laughed quietly to himself remembering the title of her new book Sometimes in December. It was true that sometimes in December something that was presumed dead could suddenly sprout new life. He knew that the presumption of his death had created its own season of cold bitter pain for her. And now here he was - here they were experiencing the warmth of love.

"What?" She could tell that something was running through his mind.

He kissed her forehead, nose and lips softly, then spoke, "Once a snowflake fell from the sky and I loved it until it became you."

The End!

About the Author

Dorian Mendez-Vaz, a native of Camden, NJ, is an ordained minister in the American Baptist Churches-USA and the President and Founder of Within Her Reach, Inc. a non-profit organization that provides programs and counseling services for women and girls. Rev. Mendez-Vaz has combined her pastoral ministry with human services believing that faith in God, a Christ filled spirituality with prayer at the center of personal empowerment, compassion for others and good education are the means to living a purposeful and prosperous life.

Her ministries, workshops and writings have focused on women, youth, sexual abuse and recovery, and family life support. A creative writer and workshop leader, past workshop topics include: Breaking the Silence: Adult Recovery from Childhood and Adolescent Sexual Abuse, In the Company of my Sisters: There is Love, Sister to Sister: Loving and Caring for Our Sisters and Ourselves.

Mendez-Vaz has a Master of Divinity from Drew University Theological School; a M.A. in Religious Studies, Chicago Theological minary; a M.Ed. in Counseling and Psychological Services, Springfield College (Massachusetts); and a B.S. in Elementary Education from American International College. Mendez-Vaz currently resides in New Jersey.

Connect With Dorian

Web
www.hawkinspublishinggroup.com/ldorianmendez-vaz.html

Facebook
https://www.facebook.com/hawkinspub

Twitter
@DMendezvaz